———————— ★ ————————

"You haven't told me the important bit yet, Nick. You said she was trying to say something. What exactly did she say?" I watched him carefully.

"She said only one word and I could be wrong. There was blood in her mouth and it was sort of gurgly. But I thought she said 'bullocks.'"

I stared at Nick. "You're not winding me up?"

"That's what I heard and that's all I know."

Did I believe him? One more thing worried me about Nick's recall of the night's events, and I couldn't not think about it. He had thought she gasped, and although I knew this could happen after death, did Nick? Because he had after all still tried to set the car ablaze.

———————— ★ ————————

"This is a saucy modern mystery in classic British vein."

—*Publishers Weekly*

CHRISTINE GREEN

DEADLY PRACTICE

WORLDWIDE®

TORONTO • NEW YORK • LONDON
AMSTERDAM • PARIS • SYDNEY • HAMBURG
STOCKHOLM • ATHENS • TOKYO • MILAN
MADRID • WARSAW • BUDAPEST • AUCKLAND

DEADLY PRACTICE

A Worldwide Mystery/March 1997

This edition is reprinted by arrangement with Walker and
Company.

ISBN 0-373-26232-9

My mother and father, sister Gwenda and James,
who all love books

ONE

IN LONGBOROUGH during the recession my landlord Hubert Humberstone is the only person doing really well. He's an undertaker.

As proper shops close, charity shops open on short leases and thrive. Even the video shop has become, grandly, The Re-user's Emporium. It's full of unfashionable frocks which manage to be matronly even in sizes eight and ten, which seems very strange. Anything over a size twelve is even worse and usually looks like curtain material from some bygone age. I take a size fourteen, but then I have a penchant for jam doughnuts and cream cakes.

There is now a trend towards bartering and people are recycling almost anything—even tea bags. Payment is often in exchange for goods and services: a few dozen eggs, firewood, a few hours' babysitting, a bit of plumbing. For the funeral business, cash is still the only respectable way to pay. And I should be grateful for that because Hubert hasn't had any rent from me for some weeks.

On the side door of HUBERT HUMBERSTONE—FUNERAL DIRECTORS, is placed my sign, KATE KINSELLA—MEDICAL AND NURSING INVESTIGATIONS. My part-time nursing subsidized my investigations, the odd night here and there used to pay Hubert's rent. I'm beginning to think I should add 'Criminal' investigations to my sign; just lately the only enquiries I've had have been from people desperate for hospital beds and treatment. It seems as if nowadays a private investigator really is needed to track down the mysteriously disappearing bed plus medical expertise. The local hospital, Longborough General, is now a Trust. Trust is a funny word; does it mean trust to luck? Anyway I do manage to give my enquirers appropriate telephone numbers, tea and sympathy, and instil into them the notion that it's he who moans loudest and longest who gets the treatment. Those who suffer stoically just get the repeat prescriptions.

My mother, who now lives in Australia and is trying to find a man with the money of a sheep farmer and an IQ just above a sheep's, said, when I decided to become a nurse, 'Well, dear, at least you'll never be unemployed.' She was wrong. I am. I'm doubly unemployed—as a nurse and a private investigator. No one, it seems, can afford either.

Longborough does now have a job centre. What a misnomer that is. Last week I paid my first visit to claim a job and unemployment benefit. Both, it seems, are riches beyond my grasp. Being an unemployed nurse is one thing, being an unemployed PI quite another. The harassed staff were so pleasant that I began to feel a bit tearful, but they couldn't really help other than give me the forms to fill in.

I peered at the notice-board. I could choose between cook in a residential home at £2.50 per hour, abattoir worker at £3, trainee estate agent (under twenty-five—I'm just over thirty) no wage specified, or sandwich maker—must be clean and healthy—at £2 per hour. All nursing jobs, private and NHS, seemed to have gone the way of those esoteric financial services jobs—up the Swannee.

Hubert, I must admit, has been very good about my non-payment of the rent. He's tall, thin and quite ugly with skin the colour of unrolled pastry but he's kind, although somewhat kinky about feet. He is at the moment going through divorce proceedings, his ex-wife having found a well-heeled scrap metal merchant after years of alimony from Hubert. Although Hubert is a bit depressed, there is a glimmer of hope for him. A new shop assistant seems to have taken a liking to him. As she works in a shoe shop, wears four-inch heels and has good legs this may bode well for a new and successful relationship.

My love life and social life are like work—non-existent. I do have my own small terraced cottage in the village of Farley Wood plus the office and box-room I rent from Hubert. Just lately though I've spent less and less time at the office and more and more time at home. More time watching morning television. I realized the other day I was actually beginning to enjoy the programmes. That really scared me. Now I go to the job centre each morning where I'm getting quite well known. I then visit the local library, plus I also ring my friend Pauline Berkerly, who runs a Nursing Agency. She's as worried as I am about the lack of nursing jobs and I suspect she's finding making a living tough too.

This morning Hubert did make me a proposition. One of his part-time assistants was off sick—would I like to prepare the corpses for burial. No I would *not*. He stomped downstairs but came back to my office a little later.

I was staring out of the window at the High Street bathed in May sunshine. I'd turned my office chair to face the sun, and put my feet on the window-sill, and I was almost in Bermuda...

He didn't even bother to knock, just came right in. I could sense him behind me, just standing there.

'Just because I'm unemployed, Hubert, doesn't mean I don't need some consideration.'

Silence.

'You're getting to be a miserable old bag just lately, Kate. You're not the only one unemployed.'

'I know, Hubert,' I said swinging round in the chair, 'but worrying about the three million others will make me feel even worse.'

'I've bought you the local paper,' he said. 'There's something in the stop press.'

'Don't tell me—let me guess. Uprising in the dog pound or mystery of neutered cats...'

'Very funny, Kate,' said Hubert, not amused in the least. The *Longborough Echo* seldom carries anything remotely interesting in the way of new stories. Dogs, cats, flower shows and the odd burglary forms most of its copy and it gets thinner by the day. 'Do you want to know or not?'

'Fire away, Hubert. Shock me.'

Hubert looked upwards mournfully then lowered his eyes and began reading. 'Woman's body found in boot of burnt-out car. Thought to be that of nurse Jenny Martin, 34, from Dunsmore.'

'Yes, Hubert?' I said, meaning I was totally mystified. He didn't answer, as if merely waiting for the penny to drop. Finally I said, 'Oh, you mean the local CID might want me to rush over there and give them the benefit of my two-case experience. Anyway just because nurses in dire trouble seem to be my forte doesn't mean I wouldn't like a change.'

He shook his head. 'You call yourself Medical and Nursing Investigations, Kate, so what do you expect—stevedores?'

I looked him straight in the eye. 'Now that could be interesting. Big muscly men in vests with hairy chests and arms—I might meet the man of my dreams.'

'I thought you were a confirmed spinster Kate,' said Hubert, trying to wind me up. I didn't answer so he carried on, 'No doubt there's someone out there who would find your red hair and cheeky face attractive.'

'Thank you, Hubert.'

'I was going to add...but he could be in the Sahara Desert.' I managed to smile. 'That's better,' said Hubert. 'Now back to the stop press. This could be a job for you.'

'As PI?'

'No. She's a dead nurse... So there might be a job going.'

I laughed. 'That's a bit tenuous, Hubert. She might not have been working.'

'Ah, but she was. I heard she was the practice nurse over at Riverview Medical Centre in Dunsmore. They'll need a replacement.'

'Dunsmore is twelve miles away,' I answered plaintively.

'You drive,' said Hubert, 'so don't whinge.'

'I'm not whingeing. Why should they employ me, anyway? I've had no experience as a practice nurse.'

'Don't be defeated before you even start. You can give injections and bandage bits and pieces.'

'There's more to it than that, Hubert.'

'You'll have to take yourself off to the library, then, and make yourself an expert.'

He went back downstairs to do whatever undertakers do when they're not actually at funerals and I daydreamed for a while. Not about being a practice nurse but about being called in to help with the case. Called in by whom, that was the question. Private investigators are not viewed kindly by the police, especially young female ones (relatively young anyway), and to the more senior members of Longborough CID I am most definitely *persona non grata.*

Poor Jenny Martin. I wondered how she'd died. Was she married? Where did she die? Perhaps tomorrow's *Echo* would have more details. Naturally nosy though, and bored to tears, I decided not to wait. I'd drive out to Dunsmore and see what I could find out by a process of lies and deceit. This may not work for normal law-abiding people but seems to work well for newspaper reporters and private investigators.

On my way out I called in at Hubert's rather splendid office. 'I'm off home,' I said, 'not much point in hanging around.'

He looked a bit disappointed. 'You never know, you could miss a big case by not being in your office at the right time.'

'And then again I might just find a piece of the action in the big world outside this grim place.'

Anxiety flickered in his brown eyes.

'It's not that grim, is it?' he asked. 'I mean, I don't see it like others see it. This is my home.'

I smiled. 'Sorry, Hubert, I didn't mean to upset you. My staircase is a bit grim, but I quite like all that purply gothic atmospheric stuff.'

'You're winding me up.'

'Just paying you back, Hubert.'

His face crinkled a bit, halfway between a smile and a grimace.

'Hubert,' I said, 'as a funeral directors' this establishment does, in my humble opinion, provide a sympathetic, splendid service. You manage that air of gravitas without being unctuous.'

'You've been studying the *Reader's Digest* again, Kate. Doing the word-power page.'

'You buy it, Hubert.'

He shrugged. 'See you in the morning?'

'At the crack.'

As I opened his office door to leave I couldn't resist asking, 'How's Dolly Two-Shoes?'

He scowled. 'It's Dorothy Tweedle, as you well know. And she's fine. I'm taking her out to dinner tonight to the Grand.'

'Just you behave yourself then,' I said as I closed the door. I could still hear his retort, though. 'You just wait, Kate Kinsella—one day you'll fall in love again.' 'Not if I can help it,' I muttered. But what really worried me was Dolly Two-Shoes—was she good enough for Hubert? Was she after his money or his body? Even more worrying was that it might not be either. Perhaps she was just a shoe exhibitionist, if there is such a thing.

Driving to Dunsmore in my clapped-out purple-sprayed car I tried to dwell not on Hubert's problems but on exactly how I was going to find out more about Jenny Martin. First I had to find out where she lived. Once more the public library would be the best place to start. There I would be able to get the council tax listings and from the telephone directory her phone number. That is of course if the library was open.

Dunsmore was not aptly named—it couldn't have done less. It was a dull, dreary market town that had been pedestrianized, no doubt to keep people from driving straight through. It was a defeated sort of place, empty or closed shops lining the precinct. It did, however have a rather splendid spired church, flanked by lawns and flower-beds. And it did have free parking.

I found the library quite easily just off the High Street, as grimly Victorian on the outside it was as grim inside. The dark green paintwork in the entrance, the stone floors and smell of disinfectant that seemed to emanate from both reminded me of a public lavatory. There were two available librarians, one, middle-aged, well scrubbed and dressed in navy blouse, navy jumper, navy skirt, only needed a toggle to be an akela in charge of a pack of cub scouts. The other wore a long floral skirt and a white lacy blouse, with a small purse slung at waist level from her shoulder. I presumed this was to deter muggers with scissors at the ready. She, in particular, had a wary pinched look but they both eyed me somewhat suspiciously when I asked to see the council tax register. I smiled a lot and said I was desperate to find an old school friend who I was sure was living in the area.

I was directed to a table by Akela who seemed very pleasant to her regular borrowers and was frequently ap-

proached by elderly people requesting help to find them a
'good read'.

I found the Martins in the register. There were six. I
quickly copied down the addresses. Then I searched the
telephone directory. There were five. I couldn't be so crass
as to telephone and ask for Jenny so I'd have to think of
another strategy. As I sat there wondering quite what to do,
I remembered I wasn't on an investigation, well not a paid
one, and I really couldn't afford to satisfy my curiosity at
the expense of missing out on a possible job. I could, if I
had the brass neck, simply find Riverview Medical Centre
and ask for poor Jenny's job. Did I have that sort of courage, though? Of course I did. They could only say no.

Undoubtedly there would be a practice manager to deal
with. They're usually a fearsome breed who hold a Chan-
cellor of the Exchequer's power, especially when the GPs
are budget holders. Why GPs should be expected not only
to take responsibility for the sick but also have to find the
cheapest treatment and then compete for that treatment is
beyond me. It all seems so devilishly cunning.

Akela informed me Riverview Medical Centre was on
the outskirts of town. Or to be exact, 'Go out of here, turn
right, past two small roundabouts, collect car,' she smiled
as she said that, 'drive for about one hundred yards, sharp
right, carrying straight on, then take the fourth left, then
second right. It's a fairly new estate—Riverview Medical
Centre is at the bottom of Riverview Lane.'

Confused I certainly was, but I didn't want to appear
stupid so I thanked her and left hurriedly. As I walked away
from the library I tried hard to remember the directions. I
hadn't really concentrated properly, I'd been too busy being
mesmerized by the woman's flaring nostrils and the soft
breathless quality of her voice. Anyway, I did remember to
turn right and pass the two roundabouts which would at
least return me to the car park.

On the way to the medical centre, I tried to concentrate on actually finding my way but I also had to formulate some sort of opening for applying for a job that hadn't been advertised and might not exist. Then I remembered I was wearing jeans and a sweatshirt. The jeans were at least black. Did I in fact look like practice nurse material? Would my car be seen? Was this down at heel approach one they wanted to foster?

Once in Riverview Lane I decided that my image was most definitely wrong. The lane was bordered by large neat bungalows. A newish estate where lawns undulated in smooth mounds, where garden gnomes guarded small ponds, where weeds only peeked up through the earth momentarily to be killed with speed and precision. Where the world was evergreen and *Gardener's World* the voice of God. I drove very slowly. I'd have to think this one through.

TWO

I'D ALMOST DECIDED to turn back when I realized it was too late. I'd come to the end of Riverview Lane and although what I saw didn't look like a medical centre there were so many police cars and uniformed police about I knew that I must have found the place where Jenny had worked. Parking was going to be difficult, if not impossible. I had two options, reverse back at speed or brazen it out. Deciding not to do either, I stopped, lowered my head and pretended to be rummaging through my handbag.

Not many of the uniformed branch know me but if the CID from Longborough were in evidence they would wonder what the hell I was doing there. I hoped that Dunsmore CID hadn't joined forces with them.

Somewhat furtively I glanced up. The river was more of a stream really, some way behind the two bungalows, which were separated not by a wall or bushes but by a low plaque on a wrought-iron stand saying RIVERVIEW MEDICAL CENTRE. A weeping willow stood to the left of the bungalow on the right-hand side; vertically challenged conifers lined the frontages. The small lawns between bungalows and conifers were as neat as carpets. It was all very discreet, as if being a medical centre was something not to be too well advertised, especially in a lane that had garden gnomes and waterfalls. Did I want to work in such a place anyway?

The police still milled around. I could ring from home, I decided. I started the engine, urging it gently not to make any unforgivable exhaust noises. It complied, but then had the temerity to stall as I tried to do a perfect three-point turn. A young constable watched me eagerly. Luckily he wasn't quite near enough to see that my tyres verged on bald and my tax disc was out of date by two weeks. But he did begin to walk towards me. In my rear-view mirror I saw his face drop as I completed my four-point turn and drove off.

It was by now three thirty. I could I supposed go back to Dunsmore and ring from a phone box there; then have tea and a bun in a café and hone in on the locals talking about the murder. Or I could drive round to the Martin house and pretend to be from the press. I like to think it was moral conscience that stopped me doing the latter but it wasn't—I'd noticed my petrol gauge was nearly on empty. I could just about get back to Longborough. Anyway mere nosiness didn't pay any bills. I had no reason to get involved at all.

Hubert was just returning from a funeral as I arrived back in Longborough. He wore his usual black ensemble and sombre expression but he smiled and waved as I drove into my parking space at the back of Humberstones. He came up to the car as I was getting out. His smile hadn't lasted long.

'Your tyres are bald,' he said. I tried to block his way so that he couldn't see the front of the car but that didn't stop him. 'And you shouldn't be on the road. You're not legal.'

I muttered something about getting an MOT done soon but I could see he wasn't convinced. 'You're off the road from now on then, aren't you?'

I nodded. Poverty and unemployment does that to you— makes you meek! Takes away your bargaining power. 'The meek shall inherit the earth,' I said.

'I won't be holding my breath, then,' said Hubert, as he passed me by on his way to the front of the building.

I walked up the two dark and narrow flights of stairs to

my office. Day and night the light bulb glowed from inside a purple-fringed lamp. All it needed at the top of the stairs was a picture by Munch—*The Scream*. I didn't feel like screaming but I did feel ready for a good mope. If I couldn't drive then I couldn't get back to my cottage in Farley Wood. I checked my purse for money—a fruitless pursuit. I had enough for about half a gallon of petrol or a bar of chocolate and a doughnut or two. I checked again, unbelieving, peering into the side compartment—which was empty except for two receipts and a book of second-class stamps.

I made myself a cup of instant coffee and sat staring out at the High Street, watching somewhat enviously as the day-time population of Longborough made their way home to cooked meals, a bit of gardening and TV. In my spartan office I had no stove to cook on, no TV to watch and only a camp bed to sleep on. I've often been told life isn't a bed of roses, as if that's a consolation. Of course life is a bed of roses; roll over on one and you get a thorn in the back-side.

I tried then to contact Riverview Medical Centre. The line was engaged. I tried again and again and again. Then I slammed down the receiver in irritation.

My good mope had turned into an 'Is life worth living?' scenario by the time I saw Hubert again. He appeared in my doorway wearing a smart grey suit and blue tie. The hairs on his head had been carefully arranged in an attempt to hide the baldness beneath. It hadn't worked but he did look very presentable. Dolly Two-Shoes should be impressed.

'Well?' he asked.

'You look very nice, Hubert.'

'Nice? Don't I look a bit sexy?'

'In a Norman Tebbit sort of way, yes.'

'I'd rather look like John Major.'

'Tough,' I said. 'I'd rather look like Princess Di.'

That silenced him for a moment. Then he said, 'If you're quick you'll find fish and chips in the oven and a bottle of wine on the table in my flat.'

'And if I'm slow,' I asked, smiling.

He shrugged. 'If she stands me up I'll be back to share it with you.'

'She won't stand you up, Hubert.'

'It's happened before,' he said.

'Well, it won't happen this time.'

'You're not right about many things.'

I ignored that remark. 'Thanks for the fish and chips. I was sinking into the proverbial doldrums.'

'I've a feeling about the Martin murder,' said Hubert. 'It could be a lucky break for you.'

'How?'

'Just a hunch.'

I managed to laugh. 'I'm the one who's supposed to have the hunches.'

'Huh!' said Hubert as he left.

I decided to dress down for my meal. I changed into a black track suit. It's hard when you're not working to *want* to look smart. You feel all dressed up with nowhere to go. Tonight I wanted to feel relaxed.

Compared with my office and box-room Hubert's flat was palatial. His kitchen boasted a state of the art cooker and with its lights shining and the smell of fish and chips permeating the air it made me feel a lot more cheerful. He'd opened a bottle of Australian red for me and the table was laid. I switched on his portable TV, drank a glass of wine and counted my blessings; Hubert was most definitely amongst their number.

Halfway through my fish and chips the local news came on. The murder of Jenny Martin was, of course, the top news story. She was thirty-four years old, married and the

police had a good description of the man who could help
with their enquiries. And they had a name for him too. A
joyrider aged nineteen who was known to the police in
three counties as Nick 'the Ace' Fenny. It seems he had
been stealing cars from the time he could reach the pedals.
He was also keen on arson and nearly always managed to
leave his stolen vehicles burnt out.

The cause of Jenny Martin's death had not yet been dis-
closed but I got the distinct impression from the police
inspector who was interviewed that he thought Nick 'the
Ace' was capable of any crime, was as dangerous as a
Rottweiler on heat and should not be approached.

Car theft and joyriding has become a bit of a problem in
Longborough. The large council estate on the outskirts of
town is constantly blamed as being a haven for psychopathic would-be car killers. In reality most car stealing in
Longborough is committed by bored little boys who doubt
they will ever grow into big boys earning enough to buy
their own cars. Probably they think they're such good drivers that not only do they live charmed lives but other drivers and pedestrians do too. Drunk drivers seem to think
likewise.

I drank most of the wine then moved into the lounge,
switched on Hubert's huge TV and curled up on one of the
plush cream sofas. The black-stemmed lamps with their
cerise shades were alight. I felt warm and cosy. I waited to
be entertained. It wasn't to be. It was one of those evenings
on TV when you can't escape worthy programmes. Programmes you think you ought to watch out of misplaced
masochism. Programmes that leave you wondering how
you dare to be so complacent about just being alive. In
those few hours there were so many things to take a smile
off anyone's face. There was bereavement, homelessness,
war, famine, gun-running, bombs, Aids, ecological di-
sasters. Followed by unemployment and *Crime Watch*.

By the time Hubert came home at midnight I was never so pleased to see anyone. Not that he reciprocated. He had a face like thunder. 'You haven't even washed up,' he said as he peered into the kitchen.

'I'll do it now,' I said, 'I didn't expect you home so early.' He didn't answer but stomped into the kitchen and moved about noisily for a while. Then he came back into the lounge with half a glass of red wine in his hand, saying, 'You could have left me a whole glass.' Then he sat down heavily on the sofa opposite mine; held the glass in his hand as if it were a crystal ball and stared into it.

'Hubert, are you going to tell me what happened or do I have to guess?'

He looked up at me warily. 'I'm in love,' he said.

'Oh,' I said, 'is that all? I thought it was serious.'

'You've got no feelings, Kate. It's worse at my age.'

'Why?'

He shrugged. 'I dunno. It feels like your last chance. I'm so scared I'll botch it.'

'What happened this evening?'

He stared down into the wine again and mumbled: 'We had a nice meal at the Grand, went for a drive, walked along the canal. Then when we got back to her place she didn't invite me in for coffee...' He paused to take a swig of the wine.

'Perhaps she didn't have any Gold Blend.'

Hubert nearly choked. 'That's typical of you, Kate. It's no wonder you haven't got a man.'

That hurt, but I didn't let it show. 'Hubert,' I said quietly, 'just because she didn't invite you in doesn't mean she doesn't fancy you.'

'It doesn't?'

'No. I take it you've arranged to meet again.'

'Yes.'

'Well, then. She must like you. She probably doesn't want to rush you.'

He thought about that for a few moments. 'What should I do?' he asked.

'Take her out and then ask her back here. If she wants a chaperone tell her I'll sit between you.'

He managed a half smile. 'That won't be necessary, Kate.'

I made us both cocoa then and Hubert lost his stricken look. We sat for a while watching a late-night chat show.

'By the way, Kate,' he said, 'I nearly forgot. I found out something at the Grand. Of course it could only be rumour...'

'Yes?' I said eagerly.

'The murder victim's car could have been stolen from outside the adult education centre. Jenny Martin was taking evening classes.'

'So?'

'Well, that particular evening the centre wasn't running her class, the tutor was ill.'

I didn't quite know what to say to that. 'How exactly did you find this out, Hubert?'

'I listened to the conversation at the next table.'

'I hope you didn't neglect Do—Dorothy while you were eavesdropping.'

'Of course not.'

'Good, I'm glad to hear it. I'm going to bed now, Hubert. I'll see you tomorrow and as soon as I'm working again I shall buy you a present.'

'What?'

'A large jar of Gold Blend coffee—then all the coffees can be yours.'

'You're not funny, Kate. Goodnight.'

THE NEXT MORNING I began ringing Riverview at eight

twenty-five. At eight thirty exactly I struck lucky. A pleasant voice answered my query.

'The practice manager isn't in until nine but if you'd like to leave your telephone number I'll get him to ring you back.' Him! I thought. General practice was changing. I stayed by the phone hopefully all morning. I dusted my two rooms, cleaned the sink, polished my desk, tidied the filing cabinet, made my bed, bit my nails and still had change from an hour. Unemployment was making me demented.

At one o'clock the phone rang.

'Hello, Miss Kinsella,' said a smooth deep voice. 'Riverview practice manager here. I believe you were making enquiries about a job here as a practice nurse. Do you have any experience?'

'Of nursing?'

'Of practice nursing.'

'I do have accident and emergency experience and I'm quite well versed in preventative health care.' (A slight exaggeration.)

'Hmm,' he said, then there was a long pause. 'We do need someone, as you've probably heard. Our last practice nurse...was tragically killed.'

'Oh dear,' I murmured.

'It could be an awkward time for anyone new but as I said we do need someone pronto. I'll have to take up references before the interview. When would you be able to start?'

'Whenever you want.'

'I see, you're not working at the moment.'

'I have done agency work until fairly recently but there isn't any work at the moment.'

'Quite. What's your UKCC number?'

'Hold on, please.' I rummaged in my desk drawer like a deranged mole and eventually found my card. I gave him the number. Luckily the expiry date was a year hence. Otherwise—no payment, no nursing work.

'I'll make a provisional date for interview tomorrow, that's Wednesday, at 2 p.m. Tonight I'll pop an application form in the post to you. Please bring it with you to your interview.'

'I will, thank you.'

As I put down the phone I realized I was wary of the practice manager with no name. He sounded a real smoothie—not in what he said but the way that he said it. And I got the impression that he thought Jenny Martin had been somehow disloyal in getting herself murdered.

THREE

JUST BEFORE 2 p.m. on Wednesday I arrived, by Daimler, in Riverview Lane. Hubert insisted on driving me but I insisted no one saw us. I sank as far down in the front seat as possible and asked Hubert to drop me at the top of the lane. Arriving in a hearse was the way not to get a nursing job. Hubert had, in ways he often keeps secret, managed to glean a few more bits of information about the murder: Jenny Martin had, according to him, been hit over the head then strangled, and Nick 'the Ace' Fenny, the chief witness and suspect, had gone to ground. That was all; and although I was interested I told myself it was none of my business.

I slunk out of the Daimler and hurried down the lane at a brisk trot. I saw the large backsides of two residents who seemed to be grovelling in the soil as if praying to the deity responsible for handsome petunias. I hoped no one lurking behind lace nets saw me.

Today there were no police in evidence and as I neared the medical centre I slowed right down so that I wasn't puffing. I had a choice between the right bungalow and the left. I chose the left. The front door merely said 'Enter' so I did. The receptionist sat at a desk in the hallway. Health promotion leaflets decorated the walls and a further selection was housed in a plastic stand near the receptionist's arm. She was in her twenties with a cheerful smile and blue eyes that were slightly crossed. She asked me to wait in the adjoining waiting-room.

A plastic-coated bench lined one wall and there was a variety of straight-backed chairs along the other two. In one of them sat a middle-aged woman who was staring out of the window. She looked up once, I smiled—she didn't. She had a face as long as a frosty bucket. If she was the only other candidate then I was in with a chance.

In the middle of the room was a coffee table scattered with more leaflets and some magazines: *Acupuncture Today*, *Reflexology News* and *Aromatherapy Update*.

These magazines worried me. I know hardly anything about alternative therapies and although I had spent a week reading through a book on practice nursing in the local book shop (I couldn't find one in the library) it had merely covered 'straight' issues. Hubert had taken a passing interest in *Reflexology News*, but only because he's excited by feet.

There was a corner table in the room too with upright books and above that certificates mounted in glass on the wall. Two names cropped up: Amroth and Holland. Dr. Amroth, it seems, had been in the army and had acquired a first-aid certificate in 1956. That was disquieting. Somehow you feel first aid should have been incorporated into medical training.

The woman in the corner continued to glower towards the outside world. Perhaps she was nervous I thought. It was then that I heard more footsteps and into the room came—the real competition. She was so...smart and pretty. Fair hair tied back with a black bow, grey suit, crisp white blouse, tall and slim as a model. I hated her! Then she smiled a ravishing smile. 'I'm Gina,' she said. 'My appointment's for two fifteen—when's yours?'

'Two,' I mumbled. I glanced at my watch. It was now two fifteen. She smiled at me again and sat down next to misery personified. Within minutes they were chatting together. Not only was she stunning looking she was also *nice*. The practice nurse's job was slipping away from me as fast as an eel down a drain. Already I'd begun to justify not getting the job by telling myself I'd have hated it anyway.

The sound of heavy male footsteps made the three of us look up. A tall man in his early thirties stood there, craggily good looking and dressed in a sharp blue-grey suit. His black hair was close cropped, his eyebrows thick and bushy. I'm a sucker for intrepid-type men and he looked pretty intrepid to me. When he said in a deep, smooth voice 'Miss Kinsella?' I didn't budge. 'Miss Kinsella,' he said again. This time I found my voice. 'That's me,' came out in a high-pitched croak. He smiled a smile of dazzling white. 'Follow me,' he said.

I will I will, I thought.

Once in the consulting room he shook my hand saying, 'I'm Alan Dakers—you're...Kate, I believe.'

I would have been anyone he wanted.

'I'm the practice manager. Do sit down. The senior partner, Dr Charles Amroth, has been delayed but he'll be with us shortly. In the mean time perhaps you could tell me a little bit about yourself.'

The next few minutes were just about the most embarrassing of my life. I babbled on, unable to think or talk in sequence and all the time trying to avoid any mention of Medical and Nursing Investigations. I told him I'd come to Longborough to nurse an elderly aunt who had subsequently died and I'd decided to stay on. All lies of course but now I'd got into the swing, I almost believed in dear old Aunt Edie myself.

'I see,' he murmured encouragingly and there was even the occasional 'Good—good', and 'Fine, fine.'

Dr Amroth arrived then, looking harassed. I guessed he was in his fifties. His thin tall body was bulked out with a padded floral waistcoat. His hair was greying but still thick and he wore gold-rimmed glasses which failed to hide the bags beneath sad grey eyes. I didn't like the look of him.

He lowered his glasses to the end of his sharpish nose and stared at me. I liked him even less then.

'You're single?' he asked.

'Yes.'

'Likely to get married?'

'Not in the foreseeable future.'

'On the pill?'

'Well...' I blustered. 'Only when...necessary.'

'Good, good. I prefer not to lose our practice nurses through pregnancy and we're really looking for someone who is likely to...stay for some time.'

That made me feel about as desirable as an elderly nun with a peg-leg. But I smiled and nodded.

'Now then. To business.' He then proceeded to fire questions at me ranging from pre-birth to the grave. He even went beyond that by asking if I believed in life after death.

'No,' I answered firmly.

'I do,' he said coldly.

Well, that's it, I thought, but he managed to smile at me once or twice especially when he heard I could do cervical smears and was willing to immunize babies. He smiled quite broadly when I said I was also willing to do nursing assessments on the elderly. He rounded off the interview by asking me what I knew about alternative therapies.

'I do think they are very valuable for treating stress. Reflexology and aromatherapy in particular...'

I mumbled on for a while longer. Well, I had once had lavender oil on my pillow and I'd experienced reflexology at Hubert's hand. I was quite an expert really.

He then explained that competition and budget holding was now the name of the game. He'd started the practice eight years ago with doctors Thruxton and Wheatly, Holland joining them three years ago. But now times had changed, it was no longer doctor versus doctor who were in competition with each other. It was patient versus patient.

'We no longer talk about the deserving poor, we now talk about the deserving sick. Unfortunate as it may seem, that is the trend. The elderly, the mentally ill, smokers, the overweight, even those with genetically determined diseases are all the undeserving sick. You see, the government can quite easily say that ill health is simply down to the individual. They have only themselves to blame, don't they? If they worked harder and dragged themselves out of poverty, ate plenty of carrots and oranges and did more exercise—the elixir of life would be theirs. The NHS could then run at a fraction of today's cost.'

Was he serious? He watched me carefully. I didn't respond and, he went on. 'That is why we do offer alternative therapies. Often there isn't anything else.'

I began to feel really depressed then.

There was silence for a few minutes whilst Dr Amroth read through my application form as carefully, if not more so, than a barrister reading evidence. Alan Dakers winked at me. Dr Amroth looked up and fixed me with a somewhat worried stare.

'As you know, our last practice nurse has died in tragic circumstances. We've all been very distressed—particularly the patients. Jenny was a good listener and a very good nurse. Anyone who takes over will find they have a lot to live up to. The police have been much in evidence and generally we all feel rather upset. It will be a difficult transition period for any newcomer. Would that bother you?'

I thought about that for a moment. I couldn't afford to be thought wimpy. 'I'm very resilient,' I said, 'and hopefully, in time, any successor will eventually become an accepted part of the team.' I smiled feebly. Did what I'd just said make sense? Dr Amroth didn't smile back. He shook

me by the hand. 'We'll let you know,' he said, 'by the end
of the week. Thank you for coming.'

Alan Dakers showed me out. He *did* smile at me, said,
'Nice to meet you, Kate,' and shook my hand. Was it my
imagination or did he hold it for longer than necessary? I
was definitely smitten.

It was only when I began walking up the lane that I
thought of all the things I could have said. I could have
been more dynamic, used more jargon, talked more about
holistic approaches. But then since ill health was caused by
people being people it wouldn't have made much difference.

'How did it go?' asked Hubert.

I shrugged. 'There is something wrong with a society
that tries to make people feel guilty about being ill, isn't
there?'

'Of course there is, Kate. Don't worry about it, doctors
are the first to take to drink and then top themselves...no,
farmers are the worst.'

'I don't think I've got the job anyway. There was a gorgeous blonde waiting to be interviewed. I bet she gets it.'

'She might be too good-looking, then. You could well
be in with a chance.'

Was that a sort of compliment? I wondered. I decided it
wasn't.

The drive back was smooth and leisured. A Daimler, I
decided, was quite the most comfortable way to travel.

'Did you find out anything about Jenny Martin?' Hubert
asked.

'I found out she was a good listener, a good nurse and
that she'd be sadly missed.'

'I found something out.'

'How?'

'I just walked down the lane and praised one or two
gardeners. They were quite forthcoming.'

'What was your angle? Journalist on the *Sun*, or old friend of the family?'

'Neither,' said Hubert. 'I was more subtle than that. I just told the truth—that I was an undertaker.'

'And?'

'And I'd been privileged to deal with the Martin family in the past.'

'I have to hand it to you, Hubert. It's not imaginative but if it worked it's not only subtle, it's brilliant.'

'Are you taking the mickey?'

'Would I, Hubert? Just keep your eyes on the road. All this excitement could be too much for the both of us.'

Hubert grunted in annoyance. After a while he said, 'Do you want to know what I found out?'

I nodded half-heartedly. 'I only wish I had a vested interest. I feel I'm just being nosy for the sake of it. After all, the police do seem to know who did it.'

'Ah,' said Hubert, 'but do they? My gardening friends seem to think the police are barking up the wrong tree. Quite soon I think you might be a bit more...involved.'

'Come on, Hubert, stop...well...trying to be mysterious, it doesn't suit you.'

'You'll see,' he said. 'Now tell me a bit more about your interview.'

I omitted to tell him how attractive Alan Dakers was. Hubert is the sort who sees future heartbreak around every corner so I thought it better to gloss over Alan's potential in the romance stakes.

Hubert drove me back to my cottage in Farley Wood. I prefer cottage to terrace—it sounds detached. Actually my place is one of a row of four opposite St Peter's church and the patch of village green. Now it's May and the oak tree by the church is in leaf, fresh blooms have been placed on the graves and front gardens have suddenly sprouted flowers—it really does look very attractive. In summer I think everyone should live in a village but in winter surely people need the comfort of warm shops, Chinese takeaways and the bustle of others around them. I've never seen anyone bustle in the winter in Farley Wood. The small population simply hibernates.

Hubert made it quite clear he wanted a cup of tea. He looked round my small front room somewhat disparagingly, then slipped me a tenner. I stared at the note.

'What's this for, Hubert?' I asked.

'Spot of polish and a bottle of Windowlene,' he said, without a trace of embarrassment. I tried to give him back the money.

'It's not that bad,' I protested. 'I'm quite insulted.'

'Come off it, Kate. It does need a bit of a spring clean.'

'I did it in the spring.'

'Which spring?'

Now that the sun shone in I could see the windows were smeary, the curtains less than fresh and there were one or two cobwebs in the corners. But generally, as my gran used to say, a blind man would have been glad to see it.

'Life's too short for worrying about a bit of dust,' I told him firmly, 'but I'll pay you back ASAP.'

I made him tea and hot buttered toast spread with honey and this seemed to restore his faith in me. When he left he said mysteriously, 'Be in the office early, Kate. I think there could be a phone call for you.'

'You're up to something, Hubert,' I said.

He shrugged, gave me a knowing smile and left.

FOUR

I WAS IN the office by eight thirty the next morning. I expected the phone to ring. I did, after all, know Hubert was up to something.

The day was already quite warm and sunny and I felt restless. There was nothing to tidy, nothing to do. I searched in my drawer for a novel to read. I found one, the rise and fall and rise again of a young girl in Victorian England. It passed the time until Hubert appeared at ten thirty.

'Had a phone call yet?' he asked as he thrust two jam doughnuts on paper plates into my hand.

'Several. One from New Scotland Yard asking me to investigate sightings of Asil Nadir in Scunthorpe, another one from *Penthouse* magazine wanting me to be centrefold of the month, another from...'

'That's enough sarcasm, Kate. There will be a phone call, I'm sure. Lunch time we can go down the pub. Dorothy will be there in her lunch break, it's about time you two met.'

'Sorry, Hubert, I'm not up to that mentally at the moment and I can't afford to buy a round so I'd be embarrassed.'

'Even when you had money you rarely bought a round...'

'That's not fair—*you* insisted on paying. And I *could* have bought a round—that's the difference.'

The phone rang then. It was Pauline Berkerly from the Berkerly Nursing Agency saying she might have some work for me. A woman who'd had a heart attack was being sent home on Monday and she lived alone. Would I like two nights looking after her?

'Great. Thanks. I'll do it.'

'I'll ring you Sunday. How are you, Kate?'

'Fine…but—'

'Bye, speak to you soon.'

The phone went dead. Just as well I didn't have a burning issue to discuss. I smiled at Hubert. He, at least, was always available. His face registered disappointment that it wasn't his caller. But when the phone rang again his mouth lifted somewhat in triumph.

'Is that the private tec?' asked a voice—female but with the throaty deepness of a smoker and probably drinker.

'Yes, Kate Kinsella, Medical and Nursing Investigations.'

'Do you do murders and that sort of thing?'

I hesitated. 'Well, yes, but usually it has a medical connection. Could you tell me something about the case?'

'That nurse in Dunsmore.'

'Yes?'

'Yeah…well…see, my boy. They want to do 'im for that. I mean he didn't do it. I'm telling you now he didn't do it.'

'How can I help?'

'You get 'im off. Find out who did kill 'er.'

'Private detective work is rather expensive and of course I may not be successful.'

'You better bleedin' had,' she said with a smile in her voice. 'Just cos I don't talk posh don't mean I can't pay.'

'Would you like to come to my office—Mrs…?'

'Rose Fenny. Yeah, OK. When?'

'This afternoon about two thirty?'

'Cheers, love. See you then.'

Hubert's initial look of triumph had become a positive gloat. 'Told you,' he said. 'I wangled that one for you. It's your lucky day. Just to cheer you up even more I'll bring you some chips when I come back from the pub.'

I protested somewhat feebly. 'I'll look like a chip soon. And my arteries won't just be thickened, they'll be full of crispy bits as well.'

Hubert smiled, 'You can start your healthy living when you get paid. Make sure, though, she gives you a week's money up front.'

'I will.'

As Hubert turned to go I said, 'By the way, Hubert, how exactly did you come to know Rose Fenny?'

He stood at the door for a moment and then tapped his nose with his index finger.

'Have a good time,' I said.

Rose Fenny arrived late. She burst into my office at three.

'Sorry love, I missed the bleedin' bus. You can't win, can you?' She smiled a crooked yellow smile, hitched up her black short skirt and sat down. She wore a tight red vest-style T-shirt with off-white high heels and bare legs. She was, I supposed, about forty, her hair had cork-screw curls dangling by her ears and her blusher had been applied in a thick brown triangle on otherwise pale cheeks.

'Mind if I smoke?'

I shook my head and found her an old saucer for an ashtray. She fumbled in a battered-looking clutch bag and brought out a packet of tobacco and some papers and care-fully rolled herself a thin cigarette. 'D'you want one?' she asked.

I shook my head. 'I don't smoke.'

'I can't do without a ciggie. Well it's either smokes or Valium in' it?' She lit the cigarette, inhaled deeply and murmured, 'That's better.'

'How can I help you, Mrs Fenny?'

'Call me Rose. You said you did murders?'

'I've been involved in murder cases but I'm not police and I don't have access to their information.'

'Yeah, but you know the people to ask—whose keyholes to look through.'

'Oh, yes, of course,' I said, trying to sound totally sure of myself without being cocksure.

'My Nick's in real trouble. Nick is where he's going to land up if he's not careful.'

'He hasn't been in trouble before, then?'

Rose chuckled throatily. 'Course he has, love. Never out of bleedin' trouble.'

'In what way?'

'Taking and driving away mostly. A bit of shop-lifting when he was younger.'

'How young?'

'Ten. He got in with an older crowd. He's tall, see, people think he's older than he is.'

'What about his father?'

'Him! The bastard! Where d'you think he learned how to drive away anything on four wheels? My old man taught Nick every crime in the book...you know, like some men take their sons to football matches. Well, instead of that, he took him on jobs. Small ones at first, house clearance he called it. But he got a bit ambitious, decided to do a ram-raid on a post office. The bloke in the post office whistled and let loose this bloody great big Dobermann. My old man's even scared of terriers so he froze and the others did a runner. He just stood there, the great prat, until the police came. The dog never even touched him.'

'Where is he now?'

'The Dobermann?'

I smiled. 'No, your husband.'

'Oh, yeah. He's inside. He got ten years. He's done four. He's happy enough. He's got no worries, has he? Mind you,

I don't look forward to him coming out. I mean he won't be out long enough for me to get used to it, will he?'

'Tell me about Nick. Is he your only child?'

'I've got a girl as well. She's seventeen and useless. I mean I think I'd have preferred it if she took to crime. She took to sex instead. She's expecting her second kid. She's only a few weeks gone but she won't hear of getting rid of it. Still, she's not a bad little mum...we'll cope, I suppose.'

'And Nick?'

'Yeah, well. He's not a bad kid really. He's not violent, I'll tell you that from the off. There's no way he'd hit a woman, especially one he didn't know. He's never laid a hand on me and he's bin ever so good to his sister. Her kid's never gone without and never will.'

'Where's Nick now? I mean if he didn't do it, surely he should come forward and explain.'

'Don't be sodding daft,' said Rose, smiling and relighting her cigarette. 'The police have already decided it's him. They think she found him trying to get into the car. He was supposed to have killed her, they won't tell me how, and then bundled the body into the boot.'

'What do you think happened?'

'Well, I don't know exactly, do I? But I think he saw the car—it was a Golf. He quite likes them but he's not mad on them. He prefers Jags, Mercs, and he quite likes them Jeep things but he's a lazy git and he doesn't like a lot of effort—so if the owner turned up he'd just do a runner. He's a coward like his dad. Nice, easy crime, that's what they like.'

'Why then are the police so convinced he murdered Jenny Martin?'

Rose stared at me closely for a while. 'You had much experience of the police, 'ave you?'

I smiled. 'Not as much as you.'

'I've had a lifetime. I'm telling you they're lazy gits,

most of them. They want a result the easiest way possible, especially with a one-off. Now serial killers there's something they get down to. But one-offs, that's different.'

'So you think just for the sake of expediency they'll convict Nick?'

'You talk like a bleedin' lawyer. But yeah. They'll find him eventually and they'll put him away for years and years for something he didn't do. And just because they couldn't get off their fat arses.'

Rose began to roll another cigarette. For all her bravado I sensed she was really upset but so far she hadn't managed to convince me of Nick's integrity.

'Let's go back over what you've just said, Rose,' I suggested, like a Relate counsellor coming to a sticky patch. 'You say Nick isn't a violent type. What about girlfriends? Could he be staying with one of them?'

'He's had a couple, but nothing serious and he treated them well. The Old Bill have already checked them out.'

At this point I was stumped. I sat back in my swivel chair and stayed silent. Another ploy—someone has to speak to break the uncomfortable silence. Rose watched me intently and then stared at the deceased cigarette in her fingers as if her life was already down to a fag end. She relit the end, took a drag and said, 'If there was any blood he couldn't have coped. My Nick is ever so squeamish, he vomits and passes out at the sight of blood. And anyway, he's never been one to fight his way of trouble. He's like his dad. If they catch him he'll—well, he'll just put his hands up, keep his mouth shut and do his bird. That's what a man does—or so his pillock of a father told him.'

There was another silence while I thought about what I was going to do.

'I've got money,' said Rose. 'I've been told you charge two hundred a week plus expenses and another two hundred when you get him off.'

I raised my eyebrows slightly as she produced a wad of notes.

'No need to look so surprised, love. My old man may be a stupid sod but he was quite successful in his own way. If that Doberman hadn't cornered him he'd still be providing.'

I hesitated for only a moment. I liked Rose. She had a sense of humour. 'I'll take the case on one condition.'

'Yeah?'

'If Nick contacts you, you have to tell me. He may have seen something that night and I'll need to know. Will you promise me?'

She smiled. 'I trust you. He won't come near our house though, he knows the police will be keeping an eye on the place.'

'But he'll ring you?'

'He'll do that, all right.'

'When he does, I want to arrange a meeting. I'll leave where and when to you.'

She looked undecided, then shrugged. 'Yeah, OK. It's a deal.'

We shook hands. And then she pressed the wad of notes in my hand.

'There's more where that came from, luv, so don't worry about being paid.'

When she'd gone I did a little jig around my desk and then felt guilty that I should benefit from someone else's misfortune. Then I remembered Hubert and debt collectors and judges and bailiffs. Lots of jobs were based on that premiss. And now I could pay my rent, buy Hubert a round in the pub, even tax the car.

I stopped jigging. I hadn't won the pools. The first week's money was already spent. All I could hope was that finding Nick would take some time.

FIVE

Being comparatively rich now I put my car in for its MOT and unbeknown to Hubert persuaded one of his drivers to loan me his Mini.

The journey to Dunsmore the next day was somewhat blighted by the memory of the mechanic's face when he saw my car, the sort of face surgeons put on when telling someone devastating news.

I spent some time wandering round the Dunsmore council estate, trying to find out more about Nick 'the Ace' Fenny. Local school children, I hoped, would be the most helpful. Especially those who weren't actually at school.

I met a group coming out of the fish and chip shop just after one thirty. I suppose they were thirteen or fourteen. My guess about them being helpful was incorrect. Perhaps interrupting boys with bags of chips and cans of Coke was a stupid move. I did say, 'Excuse me—I'm enquiring about Nick Fenny,' which I found didn't have the desired effect.

'Get 'er! Want a chip?' A bag of greasy-looking chips was thrust menacingly under my nose. 'No thanks—but I'll buy you some more if you can tell me a bit about Nick.'

'Take more than a bag of chips,' said the tallest of the four boys. He had a quarter-inch of shaved fair hair, a gold earring and a round pugnacious face. 'You from the papers?' I nodded. 'What's it worth, then? How much are you going to pay us?'

The other boys were now standing round me—waiting. 'I don't expect you know anything,' I said, adding, 'and why aren't you at school?'

Pugnacious-face didn't even blink but continued eating

his chips. 'How much?' he asked, bringing his face close to mine so that I could smell the vinegar on his breath. 'Forget it,' I said nonchalantly as I shrugged my shoulders and started to walk away. 'Tell you what,' said pug-face following me quickly and then standing splay-legged in front of me, 'make it a fiver and we'll tell you what we know about Nick.' I felt in my pocket and held out the fiver. He snatched it from my hand.

'Ta,' he said. 'I'll tell you about Nick. He's a fucking good driver.' Then he laughed. They all laughed. 'See yer,' he said. In a body they threw down their empty chip packets and ran off.

I put the fiver down to experience, thanked my lucky stars I wasn't involved in teaching them the National Curriculum and made for the post office which was further along a dismal row of five shops which the estate had the nerve to call 'The Shopping Parade.'

I'd failed dismally with the young but perhaps the elderly could tell me more. On a metal bench near the post office sat two white-haired ladies, obviously waiting for it to open at two. One smiled and moved along the bench as I sat down. She had a wizened little face, thin wispy hair and sparkling white teeth. 'Nice day today. Hasn't been a good start to the summer so far, has it?' the woman beside her said. 'We shouldn't complain, should we?' She had a round face with purple veins on her cheeks and a gash of red lipstick that clashed. Both wore winter coats.

'You just don't know what to wear this weather, do you,' she asked looking straight ahead. It wasn't a question of course so I gave a non-committal little laugh and muttered. 'That's true.'

There was silence for a moment as we all stared ahead at the post office door. Then I asked, 'Do you both live round here?'

'It's not what it used to be. It was quite nice once,' said

the lady with well-bleached teeth in a high squeaky voice.
'I've been here ever since I got married. I lost my husband
five years ago this Christmas. I'm glad he didn't live to see
it. Terrible it is sometimes round here. Terrible—' She
broke off, as if I should know exactly what she meant.

'In what way?' I asked.

In unison they answered. 'Yobbos.'

'Fighting?'

'No. Not down my way. It's stealing cars and racing up
and down the road. Betty's is worse.'

Betty laughed. 'They don't start till late at night. I've
called the police several times but they say they're just kids
and there's not much they can do. In my day kids played
kick the can and knock up ginger. I know we got up to
mischief but we never did no one any harm. Nowadays
some poor so and so gets killed every day by kids in cars.
And the parents—well, they don't seem to care. Too busy,
most of them, watching videos or drinking.'

'What about Nick Fenny? I hear he's the ring-leader.'

'I don't know about that. I know his mum. She's a nice
woman. Always has the time of day for you. Not like some
of them round here. Nick, I knew him when he was a tod-
dler. Nice little chap, always liked cars. I blame his dad.
His idea is pay for nothing and take what you want. That's
why he's in prison now. Still, Nick's never given me any
lip, not like some of them. What do you think, Maise?'

'He likes cars but he can drive,' she answered, 'even
when he was twelve he could drive. I don't think he's
caused any accidents—'

'He did, Maise,' interrupted Betty. 'Don't you remember,
he hit that tree once?'

Maise nodded slowly. 'I remember. That was the only
time around here. At least he doesn't cause any problems
on his own doorstep. He goes up Birmingham way. I don't

think his mum would put up with him upsetting the neighbors.'

'So you don't think he had anything to do with murdering that nurse?'

Betty laughed. 'Nah. I don't think so. What do you think, Maise?'

Maise shook her head. 'He's not a bad lad, really. He's just obsessed with cars. He's not one for fighting. I'm surprised he's run off like that. His mum was ever so upset.'

'What about the police?' I asked.

'What about them, dear?' asked Maise.

'Would they...well, would they be fed up with him and want to charge him with it, just to get him off the streets?'

Betty answered me. 'Dunno about that. When he did get caught he didn't give them any trouble. Believe you me, he's not as bad as some. The younger ones are the worst—little buggers, they are.'

The post office doors opened then and they both got up stiffly. I pressed a fiver in Betty's hand. 'Get some chocs for yourselves,' I said. She stared at the money in surprise.

'You from the papers?'

'Sort of,' I said.

'Well, much obliged, but don't put our names in, will you. We might get fire bombed.'

She smiled as she said it. I certainly hoped she was joking.

I went from there to 19 Cornwall Close, home of Rose Fenny. So far, in the realms of criminality Nick seemed somewhat of a paragon. There were a few things I still needed to find out. I knew the car had been stolen from the Dunsmore Adult Education Centre but I didn't know where the burnt-out car had been found or how the police had managed to identify the body so quickly.

Number 19 was easily the smartest terraced house in the close. Sparkling white loops of net curtains festooned the

windows, the small front lawn had been recently mowed
and a model stork sat staring into a square pond—at least
I thought it was a square pond until I realized it was a
mirror set in the lawn. Rose greeted me cheerfully at the
door. 'Come in, luv. I'm having a tidy up but I expect I
can find you a seat. Mind me carpet, I've just given it a
scrub.'

Various bits of cloth had been arranged in 'stepping
stones' over the hall carpet and it felt distinctly squelchy
underfoot. A strong smell of pine disinfectant mixed with
tobacco filled the air.

'Keep going luv, turn left,' urged Rose, who wore one
of those thick plastic aprons over cut-off blue jeans so that
for a moment I thought she wasn't wearing anything on her
bottom half. I opened the door to the through lounge which
was most definitely in the middle of a cleaning siege. The
dining-room table had upturned chairs on it, the three-piece
suite had been moved into the middle of the room, the
vacuum cleaner round and black as a cartoon bomb was
plugged in and obviously raring to go. A large plastic tub
had been filled to the brim with baby toys and Rose picked
up a feather duster from the coffee table and began flicking
it seriously along the top edge of the door. So this was
spring cleaning. Hubert would have been impressed.

'I've come at the wrong time, Rose,' I said. 'I should
have rung.'

'Don't you worry. I'm a cleaning fanatic. Today's my
day for downstairs.'

Day, I thought, *day!* 'You're not spring cleaning, then?'

She laughed throatily. 'I'm always fussy. We've been
done over by the police so many times I have to keep
everything under control.

'Done over?'

'Yeah—you know. Searched. There's no way I'm going
to have them going back to the station saying I'm filthy.'

I smiled and stood around while Rose finished vacuuming and dusting, then together we righted the furniture. She talked all the time. 'He hasn't rung me yet. He will though. The police came round yesterday—they weren't so bad, the inspector said he didn't think he'd done it, although he could have been saying that to butter me up—'

'I'm a bit confused, Rose,' I interrupted.

'Yeah?'

'Where exactly was the car found? I know Nick was supposed to have taken the car from Dunsmore, perhaps from the adult education centre, but where did he go from there and why did he set it on fire? And how do the police know it was Nick who took the car?'

'There's no mystery there—they clocked him driving it. I don't know what really happened, only what the Old Bill have told me. I do know he'd been on the lagers with his mates and I suppose he just thought he'd take it for a spin. A police patrol car clocked him going up the M1 towards Birmingham. They gave chase of course—they're as bad as the young lads, y'know. Just out for a thrill. Anyway they chased him, going bloody fast, but he outdrove them and then he came off the M1, drove the car into a field, set it alight and did a runner.'

'Did the car burn out?'

'No. The police were right behind him. They thought he was still in the car. They were ever so brave and managed to put out the fire. Then the boot shot open and they found the body of that woman—poor cow. Of course by this time Nick is well away.'

'So the body wasn't burned?'

'Not according to the Bill.'

By now the furniture was straight, the glass coffee table cleaned, the cushions plumped and a vase of dried flowers placed on the shiny black dining table. She gave a final dust over the television set and video which were secreted behind the doors of a TV cabinet. I was most impressed.

Rose could have given lessons in housewifely skills. 'Come on into the kitchen and we'll have a coffee,' she said.

The kitchen was small but gleaming with white Formica, the sort that's more suitable for surgery than eating or cooking in, but she produced strong coffee and chocolate biscuits which I ate while she rolled herself a cigarette.

My first impression of Rose had been totally wrong. I'd assumed she was the Bingo and Pernod with blackcurrant type but she wasn't. She seemed more like the dusting and Domestos paragon of TV ads.

After eating a chocolate biscuit I asked, 'You are sure Nick didn't know Jenny Martin?'

'I couldn't swear to it on the Bible, luv, but it's doubtful, isn't it? I mean he's only nineteen. Most of the girls he knows are from school days. They're like groupies. Some hang round bikers and joyriders. The bike girls are all gold earrings in funny places and black leather with big flashy zips from kneecaps to tits. The joyriders' molls are all short skirts, legs and bum and skimpy tops—like tribes, they are.'

I got the picture, finished my coffee, thanked Rose and asked if she had any of his friends' addresses. She thought for a while and muttered something about not knowing most of them.

'I know one though,' she said as she wrote down the name and address. I glanced at the name, said I'd be in touch soon and left.

The name was Karen Toohey. She lived on the edge of the estate in a run-down house with a front garden that housed an old bike, a pram on its side, bits of a car engine at the edge of the front path and a snarling Alsatian dog. I sussed out the back gate first. It looked strong enough to hold the salivating dog behind it. As I knocked on the door I rather hoped no one would reply, but it opened almost immediately, the occupants obviously primed by the dog.

A burly man, middle aged with black hair almost everywhere but mostly sprouting from holes in his string vest, stood at the door eyeing me suspiciously. 'Is Karen in?' I asked. He turned his head and shouted loudly: 'Karen!'

'Who is it?' came a voice from above.

'How the fook should I know,' he shouted back. From inside the house came the sound of squabbling and a steady thump-thump of heavy metal music.

'Jasus!' he shouted. 'Turn that off, you little bleeders.' Then turning to me he said, 'You'd better come in, missus.' I had one foot in the door when he thought better of it and raised one hairy arm to bar my way. 'You're not a fooking bailiff, are you?'

'Do I look like a bailiff?' I asked. He didn't answer but he didn't look too sure. He muttered something then about devious bastards. 'You're not from the poll tax office?' I shook my head. 'Every booger's on my back,' he said. 'Fooking last year's arrears.'

I put him out of his misery. 'I just want to ask Karen about Nick Fenny. I'm trying to trace him.'

He lowered his arm. 'You're not the police?'

I shook my head. 'My name's Kate Kinsella.'

He walked me through to the kitchen and as he walked he shouted 'Get fooking out!' to various children who scattered as requested, nearly knocking me over.

'How many children do you have, Mr Toohey?'

'Too fooking many,' he said. 'I've lost fooking count.'

In the kitchen it looked as if they had just been burgled but unconcerned he wiped his hairy hand over a plastic kitchen chair so that comics and pencils fell to the floor to join the odd bone, crust and screwed-up pieces of paper already there.

'Karen!' he shouted once more. 'Jasus, I won't tell you again.'

I stared around me. A hologram of the Virgin Mary stared eerily at me from the kitchen wall. 'Do ye want a drink?' he asked as he opened himself a can of beer. I smiled and shook my head. There were several cracked tea-stained mugs on the table and I thought it best not to reduce my life chances by risking a drink from one of them.

Heavy thumping from the stairs preceded Karen's appearance. She stood at the kitchen door, the clink of chains coming to rest as she did so. Her black hair was close cropped, shaved into her neck. Her ears were a riot of piercing, a gold earring hung from her left nostril, she had a ring on every finger and chains hung from her black leather trousers. She was heavy breasted but wore a skimpy black tank top. Her face looked as if she had applied talcum powder with a heavy hand and her lips were a cyanotic blue.

'Yeah?' she said. 'Who are you?'

I explained I was trying to trace Nick and hopefully prove his innocence. She laughed drily. 'Innocent? Him! He's about as innocent as the Yorkshire Ripper on a night out with the boys.' She sat down heavily on a chair with a wonky back and eyed me warily.

'I've been told you and Nick were quite close,' I said. 'Surely you don't think he had anything to do with the murder of Jenny Martin?' She shrugged and said nothing. 'Well, do you?' Her top lip curled. 'Look. Nick is, well, he used to be a friend. Bikers and joyriders are like...they're different—they don't mix. It can be dangerous, starts fights, real gang warfare... I always preferred the bikers. Nick and I should never have been friends in the first place.'

'Why's that?'

She shrugged again as if I was being painfully stupid. Then she said, 'Look, you're just wasting your time. If he's missing he'll stay missing till they find the bloke that killed her. Nick's no fool...'

'But is he a killer?'

'Look, Kate...whoever you are. I don't know. Perhaps

we could all become killers. I mean look at the Ten Commandments…Thou shall not kill. That's the first one. Now if God didn't think it was bloody likely He wouldn't have put it first, would He?'

'I suppose not,' I said and I couldn't argue with her about that commandment being the first because I wasn't sure.

It was as I was leaving I heard a baby's cry. The sound, strong and lusty, came from upstairs. Karen flicked her head towards the noise. 'That's Sammy,' she said. 'Starving again. It never stops, his stomach is like a soddin' well.'

'He's yours?'

She laughed drily. 'Yeah. Guess who the father is?'

I raised an eyebrow, wondering if Rose who thought Nick had no serious relationships knew about her extra grandchild. 'Does he help with maintenance?'

'You must be joking,' she said. 'No, I tell a lie. The first week he was born Nick came round with a crate of toothpaste—said it fell off the back of a lorry.' She laughed again. 'At least when he does get teeth he'll have enough soddin' toothpaste for the rest of his life.'

As I walked past the obstacle course in the front garden I tried to work out if I'd learnt anything more about Nick today. He was a father, a petty criminal, a 'good' driver and maybe he was capable of murder. But no one had suggested he was likely to kill just for the sake of it or even in the pursuance of his trade. As far as I was concerned he was still innocent. But not that innocent, a little voice murmured to me.

SIX

THE NEXT DAY the garage mechanic summoned me to his oily palace. He wore a black T-shirt and black jeans and he waved his spanner dramatically about over the open bonnet. I didn't really understand a word he was talking about. There was trouble with the carb, the points, the plugs, the brake pads, it needed tracking, a spot of welding and for good measure there was an 'emission' problem. After all that he gave me a quote. I leant against the car door to keep myself upright.

'You're joking,' I said. He shook his head mournfully. He was only in his late twenties, but he had the seriousness of a much older man. 'I wish I was,' he said. 'You haven't had her regularly serviced, have you?'

'No,' I answered glumly. 'I couldn't afford to have him done.' Why should cars be females? I thought. Mine was a he.

'It's up to you. With these bits seen to she could last you another year or two. She's not really in bad nick.'

'Do you do terms?' I asked hopefully.

'If you do it through Humberstones then yes, otherwise no.'

'I'll get back to you,' I said. He gave a quick sort of grimace as though he'd had a sudden attack of anal pain and I left to find Hubert and grovel.

Hubert did agree providing I went to the pub with him at lunch time. I needed no added inducement especially when he told me he had news about the case. As we walked along Longborough High Street I tried to prise it out of him.

'You'll just have to wait,' he said. 'And anyway I want your advice on—'

'Alienated youth, sex and the older woman, managing—'

'I wish you'd take me seriously, Kate. I do try, I really do.'

I stopped in my tracks. He sounded quite anguished. I stared at his face.

'What's up?' he asked, looking around anxiously, as if passers-by would notice. 'What's the matter? Why are you looking at me like that?'

He sounded quite paranoid at that moment. I tried to lighten the mood. 'I was only trying to assess the damage, Hubert. It looks like a three pint and chicken in the basket job—with chips!'

'That does it!' he said. 'That does it. Pay for your own car. Start paying your arrears of rent or you're out. My feelings are just a joke to you.'

'I'm sorry, Hubert, I didn't mean to upset you...' My voice tailed off as he strode off in the opposite direction. I couldn't have felt worse. Normally he would have managed a smile at my little quip. But then I remembered he wasn't normal at the moment. He was in love.

I went to the pub on my own. Now that Hubert had huffed away I didn't feel much like eating so I drank two pathetically warm ciders and sat staring ahead of me in a dim booth. Outside it was just bright enough to sit at the wooden picnic tables but I've always preferred drinking inside. Somehow even warm cider tastes better then. No one spoke to me, or even looked in my direction so after half an hour and my solitary pint I walked back towards Humberstones.

On the way I bought Hubert a cream horn and a sandwich. Then I sneaked into reception, stole a rose from the display, slipped out again to the side door and made my way up to the office.

I listened for him on the stairs all afternoon but he didn't come up. Finally I went down to reception, and there were relatives in the office so I wasn't able to ask where he had gone. Miserably I drove back to Farley Wood in my borrowed Mini. If I lost Hubert's friendship and his goodwill I was sunk, I knew that.

In my front room I stared out over the graveyard for a while and then to avoid becoming totally morbid I made myself a childishly comforting jam sandwich and a mental list of foods which are and which aren't, like U and non-U. Sun-dried tomatoes being the first on my list for not being comforting. Apple dumplings and jam rolypoly came high on my comfort list—but who can say they have eaten either of these things during the last year, or indeed, ever.

Then the phone rang. I rushed to answer it hoping it was Hubert. It was Pauline Berkerly from the nursing agency saying unfortunately my would-be patient had died. Moments later, it rang again. This time it was the Riverview Medical Centre saying I hadn't got the job. I could have cried and I did.

I was still a bit snivelly when the phone rang a while later. It was Hubert. 'I'm in Dunsmore,' he said.

'Oh. What for?'

'I'll tell you in a minute...'

'I didn't mean to upset you, Hubert. I was just trying to cheer you up.'

'You don't sound very cheerful yourself.'

'I've got a cold coming.'

'Oh.'

'And I've lost two jobs this afternoon.'

'Well, you can't have lost what you didn't have in the first place.'

'I'm still disappointed. I was banking on that practice job.'

'I've just been to the Dunsmore Adult Education Centre. I know the caretaker.'

'And?'

'He saw something the night Jenny Martin was murdered.'

'What?'

'I'll tell you tomorrow.'

'I could come back to the office.'

'You must be at a loose end.'

'Hubert, sometimes I think my life is one long loose end.'

'You, Kate, need a man.'

'Hubert, you keep saying that. Just because you've got someone now you can't bear to think of me being left out, can you? I'll advertise, shall I?'

'You'd have to lie.'

'Thanks.'

'I'll see you in about an hour, Kate. Bye.'

I washed my face, brushed my hair, changed into a black track suit and trainers and mused on Hubert's life amongst the dead. He showed so much interest in my cases he was surely in the wrong job. But was I in the right one?

THE NEWS FROM the caretaker at Dunsmore, Bill Stone, was that he had seen the car being driven away some time after midnight. Hubert told me this as he cooked pasta, wearing an apron and a serious expression.

'Did he see the driver?' I asked.

'From a distance.'

'And?'

'Pasta's ready,' said Hubert, pointedly ignoring me whilst he drained tagliatelle on to the plates and thrust the tomato sauce under my nose for me to sniff appreciatively. Then he poured it over the pasta and signalled that I should sit down and eat. Although I was grateful for some food I couldn't help thinking that pasta is overrated. Anything that doesn't need a knife seems to me to lack the essentials of a proper meal. Hubert has taken to watching *Master Chef* of late and occasionally gives me the results to sample. His choice usually revolved around dishes like polenta, gnocchi and couscous. The polenta often looks like a half brick and the couscous is normally a flavourless mush. Still, with a good bottle of wine, most things are acceptable.

'Kate?'

'Yes.'

'Don't you like it?'

'It's delicious,' I said. 'And the wine is great. Tell me about the caretaker.'

'The centre closes at nine thirty most nights. Ten if the classes finish later. Bill checked the building was all locked up at about ten. There were two cars left in the car park but he said that's not that unusual. Occasionally they're abandoned. He went home then. From the front window of his bungalow, he could see the car park. Just after twelve he heard voices...'

'Raised voices?'

'No—just voices.'

'He looked out and saw a man and woman standing together. A bit later he heard a car drive off at speed.'

'Anything else?'

Hubert sucked in his tagliatelle thoughtfully. 'I don't like to mention this during a meal...'

'Go on, tell me—be a sport.' He looked uncomfortable and I tried to guess what had been found. 'Has it anything to do with safe sex?' I asked.

'No it has not,' he said, his face colouring to match his tomato sauce. 'Bill always does a check before he goes to bed and as the car drove away he walked out and looked around.'

'Yes?'

'Someone had vomited near the bushes. Bill cleared it up of course.'

'Good old Bill.'

'Are you being sarcastic, Kate?'

I shrugged. 'Well, what a pity he didn't leave it. It could have been evidence.' He thought about that as we finished our meal, and somewhat jaded by now, I said, 'You didn't by any chance ask him what was in it?'

'In what?'

'In the vomit.'

'Oh God,' groaned Hubert. 'I'll never eat tagliatelle again.'

'You didn't ask?' I said, ignoring his touch of histrionics.

'No, I didn't, and can we talk about something else, it's making my stomach churn.'

I did change the subject then, I told him about my trip to Dunsmore and that I was fairly sure Nick 'the Ace' Fenny didn't kill Jenny. Hubert picked up on that. 'Only fairly sure?' he said.

I nodded. 'It's the victim who interests me. Why was she there if her class had been cancelled, and was the car there all the evening? What was the estimated time of death and are there any other suspects?'

'It's a pity you didn't get that job,' said Hubert. 'You could have been on the inside.'

'I know, Hubert, and more importantly I could have paid the rent and paid for my car.'

Hubert shrugged and patted my arm. 'I'm not short of a bob or two,' he said. I smiled, grateful. But that didn't stop me asking for yet another favour.

'Will you,' I asked, 'do your snooping bit and find out when she died and if the police have any leads, other than Nick?'

Hubert stood up and began collecting the dirty plates. Once he stacked them he said, 'I'll do my best, Kate, but

I haven't got as many contacts in Dunsmore as Longborough. The funeral director over there isn't a particular friend of mine.'

I nodded. I knew Hubert would do his best but he couldn't manufacture information. I'd probably have to visit the Dunsmore police myself.

The phone rang then, it was Dolly Two-Shoes. I stacked the dishwasher, cleared the table and when I'd finished doing that Hubert was still on the phone. I whispered thank you to him but he didn't seem to hear me. I crept downstairs as though if I was noisy I could wake the dead and made my way to the borrowed Mini.

It was nearly eleven by the time I got home. I didn't feel tired and so I had a bath, read a few chapters of a book, drank cocoa and thought about Jenny Martin. If she'd been at the car at eleven thirty where had she been until then? What class had she told her husband she was going to and if she genuinely had expected the class to be going on had she met someone she knew outside the centre who suggested—what? A drink? A meal? Come back to my place? Surely if no one had come forward it looked as if they had something to hide. Or had she met her lover that night? He wouldn't dare come forward, would he? It now seemed that her whereabouts from around seven to twelve were as much a mystery as her death.

I slept eventually. A nightmarish dream. I was grown up but back at junior school. My friends had stayed the same. The teacher hadn't changed. I sat at the tiny desk, big and cumbersome, and had to do a maths test. I couldn't fathom the fractions at all. Everyone was laughing at me... I woke suddenly. I blinked.

There in the doorway stood a man. All in black with just his eyes glinting in the darkness. My heart seemed to come up into my mouth and gag me. I couldn't breathe. I struggled up in bed. I didn't want to die lying down. I opened my mouth but I was like a suffocating fish—my lips moved but the banging in my throat stopped the sound from coming out. He moved nearer the bed. My legs twitched, a pulse hammered in my head, my mouth was suddenly as dry as an Australian river bed after a seven-year drought. But worse than all that—I didn't know what to do.

Then he spoke, a sinister throaty whisper. 'Don't move. Don't scream.'

Christ! What did he expect? That I was going to be raped or worse and not complain? I picked up my portable radio and threw it at him. He ducked. I wrenched the lamp from the wall and threw that. It missed. I found my voice. 'You bastard!' I screamed as if I knew him personally. I fumbled on my bed and found my book. It was a hardback. That caught him. He stumbled and fell. I was out of bed like a shot, picking up my trainer from the floor and hitting him on the head with it. He didn't like that, I could tell. He was swearing and cursing and finally he screeched, 'For fuck's sake, it's Nick.'

My hand holding my trainer was still in mid-air. I kept it there. 'Take that Balaclava off,' I demanded. Backing away, I switched on the light. Bare faced and sitting on the floor he was a lot less threatening now. My heart began to thump in the right place now. 'What the hell's going on?' I asked in a squeaky voice.

'I had to see you,' he said.

'Well, you could have bloody well rung first.' I had a strong desire to hit him again but I resisted. He was, after all, technically my client. Lowering the shoe I said, 'You'd better sit down or I'll call the police.'

'I had to come this way,' said Nick. 'Every force in the country is out looking for me. I have to play it careful.'

I looked at him more closely now that I was calmer and I could see he looked older than nineteen. He had slightly frizzy black short hair, brown eyes with long lashes that looked as if he'd used mascara and a clear complexion. He looked neat and clean cut. As I observed him he too was looking me over. It was not until I caught the gleam of youthful lust in his eyes, that I realized I was only wearing a thin T-shirt that barely covered anything at all.

Very swiftly I got back under the duvet, fixed him with a stern older woman look and said, 'Say what you've got to say and then go.'

'Yeah, OK. I didn't mean to start you off but I took a chance coming here, you know. I just wanted to tell you what happened...'

'Well tell me,' I said briskly.

Nick picked up his Balaclava from the floor and began to get to his feet.

'Just stay where you are,' I ordered, with what I hoped was a snarl in my voice. He slumped back on his heels and began to fiddle with the knitted black hood as he spoke. 'I'd been drinking with my mates, see. I wanted to go for a ride but they didn't—we were all well cut but I drive better then. I'm a great driver...'

'Modest as well.'

He ignored that. 'I'm a great driver, they don't call me "the Ace" for nothing. Anyway, one of the lads lives near the adult education centre and we was passing and I saw the car. It looked in good condition—I only like good runners. And I thought, Well, why not?'

'Why exactly were you going to your friend's house?'

'I stay there sometimes. His dad's on his own and he's a piss-artist so we thought there might be a few beers going.'

I nodded. 'But you wanted to joyride?'

'Yeah. I just saw the car as I said and I went over to suss it out. It was like it was meant to be. The door was open. I started it up—the keys were in the ignition—' He broke off to chuckle about that. 'And then I was off towards the M1. I've got a girlfriend in Birmingham, see. I thought I'd go up and stay with her. I stopped at a lay-by miles from anywhere just to see if there was a spare petrol can in the boot because the petrol gauge was showing nearly empty and I hadn't got any money with me. And anyway I suppose you know I always burn them out. Anyway I opened the boot and... Oh, God it was 'orrible...'

'What was?'

Nick stared at me for a moment. He had definitely paled and he screwed the Balaclava nervously in his hands.

'What was?' I repeated. He looked up at me, then away again.

'The body—her. Big eyes staring at me, her face all white with blue lips and bruises round her throat. It was 'orrible. She was just lying there... It was like she was accusing me.'

'Of killing her?'

'Yeah, sort of. Her eyes seemed to move and then—this was the worst bit... I thought she was dead. Well, that was bad enough, but then she started to move her mouth trying to talk. I was going to ring for an ambulance—I was—but next thing I know she's holding my wrist saying something and then a bit of blood starting coming out of her mouth and her lips had bitten through and then she let go of my wrist and her head fell to one side and I knew then she was dead.'

'What did you do?'

'I threw up again. I just stood there. I was shaking all over. I closed the boot of the car real quick. I was panicking. I would have legged it only it was pitch dark and I saw some blood on my sleeve and I thought the Old Bill won't believe this. So I got back in the car and drove off towards the M1.'

'You said you threw up "again".'

Nick gave me a puzzled look. 'Well, I did puke a bit in

the bushes by the college. I'd lost track of the pints I'd had.
I'm not a two-pint bloke, you know. It was the blood the
second time—I just kept retching.'

'And then what did you do?' I asked.

He looked sheepish. 'I've told you. I sat in the car for a
while. I felt terrible, what with the beer and the body and
everything. I was quite near the M1 by then so I thought...
I dunno what I thought. I just wanted to get rid.'

'Did anyone see you?'

He shook his head miserably. Any bravado had now
gone. 'I don't want to go down for this one. I never touched
her, honest I didn't.'

'You're sure she was dead?'

A soft groan came from his lips. 'She was dead all right.
She was...she was! I just drove then, I was in a panic. The
next thing I know is the cops are after me. I was easily
doing a ton and then I lost my bottle. They were gaining
on me. So I came off the road, drove into a field and
thought I'd set the car on fire and do a runner.'

'And did you?'

Nick gulped. 'I had to open the boot again but I wanted
to set it on fire because it would give me more of a chance,
more time—I mean they were right behind me. I moved
her a bit—she...she sort of gasped as I moved her. I was
desperate to find a petrol can and I could see the plastic
top of it. I managed in the end to get it out by sliding my
hand underneath her. I was in a right state I can tell
you...shaking, feeling sick. I poured on some petrol, flung
a match on to the front seat and I'd just got it going when
the police car appeared—but luckily it stalled in a ruck in
the field and I just ran off. I've never run so fast in my
life. I got a lift in a lorry and managed to get to Birmingham. I told the driver I was a joyrider, he let me lie down
in the back. I felt terrible, I did.'

'You haven't told me the important bit yet, Nick. You

said when you first opened the car boot she was trying to say something. What exactly did she say?' I watched him carefully.

His expression changed, he seemed more nervous, more ill at ease. 'Look,' he said, 'I was in a real state. She only said one word and I could be wrong. There was blood in her mouth and it was sort of gurgly. But I thought she said—''Bollocks.'''

'I beg your pardon?'

'You heard.'

I stared at Nick. 'You're not winding me up?'

He shook his head and then said emphatically: 'That's what I heard and that's all I know.'

Did I believe him? Maybe. If she had said that, maybe it was because she was brain damaged. Not defiance but one demented utterance. One more thing worried me though about Nick's recall of the night's events and I couldn't not think about it. He had thought she gasped and although I knew this could happen after death, did Nick? Because he had after all still tried to set the car ablaze.

SEVEN

I SHOULD HAVE SEEN what was coming but I didn't.

'Can I stay?' he asked with a slight whine in his voice. At 2 a.m. I was beginning to wish I had Doc Martens to thump him with. Then he added with a touch more whine to his voice, 'I haven't got anywhere to go.'

'Tough!'

'Oh, go on. I wouldn't be any trouble.'

'No, Nick. I'd be harbouring a criminal. I'm not held in high regard by the police, you know. Bag-ladies get more respect than I do. They wouldn't hesitate to prosecute me.'

He kept on and on. He was hungry, he was tired. Just a couple of nights.

'You can make yourself a meal,' I agreed eventually, 'and stay for a couple of hours but that's all. And anyway you do have an alternative.'

'What's that?' he asked.

'Simple. Give yourself up.'

He snorted. 'You're an effing joke, you are. You're paid to be on my side.'

'I'm just being realistic.'

He paced up and down for a while and then said, 'Got any eggs and bacon?'

I nodded. He left the room and I heard him banging around in the kitchen for a while. I didn't trust him enough not to come back to my bedroom and I knew I'd never sleep if I thought he might appear in my doorway again so I dragged a chest of drawers in front of the door and stood by the door for a while just listening. Then there was silence, I got back into bed and after what seemed like hours I drifted off into a restless half sleep.

When I woke it was 9 a.m. At first I forgot about my visitor but when I did remember I rushed downstairs. The kitchen was a shambles and the smell of bacon and cooking fat lingered in the air. He'd cooked chips as well and the peelings were left on the draining-board. For someone with such a house-proud mother I wasn't surprised she let him roam free. It was as I was clearing up I noticed he'd also carved out a circle of glass from one of the square panes in my back door. At least that was neat, though. He was obviously more house-breaker trained than house trained. I just felt relieved he'd gone and hopefully would stay gone.

I had a bath then and tried to plan my day. I'd go to Dunsmore and talk to the caretaker; after that, I'd either pay a visit to the Dunsmore CID and see what I could find out or visit Jenny Martin's husband.

I dressed suitably soberly in a navy skirt that had seen better days and a loose shirt-type blouse in peach, tried on three pairs of earrings and then decided I looked better without. It was by now 10 a.m. My weeks of idleness seemed to have slowed me down but today I felt reasonably optimistic. I was going to find out who killed Jenny Martin and my future as an investigator would be assured.

I opened the front door, sniffed the fresh, warm summer air appreciatively and walked to the front gate. I stared ahead of me into the road—at the space where the car should have been—my Mini had gone—my *borrowed* Mini had been stolen!

'The thieving little sod!' I shouted as I kicked my front gate. One of my neighbours, Mrs Godbold, white haired, spritely and a leading light of the WI, came out to see what was going on.

'Oh dear, oh dear. Fancy that,' she said excitedly. 'You'd better ring the police straight away.'

'I will,' I said miserably. I could feel tears pricking at my eyelids, partly with frustration, partly with anger at myself for allowing it to happen.

Inside the house I picked up the phone. I paused. It seemed natural to phone the police, but should I? Just imagine if Nick had been caught. They could assume I had given him permission. They might even believe I had been harbouring him for days. I rang Hubert instead. I embellished the story somewhat saying I had been prevented from calling the police and I'd been in shock, etc. etc. Hubert was brick-like, even when I told him about the hole in my back door.

'Now don't you worry, Kate. I'll get someone round to fix that and I'll tell Ted, as the owner, to report it stolen from outside his house. Fenny probably won't deny it when he's caught. You've had a lucky escape. Are you sure he didn't hurt you?'

'No, Hubert. I would have noticed. But what I am going to do without a car?'

'I'll come over for you. You can borrow one of mine.'

'I can't drive around in a hearse.'

'Stay there then, Kate. You'll just have to wait till your own car's fixed.'

'You've won me over, Hubert,' I said. 'A hearse would be lovely.'

He grunted. 'I've got a funeral soon but I'll come over straight after. Chin up!'

Do people say 'chin up' with the idea that the tears won't then fall—they'll miraculously slip back into your eye sockets? Anyway I kept my chin up for a while but gave that up in favour of a large glass of very cheap sherry which tasted medicinal and worked.

By the time Hubert arrived I felt more optimistic. Ted had been told his Mini was stolen but he didn't appear too concerned as it did, in fact, belong to his wife. Hubert patted my arm when he saw the empty wine glass. 'That's not the answer,' he said. I nearly made a smart Alec retort but I managed to say instead, 'Thanks for coming.'

For all my meekness he insisted on driving me to Dunsmore. 'I'll wait in the car,' he said. I wasn't pleased, but my options were definitely not open. At least he hadn't brought the hearse, instead he'd come in his white car, which was so flash a pop star would have been pleased with it.

I sat back and quite enjoyed the drive. Hubert would have made a good chauffeur, he drove steadily and didn't talk too much except to say, 'This makes a real break for me. You should try going to a funeral nearly every day of the week. It's no joke.'

'It wouldn't be,' I agreed and to get him off the subject of funerals gave him my itinerary for the day. 'As long as I'm back by six,' he said. 'I'm going out tonight.'

I felt a little twinge of jealousy. He was twenty years older than me, in love and now having a reasonable social life. I seemed to have made no real effort to make friends. Not that Longborough offered much—flower arranging, and rambling where the members, male and female, wore beards and great hefty walking boots. There were various worthy organizations for those with problems. But not being sporty, anorexic, overweight (well, only a few pounds), depressed (only occasionally), a single parent or a smoker, there wasn't much on offer for me.

We arrived at the Dunsmore Adult Education Centre and made a slow and stately advance past the entrance sign which announced DUNSMORE TERTIARY COLLEGE and underneath the small print previously DUNSMORE ADULT EDUCATION CENTRE. I wasn't surprised it was still called by its old title. Who knows how to spell tertiary let alone knows what it means? At the portals of the establishment

was the caretaker's bungalow. It faced directly towards the
car park.

The college itself was a low-level modern building with
Porta-cabins attached. The narrow roadway curved into the
obligatory miniature roundabout with a flower-bed in the
middle. Hubert drove round again and parked outside the
bungalow.

Bill Stone, the caretaker, had by now emerged and was
bending down and attending earnestly to his weeds. He
straightened up as we advanced on him. 'Hello, Hubert, my
old doom merchant, how are you?'

Hubert nodded and smiled sheepishly and introduced me
in such glowing terms that even Hercule Poirot would have
blushed.

'I'll get the missus to bring out some tea if you like,'
said Bill. I looked around for somewhere to sit but there
wasn't anywhere except for a tiny patch of lawn. I shook
my head but Hubert said, 'Very nice, thanks.'

I gave Hubert a warning look that was meant to convey
I didn't want to waste any time but Bill had already disappeared by then, so we both sat down on the patch of
lawn and looked out towards the car park. In a few minutes
Bill came back with mugs of tea and a plate of biscuits.
He looked overly fond of biscuits. He was round all over
with a cheerful pink face and hair so thick and silvery it
looked like a wig.

'Hubert tells me you saw the car that was stolen and you
may even have seen the murderer,' I said to Bill, who was
staring at a weed he'd missed as if it were a primed hand-
grenade. He sat down awkwardly by my side, lifted a biscuit to his mouth. 'Mmm,' he murmured, whether at the
taste of the biscuit or the memory of that night I wasn't
sure. Finally he said, 'Classes finish about nine thirty. I lock
up once everyone's gone home. There was a red Golf in
the car park. And a black car, I don't know the make. I

didn't take much notice I must admit. I came indoors and watched TV for a while and then about twelve I heard voices. I turned down the volume on the TV and listened. We do get yobs coming in and racing about from time to time. They use this place to do handbrake turns. I think we should lock the gates but it's not my decision, is it? Anyway I drew back the curtains and I saw a tall man and a woman talking by the car...'

'The red Golf?'

'Yes, the red car. They were standing beside it.'

'How did they stand—were they close together, talking, kissing?' He thought for a moment. 'Quite close together, he was taller than her. She was blonde, well...fairish, hair to her shoulders, slight build—looked ever so young to me.'

'And the man?'

'As I said, tall, darkish hair...I think. I couldn't see his face but I did notice something. He was dressed in black.'

'Trousers?'

'All of him.'

'But you didn't see his face?'

'No. A bit later I thought I heard them drive away and I walked around for a time doing my final check like I always do. The black car, I think it was black, was still there then. People do sometimes leave their cars, the houses opposite don't all have garages and some of that road outside has yellow lines. Anyway, it's not unusual to have a car left overnight. I went to bed about quarter to one and in the morning both cars were gone.'

'Your wife didn't hear anything?'

'No.'

'And someone had vomited in the bushes?'

'Yes, that's right. It happens.'

'What did you do?'

'I cleared it up of course.'

'When was that?'

'Just after I'd finished looking around.'

'What did you clean it up with?'

'The usual—sawdust.'

'Do you mind me asking if you noticed anything special about it?'

Hubert groaned, Bill looked puzzled. 'I didn't look closely at it— I mean you don't, do you?'

'No, but was it solid looking or mostly beer?'

'Now I think about it,' said Bill, staring into the middle distance, 'it was quite solid...it...'

Hubert stood up then. 'My stomach can't take any more of this, Kate. Let's be off. Thanks, Bill. I'm sure Kate will be able to deduce something from what's been said.'

'Just one more question, Bill. Have you any idea when that vomit first appeared?'

'No idea, my love. Sorry.'

Once in the car Hubert said, 'Well, that was a waste of time.'

'I don't know. I've learnt that a man in black was by the car around midnight and that the woman, if it was Jenny, was still alive at twelve, which means Nick Fenny probably didn't do it. I mean, it doesn't sound as if she was trying to stop him stealing the car, does it? I also think Bill isn't a very reliable witness...'

'Why ever not? I've known him for years.'

'How well, though?'

'I know him slightly. Years ago he lived in Longborough.'

'And his wife?'

'I know she goes to bed early and they argue a lot.' As he started the engine Hubert said, 'Why don't you think Bill was a good witness?'

'I'm not sure....I—'

'Come off it, Kate, just because he's a friend of mine you doubt his word, but that yob Nick you believe.'

'True,' I agreed, 'or at least I try to. But Bill says he heard voices, and he couldn't have from that distance—eight yards or so away—and yet he said they weren't shouting. And the vomit—the timing doesn't make sense. Why should Nick lie about that?'

Hubert switched off the engine. 'You don't think Bill did it, surely?'

'No, of course not. But it's all a bit convenient, isn't it? Almost as if he felt he had to see something.'

'I believe him,' said Hubert. 'Salt of the earth, old Bill. You're getting warped, Kate. Just because you're being paid by Fenny's mother doesn't mean you can definitely eliminate her son.'

'I know that, Hubert—be a dear and drive on.'

'Where to, madam?' asked Hubert. From the tone of his voice I guessed our trip wasn't as enthralling as he'd at first thought it might be.

The murder victim's home was our next stop. I didn't look forward to this but I had no idea what Jenny Martin was like and maybe the husband could throw some light on where she was in her final hours—if in fact he could tell me when exactly they were.

The house itself was on the outskirts of Dunsmore, a fine semidetached Edwardian edifice with stained glass at the front door and a general air of solid respectability. Hubert sat in the car and watched me walk up the front path. I signalled to him to drive on a little but he ignored me.

I raised the heavy brass knocker and knocked loudly. The sound seemed to echo through the house. I waited and waited. Eventually I heard footsteps. A tall middle-aged man, probably good looking when dressed and with his greying hair combed, answered the door. He wore a plaid dressing-gown that would have looked more comfortable on a horse. His eyes were reddened and he looked totally defeated. I'd expected a grieving husband, a confused man, but not this poor shambling wreck who actually wanted me to come inside and ask him questions.

'Come in...come in.' He said the words slowly, as if speaking was an effort. 'I'm Geoffrey Martin—call me Geoff. If it will help to find who did it I'll talk to anyone—anyone.' He led the way along the hall, walking slowly, his head down, shoulders hunched. He opened a door that led to a large back room, pointed to an armchair and I sat down.

The room was large and spacious, and would have been light and cheerful but the dark green curtains were half drawn and so the room was shadowy with only pinpoints of light. Where the sunlight did spike the mantelpiece it shimmered onto family photographs. Geoff Martin noticed where I was looking and took one framed photograph in his hand and stared at it. Then he sat on the arm of my armchair. 'This was taken on holiday,' he said. The photograph showed a laughing blonde young woman with a bucket and spade and beside her a small boy proudly showing off his sandcastle. 'That was our son—Simon. He died. He was ten years old.'

'I'm so sorry,' I said. 'Please don't feel you have to talk to me.'

'No, no, as I said, I want to talk, I need to talk. I don't want to act as if they never existed. Jenny changed after Simon's death. She wasn't the same person. I suppose I wasn't the same either. We were on the verge of separation—did you know that? Of course I'm much older than her... Simon dying affected us both differently.'

'How did Simon die?' I asked gently.

He stared at me with his empty grey eyes for a moment. 'Hit and run. He was on his way home from school, it was getting dark. A car mounted the pavement and mowed him down. He died instantly. The police never caught the driver—' He broke off, choked with his awful memories. 'And now this...my whole life...my whole life.'

His head dropped and he sobbed quietly for a while, dry racking sobs. I patted him on the shoulder and as I did so I could feel emotional tugs as real as rope threatening to drag me in. Other people's grief often seems to reflect every fear you ever had, every grief experienced. I drew back, swallowed hard. 'Mr Martin—Geoff—I know this is difficult for you, but could we talk about Jenny. The police are doing all they can but maybe I'll be able to help too.'

He gulped, passed his hands wearily over his face as though wishing he could wipe away his grief, and said, 'What do you want to know?'

'As much as possible. Just talk about her—anything.'

He paused as if remembering, and then said softly, 'I'm twelve years older than her. We married when she was eighteen, just before she started training to be a nurse. She was just over twenty when she got pregnant, she was still a student nurse so I looked after Simon with the help of my mother, she died a year after Simon's death...she never got over it. Anyway before the...accident, we were very happy. I work from home, I'm a freelance journalist. It was tough at times to meet deadlines but we managed. Jenny in those days was always cheerful. She always said there were so many sick people in the world we should just be grateful for good health...'

'And after your son's death?'

'She changed. At first I thought that once the first year was over she'd get back some of her spirit but losing a child isn't something you do get over. The pain eases a bit but the sense of loss is always there—'

He broke off again and stared bleakly at the photograph.

'Tell me about the night she died, Geoff.'

He stared at me for a moment. 'We had a meal about sixish. Jenny was quite quiet, didn't say much. She'd worked at the medical centre that day, in the morning and early afternoon. I was working on an article and she'd been annoyed I hadn't prepared the vegetables. It was her evening class night. She's doing calligraphy—she *was* doing calligraphy. She left about a quarter to seven. ''I'll be home by ten,'' she said. That was the last time I saw her...' His watery eyes gazed into space.

'Tell me about her friends.'

'She had quite a few friends, nursing friends, people she met at evening classes.'

'I hate to ask this Geoff, but did she have any men friends?'

He glared at me. 'I don't think so. I would have guessed if she'd been having an affair, wouldn't I? I know we had our problems but it wouldn't have ended in divorce, I'm sure of that.'

'But you discussed separating?'

'Yes. We thought maybe living apart for a while might help us.'

'Did you hope for more children?'

'Of course,' said Geoff sharply. 'Of course we did and we tried but Jenny refused to go to an infertility clinic. She simply refused. I think she was frightened of more suffering.'

'One final question, Geoff.' He nodded. 'Did Jenny, to your knowledge, have any enemies?'

He shook his head. 'No of course not. I've been surprised that I've not been contacted by some of her friends but it's difficult for people, isn't it? They just don't know what to say. I think she was just in the wrong place at the wrong time. There's someone out there on the rampage. Another woman is missing. The police told me. They wouldn't tell me her name. If there is a serial killer at large the CID don't want to give him the kudos of publicity. It seems this woman has been missing since the night Jenny was killed.

She didn't turn up for work after her holiday. It's highly probable, the police think, that she's dead. It's just a question of finding her body...' He stopped talking suddenly and his mouth sagged open.

'Oh my God...'

'What's the matter?' I asked, concerned, as his head dropped forward on his chest. He stared at the floor for a moment then raised his eyes slowly to stare into mine. 'How could I not have realized? That bastard's killed them both.'

EIGHT

'WHAT EXACTLY do you mean?' I asked sharply.

Geoff shook his head. 'Why didn't I guess? I thought she just couldn't face seeing me or she'd gone away...'

'Who are we talking about?' I asked, growing more insistent.

'The woman from Longborough. You live in Longborough, don't you?'

I nodded, my impatience growing.

'My wife's best friend—Teresa Haverall. She's missing. She was on holiday from the hotel—she's a receptionist at the Grand. Jenny told me she was going alone that night because Teresa was going away—so it didn't cross my mind that it might be Teresa.'

'Who told you about the missing woman?'

'A police inspector from Dunsmore. He thought he should tell me straight away—to get me off the hook, as it were. I was the chief suspect for my wife's murder, you see—husbands always are, of course. I didn't have an alibi. I was here alone all that evening just waiting for her to come home. Now with this recent...development, it seems I'm no longer their prime suspect.'

He sounded disappointed, as though somehow he'd lost a toehold on life. Perhaps being a suspect gave him willing ears and without police interest in him he felt abandoned. Even so I couldn't understand why a woman, merely missing, should have detracted from his being a worthwhile suspect. As I knew so little about what was going on, however, I decided not to suspect him.

'What time that evening did you report your wife missing?' I asked.

A slightly embarrassed look crossed his face. 'Not till very late, I'm afraid. I worked all the evening, I didn't notice how late it was getting. About eleven I sat down on the sofa and I fell asleep. I woke at two, realized she wasn't home and rang the police. I thought it was worrying when instead of fobbing me off they said they would send two officers straight away. In the morning they drove me to the mortuary to identify my wife.'

He looked about to cry again so I blurted out one more question. 'Do the police know at what time your wife died?'

'Yes,' he murmured. 'They think after midnight and before two. That's as near as they can say—time of death is never very accurate, so the inspector told me.'

'I see. And you did know her class was cancelled?'

He shook his head. 'Why the hell didn't she come home? Where was she? That's what I keep asking myself. Where was she?'

'She had no friends near the college she might have walked to?'

'Not that I know of. Husbands are the first to be accused but, where their wives' secret lives are concerned, the last to be informed.'

'So you do think your wife had a secret life?'

'I don't know, I really don't. The police seem convinced she met a lover but I think to have an affair you have to have a basically uncluttered mind. Jenny was wound up all the time. She was being treated for anxiety. Beta-blockers. They slow the heart rate, calm you down.'

'Who was her GP?'

'An old boy, a one-man band over the other side of Dunsmore—Charles Gregory. A bit past it, if you ask me.

He must be nearly seventy but she wouldn't see anyone at Riverview.'

'Why was that?'

'She said she didn't want them to know her business.'

Geoff by now looked worse than when I'd arrived. I explained I had someone waiting for me and I'd have to go. I shifted my position and was about to stand up when grabbing me by the wrist he whispered, 'You will come again, won't you? Promise.'

'Well, I...'

'Promise.'

He was actually hurting my wrist. 'I promise. Perhaps next week; before, if I have any news.'

He relaxed his grip. 'I like you,' he said. 'I want to keep in touch. I need to talk.'

'Of course you do,' I said, smiling, patting his hand.

Inside I realized I was nearly as scared of his neediness as I was of finding a Balaclaved man in my bedroom. The dim house, the photograph, the haunted expression on Geoff Martin's face now began to unnerve me. 'I must go,' I said.

'You've promised. Don't forget.'

'I won't.'

At the front door I felt released. Hubert drove alongside the house and Geoff hurriedly shut the door.

'What's wrong with you?' asked Hubert as I clambered quickly into the car. 'You look as if you've just had a cold draught somewhere very personal.'

'Mmm. A cold draught to the heart more like.'

'Where to now, madam?'

'Home, Hubert. Back to Longborough.'

Hubert started the engine, raised his eyebrows and said, 'Well?' When I didn't answer immediately he said, 'Did he do it?'

'He could have, Hubert, he could have.'

'Do you think he did?'

I shrugged. I'd been fairly convinced he was innocent until he told me about the missing woman. He'd lied to me then—but why? Anyway I was fairly sure in my own mind that given the right set of circumstances everyone was capable of one murder.

'Hubert,' I said lightly, 'you're a disappointment to me.'

He looked puzzled but he tried hard not to be fazed by my comment. 'I'm a disappointment to women in general.'

I laughed. 'Come on, Hubert, I thought you were on a new phase in your romantic life.'

He shrugged resignedly but managed a wry smile.

'Drive off and I'll tell you what I mean,' I said.

He'd nearly driven out of Dunsmore when I did tell him. 'I don't believe it,' he said, 'I'm always the first to know, after the police. I'm shocked I didn't know. Maybe it's not sinister, though, maybe she's just gone off somewhere for a while.'

'You missed this one, Hubert. I don't know any details yet but the police seem to think it removes Geoff Martin from their list of suspects. Why, I don't know. Murdering a wife is a relatively regular murder but murdering her friend takes it far beyond that. So they must presume the two women have something in common.'

Hubert sighed. 'Well, I suppose they have if they're both dead. If you ask me, there's a madman loose...'

'Or someone wanting us to think so.'

IT WAS LATER that afternoon the Riverview practice manager phoned me.

'It's somewhat embarrassing,' he said.

Not that he sounded embarrassed. 'Yes?' I answered coolly.

'As you know we selected our new practice nurse with great difficulty and now...unfortunately we've been let down. She's declined the job temporarily—on the grounds of sudden ill health.'

'I see.'

'We were wondering if you were still interested? Part-time temporary in the first instance. It was a close-run interview and you were my first choice anyway. We'd be delighted if you could start as soon as possible.'

I stayed silent for at least two seconds during which time I wondered if he had fancied me—perhaps he still did.

'When would you like me to start?'

'Tomorrow? Just the morning surgery.'

Another pause of a second or so, I wanted to seem keen but not desperate. 'Fine,' I agreed. 'I'd be delighted.'

'I'm delighted too,' he said, and I'd swear on oath he said that flirtatiously. 'We start at eight thirty. See you tomorrow.'

'Till tomorrow,' I muttered as I replaced the receiver. Then I punched the air and rushed downstairs to tell Hubert.

The receptionist who had replaced the previous Dorothy, which was just as well as it avoided confusion between Dorothys, sat at the desk putting together brochures. From the first moment I saw her I was convinced she was a man in drag.

'Hubert's popped out,' she said as she placed the hymn selection into its plastic jacket. Then she stood up to place the brochures in a filing cabinet. At least six feet tall, she had skinny legs that reminded me of a plucked dead chicken, large angular shoulders, narrow hips, no bum, high breasts and an Adam's apple that would have done credit to a Bramley. And she had a voice that wouldn't have disgraced a burly miner. Incongruously her name was Danielle. But I had heard her being called Desperate Dan by one of the drivers. She had a bouffant hairstyle of perfect black, false eyelashes and long red nails that were not home grown. Judging by her neck creases I guessed she was in her early forties. She'd only been working at Humberstones for a week and I'd spoken to her only once and then she'd called me Katie.

I must admit I did try to avoid her. Partly because she made me feel ill at ease, partly because Hubert seemed to like her. Or at least he was fascinated by her shoes. Dolly Two-Shoes was a shoe-aholic, wearing a variety of shoes, boots and sandals. Danielle only wore high heels and although she tried to wiggle her hips she actually tottered.

'Come and sit by me, Katie,' she said. 'Gravelly' would have described her voice, as though a handful of shale had become lodged in her throat. 'Hubert will be back soon. He's gone to find out more about the missing woman.'

I wasn't pleased about that. I didn't want him sharing information with all and sundry and I'd tell him so when I saw him.

I looked round the reception area. Danielle had obviously made a few changes since I'd last made reception a visit. The funereal flowers were gone and in their place was a tank of tropical fish. In fact she'd tried to give the whole of reception a tropical feel. Huge green plants in tubs as big as barrels encroached near her desk. 'Sitting by her' would have meant having a cheeseplant leaf flicking at my face. All the room needed now was a model of Long John Silver and a parrot on a stand.

'You look harassed, dear—take the weight off your pins. It's been ever so quiet here today. Must be the good weather. Shocking about that poor woman, isn't it? The local papers will be full of it.'

'You're not local, then?' I queried.

'I'm a Londoner born and bred, Katie. Couldn't you tell by my accent?'

I shook my head. 'No. Just the fact that you thought the local paper would manage to make headlines of a missing woman. ''Pig escapes from farmer's barn'' would make headlines in the *Longborough News*. I think the editor doesn't approve of crime, that's why he doesn't report any.'

'Oooh, you are a one,' laughed Danielle with a toss of her heavily lacquered hair. I perched myself on the edge of her desk and asked, 'What have you heard about the murder?'

Easing herself forward in the swivel chair she said in a whisper, 'I've heard people are pretty sure the missing woman is dead. She had a cat I believe, it's still alive but only just. And she was a friend of that murdered woman.'

I raised my eyebrows in disbelief.

'I'm telling you, Katie, that's what I heard. I do know her name—Teresa Haverall. A woman living alone aged forty.'

At that moment Hubert appeared. 'Everything all right, Danielle?' he asked with a smile.

She positively simpered, 'Yes, thank you, Mr Humberstone. I've been telling Katie here about the missing woman.'

I seethed quietly. Desperate Dan was a name that suited him or her. With a flutter of spidery lashes at Hubert as if he were Richard Gere responding to a young Joan Collins at the very least, she added, 'And we've got on really well, haven't we, Katie?'

'I have to go now,' I said archly. 'I start at the Riverview Health Centre tomorrow.'

I tried not to flounce as I left the room. I half expected Hubert to follow me but he didn't. I sat in my office and stared out at the High Street counting the ratio of hairy legs in shorts to fat legs in shorts. It worked out at 4:2 in favour of fat legs. It was only a moderately warm day but Longborough people seem to strip off the moment the temperature rises a fraction above sixty. I'd been sitting there for a while when I heard the stairs creak and knew Hubert was on his way. The door was slightly ajar and he stood there for a while thinking I hadn't heard him. 'There's no need to lurk, Hubert,' I said.

'You're in a bad mood,' said Hubert, 'especially as it seems you've now got a job. What happened?'

I swung round in my chair. 'Come in properly, Hubert.'

Hubert walked in, a slightly sheepish expression on his face.

'What's the matter?' he asked. 'Why are you miffed?'

'I'm not miffed.'

'You are. What have I done?'

I smiled. 'I'm sorry, Hubert. It's that person downstairs. Obnoxious is how I'd describe…' I balked at using the word 'her' but Hubert didn't seem to notice.

'I thought she'd settled in quite well. An asset to the business, she's very good with the clients. And she's attractive.'

I nearly choked. 'Hubert, you do realize, don't you, she, is *he*!'

Hubert's eyes widened. 'That's a wicked thing to say. You must be jealous. Just because she's got a deep voice. You should be careful what you say about people, Kate. I'm surprised at you, I really am. Danielle is a very nice woman.'

'Jealous! I'm not jealous…well only about information which *he* seems to have and I don't.'

Hubert looked genuinely hurt then, and I felt guilty, so I mumbled on a bit about anyone could make a mistake and how some women could look quite masculine.

His mouth stayed for a while in a sulky downturn, but he wanted to tell me what he'd found out because after a few moments of glaring at me, he said, 'If you make me a cup of coffee I'll tell you all about the missing woman— well as much as I know.'

Over coffee he told me that Teresa Haverall attended calligraphy classes with Jenny.

'When was she last seen alive?' I asked.

'A student at the college saw her at about seven on Monday night.'

'Nothing after that?'

He shook his head.

I tutted for a while about people being as unobservant as earthworms.

He ignored my grumbling. 'I do know Teresa lived alone in a terraced house in the middle of Longborough. She was divorced from her husband, he's working abroad—Germany. The police are trying to contact him. There's one son, he's at Dublin University. By all accounts she was a very respectable woman.'

'Hubert, you sound like the police. Even if a woman isn't "respectable" she doesn't deserve to be murdered—if she is dead, because we don't know that she is yet.'

'I didn't say she did deserve it—did I?'

I smiled at Hubert's rather stricken face. 'Sorry, Hubert. That sort of statement just makes me tetchy.'

'You're often tetchy.'

I ignored that. 'Anything else?' He shook his head. 'Well, I've got a piece of info,' I said, 'but you are sworn to secrecy because only Nick and I know about this.' He leant forward, looking eager. 'Our secret, Hubert,' I repeated for good measure.

I told him then about Jenny's last minutes on earth and about her last word. Hubert was taken aback. 'He must have misunderstood or he's saying she was still alive to persuade you he wasn't the one who attacked her in the first place.'

'I don't know,' I said, 'but you have to assume that she knew she was dying and that what she said was important. Could the word "bollocks" have been mistaken for something else—"Robert"—"Roberts"?'

Hubert smiled mystified. He was a non-swearing man himself.

'You say it, Hubert, with a gurgle in your throat—let me hear what it sounds like.'

'I'm not an actor,' he said with a shake of his head.

I took that as a refusal. 'Come on, Hubert,' I urged. 'In my nursing career I've heard more swear words than you've done funerals.'

'That's as maybe,' he said. 'But can you believe anything a car thief says? Maybe she was just swearing, like people do if they've been under an anaesthestic.'

'That's a possibility,' I agreed, 'but that's a bit of a fallacy, patients do worry about losing control but mostly when their operation is all over they just mumble things like "ouch" and "ah" and "I'm thirsty".'

This talk of patients and surgery reminded me that I was supposed to be a practice nurse the following day and I needed to read all about it. I rushed out of Humberstones' to the bookshop, leaving Hubert thinking about Jenny's last word. Walking back, I tried to revise my knowledge of topics ranging from epilepsy to contraception. It was like the night before an exam and after a short while I began to feel not only confused but worried. Could I cope? What if they found out I also worked as a private investigator? Would I be sacked?

I couldn't ask Hubert for another lift so I would have to stay at the office and sleep in the box-room cum bedroom, which was really only a step up from camping.

The phone rang later. My car would be ready in the morning—any time after 8 a.m. I pleaded for an earlier time and he agreed to leave the car out for me on the forecourt.

I ate a dull hamburger and chips from the chippy, wrote my mother a letter, re-read the chapter entitled 'Emergency Procedures' and then spent time fretting about having one on my first day. My final thoughts as I went to sleep were:

is life always going to be this exciting? Could a mad passionate affair with Mr Practice Manager be the answer to life's doldrums or would it all get far too complicated? Was he already involved with someone? More to the point, did he fancy me? Or was it all in my imagination?

Later in bed when I was at that stage of going to sleep when you think nothing will wake you, I began to wonder if there were any Roberts at the practice. And what was 'the sudden ill health' of a particularly healthy looking young woman? Did she know something I didn't?

That did bring me back from the brink of sleep. Hours later I was still awake. Maybe Riverview Medical Centre was jinxed.

NINE

HAVING MY OWN car back really cheered me up. I arrived at Riverside Medical Centre by eight and the cleaner let me in. Bent double she was staring into the murky depths of a black plastic bucket.

'You the new nurse?' she asked without looking above my kneecaps.

'I am.'

She stood upright then, holding her mop aloft like some sacred flag. Even upright she appeared somewhat vertically challenged and I could see her grey hair was thinning on top, her face was narrowed and lined and she looked about seventy. 'Well, I hope you'll like it here,' she said ominously as if she was sure I wouldn't.

'I'm sure I will,' I said lightly.

'Not many people do. I only stay because I'm past retirement age.'

'What's wrong with the place?' I asked.

'That's not for me to say, is it?' She paused to inspect the head of her mop, gave me a wry smile and said, 'Well, I must get on. Staff room's that little door at the end of the hall.'

She staggered off then, weighed down with her bucket, and I made my way to the staff room, which was pretentiously named, because it was only a lavatory and a tiny alcove with two hard-backed chairs, a well-worn card table and on the wall, five clothes hooks. I changed quickly into my blue uniform dress, which by now was creased, and hung my skirt and blouse on the one clothes hanger. I brushed my hair, flicked mascara on my eyelashes, hoping it gave me a wide awake intelligent look, took a deep breath and prepared myself psychologically to become, not Kate Kinsella private investigator, but Kate Kinsella—practice nurse.

I spent a few minutes trying various doors to get the lie of the place. Then I went into the treatment room and investigated cupboards and drawers, checked sterile packs and instruments, peered into the tiny sterilizer and felt in that moment I had returned home. This treatment room was so similar to ward treatment rooms it made me long to return to busy hospitals and the camaraderie that used to exist in them.

The sound of cars driving up and doors banging signalled the arrival of the other staff. I emerged from the treatment room straight into the chest of Alan Dakers.

'Trying to knock me off my feet already, Kate? Glad to see you made it. Finding your way about?'

I nodded, a bit flustered by being in such rare and close proximity to an attractive man. I stepped back and smiled. The space between us made me feel more at ease. He took me by the elbow and led me to the first consulting room. 'By the way, did I tell you the practice is virtually run separately although you will do clinics in each one?'

'You didn't.'

'Ah,' he said, 'then I probably didn't tell you that Doctors Amroth and Holland do not speak to Doctors Thruxton and Wheatly.'

'You're joking.'

'I'm not.'

'They communicate in writing of course and just occasionally I can manage to arrange a meeting but it usually ends in a row.'

'What happened? Why aren't they speaking to each other?'

'No one knows.'

'Someone must,' I said.

Alan smiled. 'You're the persistent type, aren't you? Everyone has a theory about why they don't get on. Mine, for what it's worth, is the God Syndrome.'

'What do you mean?'

'Thruxton and Wheatly had fathers who were both doctors; one was a top-flight surgeon. So you see they are direct descendants of God.'

'My, we are a cynic, aren't we?' I said, laughing.

Alan grinned back. 'Amroth and Holland are both first-generation doctors and are merely preparing for Godhood. Holland was a bright spark from a comprehensive school and Amroth from a grammar. Thruxton and Wheatly, of course, went to public school.'

'That doesn't really explain the animosity, though, does it?'

'It's the numbers game that creates most of the animosity.'

'What numbers?'

'Patient numbers. Especially the elderly. Amroth and Holland are by far the most popular doctors. GPs, as you probably know, get extra money for visiting the elderly, extra money for almost everything—cervical smears, immunizations, even signing insurance forms. They compete amongst themselves for patients. Amroth and Holland are by far the most popular doctors. Mostly they work very hard and don't socialize much. In contrast, Wheatly plays a lot of squash and golf and Thruxton disappears on fishing trips and attends numerous medical seminars, or says he does. And of course the "freebies" cause problems. Amroth laid down the law about accepting "freebies" from the medical reps. Mostly it's pens and mugs or notepads but just occasionally it's weekends away or the odd bottle of whiskey. On this issue Wheatly and Thruxton just ignore Amroth.'

'I see,' I murmured.

'That's only my interpretation of the problem, Kate, so don't take it as gospel. Others think the problem comes back to women. But no doubt you'll hear all the gossip on that one from the wives. They all talk to each other— though methinks they speak with forked tongues.'

I was suitably intrigued and impressed with all this but suddenly Alan said, 'I'd better get back to the paperwork. You've got Dr Amroth's clinic and tomorrow afternoon you'll be doing Dr Wheatly's baby clinic. I'll write up a roster for you.'

'Thanks,' I murmured. I was beginning to realize I wasn't going to belong in any camp and I'd have to watch my tongue very carefully.

Alan then introduced me to Dr David Thruxton and Dr Marcus Wheatly. My reception was fairly friendly given that the opposition had recruited me and I was only second choice anyway. David Thruxton was in his early forties with straight fair hair that flopped over his forehead and which he flicked back at regular intervals. The sort of hair that remains boyish. I could easily imagine him at prep school, pretty and blue eyed and even then flicking the hair from his eyes.

Marcus Wheatly was younger, in his thirties, darkly attractive but too neat featured for my taste. His hands were small and womanish and moved constantly.

His voice was low but had a quality of assurance that could be comforting or patronizing depending, I supposed, on whether he was imparting good news or bad.

'Ours is a very middle-class practice,' he said, signalling that I should sit down. 'And we don't have too many problems...at least we didn't, but with the recession I'm afraid we are catching the middle classes on the slide, as it were.'

'Tumbling headlong into the working class?'

He looked at me sharply as if he knew I was being sarcastic. I had already taken a dislike to Marcus Wheatly. 'Health problems are growing,' he continued, 'mostly on the psychological front—depression, heavy drinking, eating problems, sexual problems. I did off-load quite a bit of that on to Jenny. It's so time consuming. I hope you feel able to deal with that sort of thing.'

'I'll certainly do my best.'

I'd fondly imagined I'd be doing mostly dressings, injections and dealing with cuts and bruises, even the odd bit of minor surgery. I already sensed that any drama was more likely to be in the psychological mode rather than blood and guts.

After that, Alan introduced me to 'the diary'. Scrawled in red pen in what looked like a doctorly hand were the names of four patients to see me. Two for tetanus injections, two for dressings. That was more like it. Moments later Dr Amroth stood at the open door of the treatment room. He seemed slightly surprised to see me and said, 'There'll be quite a few this morning. I'll send a short note in with each one.'

Short was the operative word. One note simply said: *Advise!*

The morning passed quickly. One of the regular patients, an elderly lady with an infected toe, mentioned Jenny. 'Jenny always made it nice and comfortable. Such a pleasant person, she always did my dressing just as I wanted it done.'

'I'll try to do the same,' I said. That comment seemed to do the trick, but afterwards I couldn't seem to get the conversation back to Jenny and I doubted that she had ever given much away. But of course that didn't mean that a patient didn't confide in her and then regret it enough to have to silence her. Or, of course, the same could be said for a staff member.

Once all the patients had gone I chatted for a few minutes

to Michelle Rushmore, the receptionist. We sat on the chairs outside the toilet, drinking coffee. 'Do you think you'll like it here?' she asked.

'Oh, yes,' I said, as if there could be no doubt. 'It's all a bit strange at the moment but I was lucky to be offered the job.'

Michelle smiled. 'I suppose you were. The girl they offered the job to came off her bike and broke her leg.' Then she added quietly, 'I suppose that was lucky compared to poor old Jenny. I really liked her. She got depressed at times, don't we all, but she always put on a brave face for the patients.'

'Have you any idea who could dislike her enough to kill her?'

Michelle shrugged thin shoulders. 'Not exactly, but I can't help thinking her husband might have had something to do with it.'

'Why do you think that?'

She began to look embarrassed. 'I shouldn't have said anything. It's not my business, is it? I'm sure the police know what they're doing.'

'Yes, but they do need all the information they can get.'

She sipped at her coffee thoughtfully. 'It was only once or twice, anyway... She was changing in here early one morning. I saw—I couldn't help it—bruises on her arms, and once she came in with a bruised face.'

'Perhaps they were just under a lot of stress.'

'Maybe,' agreed Michelle. 'It's just that I got the impression he was very possessive. He didn't like her going out, she told me that.'

'But she went out?'

'Oh, yes. She said since her little boy died there was nothing to stay in for. Her husband used to work in the evening so she said there was no point staying in to watch.'

'Did she go out with anyone from here?'

'What do you mean?' asked Michelle sharply.

'Well, I just thought that she might have socialized with colleagues at work, lots of people do.'

Michelle gave a brief little laugh. 'You'll understand why I laughed when you've been here a bit longer. Although she wasn't that friendly with anyone here, she was quite friendly with the doctors' wives.'

'All of them?'

'I don't know about that, but the wives are a friendlier bunch than their husbands. There's only three wives in the practice—Dr Amroth's wife left him four years ago. About once a month they used to have a lunch, alternating houses, when their husbands were doing other things. It was all girls together and Jenny seemed to enjoy herself.'

'You didn't go?'

Michelle smiled. 'I'm only a lowly receptionist. You'll probably get invited, though. I think the practice nurse is invited so that they get to know what their husbands are up to.'

'And are they up to anything?'

'Not that I know of. Mind you, one of them drinks quite a bit.'

'Which one?'

'I'm not telling you that,' she said standing up. 'You'll find out soon enough.'

She was opening the door to go when I plucked up enough courage to ask, 'What about the practice manager, Alan, is he married?'

She smiled, knowingly. 'Divorced, two kids, thinks he's Jack the Lad.'

I wanted to ask more but the knowing smile put me off. She probably fancied him too.

Before I went home I tidied up the treatment room and checked my diary. I flicked back to look at my predecessor's handwriting. It gave me an eerie feeling—everything

Jenny had written was work connected, yet I still felt I'd somehow encroached on her privacy. I also knew that I would be looking through her entries again and again to find a clue that might or might not be there. The diary had obviously been examined by the police anyway and as a work document they had passed it as non-vital evidence. In other words, it was no help at all. I had to assume at this stage that the murder and Teresa Haverall being missing were somehow connected. The police obviously thought so—but why? They obviously knew something that I didn't. Did they have something more in common than just an evening class—was Teresa a possible suspect?

I drove back to Humberstones relieved that my first morning was over and I hadn't had a single emergency. As I drove past the slatted blinds of reception I could see Hubert talking to Danielle. I hoped he wasn't going to get involved with her. From a mere ex-wife Hubert now had two women in his life and I was beginning to hope he'd soon settle down with Dolly Two-Shoes. Desperate Dan was likely to be the more disappointing of the two.

I made coffee, scraped the last morsel of peanut butter on to two crispbreads and was just about to enjoy the moment's feeling of virtue that eating sparsely manages to induce, when the phone rang. It was Nick's mother.

'Hello,' she said, 'I've just rung to apologize for my son. He's a scum-bag, he really is. I've told him if he pulls another stunt like that I'll personally drag him down to the Old Bill.'

'So you do know where he is?'

'I do now. I've said I'll give you another week and if no one's come up with a suspect then he'll have to give himself up. I can't keep paying out, can I?'

I murmured in agreement, wondering as I did so if on one more week's money I could keep going till the end of the month and my first pay cheque from Riverview.

'Just make sure Nick returns that car unharmed, will you, and then get him to contact me. There's a few questions I'd like to ask him.'

'Yeah, I'll try. But he only ever does what he wants anyway. I'll drop your money off in the week.'

It was only when I put down the receiver that I realized what a change of face this was. From the mother convinced of her son's innocence, who was willing to pay to prove it, she now seemed to be equally keen that he turned himself in. Did she in fact think he was guilty?

Hubert came up later to report that a glazier had repaired my window and that if I had any sense I would invest in a security system. Money was a sore point, or at least owing it was, so I answered him a bit tartly. 'Hubert,' I said, 'if I had money to invest I would invest it in stocks, shares, gilts, diamond mines or the like but a security system— never.'

He wasn't pleased. 'If he comes back you needn't think I'll get your windows fixed again.'

'Nick won't be coming back. I think he'll give himself up.'

'Not if he did it,' said Hubert. 'The sooner he's behind bars the better.'

I paused, thinking about what he had just said. 'You are a dear,' I murmured, as I gave him a hug.

'What did I say?' he asked with a grin, half embarrassed, half puzzled.

'You, Hubert,' I said, 'have given me a bargaining point for the CID. I could offer up young Nick as a sacrificial lamb in return for information.'

Hubert frowned. 'Hang on a minute, if Nick Fenny's mother stops paying you, you haven't got a client. No point in carrying on, is there?'

'Money isn't everything. Anyway, I just want to find the

bastard. He's killed once—maybe twice. It's a question of pride and it's a challenge.'

'You can say that again. Have you got one single suspect yet apart from Nick?'

'Well, no. Nick isn't a suspect anyway. Not now. If I can find the connection between Jenny and Teresa, I'll find the killer.'

Hubert shrugged, in disbelief or despair I wasn't sure. 'There may not be a connection,' he said pointedly.

'There already is, Hubert—the same evening class. But there's more to it than that. They must have had someone in common.'

'So?' said Hubert, giving me a 'What the hell are you talking about?' look.

'So, I think Jenny met her killer by arrangement. After all, who with any sense would let a strange man into their car?'

'Maybe she didn't have much choice. Maybe he came from behind and took her unawares.'

'Possibly, until we know exactly how she died we won't be sure.'

'There were no clues found in the car park even though they searched for two days. Not according to Bill, anyway.'

'No, Hubert. Maybe Jenny was attacked somewhere else and then put in the boot of the car.'

'That could mean two cars.'

'Precisely, and I think the other car was Teresa's and when it's found she will be too.'

'What about Bill's account?'

'As you know, I think he's an unreliable witness, not perhaps intentionally. And I'm not even sure the woman he saw was Jenny.'

'Who was she, then?'

I smiled at his frowning face. 'That, Hubert, is what makes this case so fascinating.'

TEN

ACCORDING TO my roster I was working three mornings and two afternoons. That suited me. It meant that the following morning I was free to visit Longborough CID. Not that I had any actual friends there but I did have acquaintances, Detective Sergeant Roade being one of them. He looked so young I think I reminded him of his mother, and so he was slightly more friendly than Detective Chief Inspector Hook, who, if he had a mother, had long since forgotten her. Roade had acne, a penchant for Mars bars, and managed to be a bit brighter than he looked.

Longborough police station seems to want to give the impression of being an upmarket dentist's and today it certainly smelt like it. The cleaner had just finished with the reception area floors and the disinfectant reminded me strongly of the smell of mouthwash. The desk sergeant was pleasant and female. I told her I was a close friend of DS Roade. She raised her neat eyebrows in surprise and looked at me with interest rather than suspicion but she showed me through to his office without any searching questions.

Roade sat alone in the office in front of a computer. The door was open and his head moved slightly as if he were conversing with the screen.

'Detective Sergeant Roade,' I said warmly. 'So good of you to see me.'

He mumbled. 'Oh...that's OK,' whilst looking very puzzled. That was a ploy I could use again, I decided. He obviously assumed now I had made an appointment and he'd forgotten about it.

Now I was on to a winner, all I had to do was win him over. 'May I sit down?' I asked, honey-tongued.

'Yeah,' he said. 'You can sit here. What can I do for you?'

'Well...I was hoping I could do something for you.'

'Such as?'

I was beginning to think any charm I was trying to drum up was being lost on him but his pupils did dilate a fraction when I crossed my legs and hitched up my skirt to expose my rather fine knees, which was one part of my body I couldn't fault.

'I thought I could be of some assistance with the Martin and the Haverall cases.'

'How?'

I could sense from his tone I'd irritated him already but I smiled sweetly. 'I've heard you're really making good progress and I thought if I could give you some information, then you might be able to tie up the loose ends.'

He stared at me. He was still playing it cagey; the expression on his small face didn't change but his nostrils flared slightly. I hoped he wasn't smelling a rat. I smiled inwardly. Roade had got an animal's face, with small eyes and a snub nose. It wasn't ratlike but it wouldn't have disgraced an anorexic guinea pig.

'What loose ends?' he asked.

I smiled knowingly. 'Nick Fenny for one. Is he still a suspect?'

'Yes. We would like a word with Nick.'

'I think I could find out where he is.'

'In return for...?'

'You're quick, DS Roade. It's no wonder you've made sergeant so young.' That seemed to please him and he tried not to smile. 'In return for my telling you where Nick is, you'll share some of your information with me.'

'How do I know you *do* know where Nick is?'

'You don't. But I'll only give the information to you and then you can do what you like with it. It's a bit of one-upmanship.'

Roade nodded. 'It's a deal—where is he?'

'Not so fast. I'll tell you in a day or two. After all, he is meant to be my client...'

'And you're shopping him?' Roade queried in a tone of mild disgust.

'It's not as simple as that. I believe he's innocent and I think it would be better for him just to plead guilty to taking and driving away...'

'Don't forget he set fire to the car as well. Those poor sods who got to it were in shock for days, you know. When the car boot flew open with the heat, there in the smoke and flames was the body and suddenly...it sat up!' He paused for the full weight of this pronouncement to affect me. I merely nodded. I did know that extreme heat can cause a body to sit up. So I simply said, 'He didn't kill her.'

'I never said he did,' agreed Roade. 'He's just a mindless yob.'

'Be an angel,' I urged him softly, 'and tell me more about Teresa Haverall.'

Roade shrugged. 'You'd better be on the level. If Hook finds out I've been giving you info he won't be pleased.'

'I'll do my best, Sergeant, to give you all the credit.'

Roade stared at his computer screen. 'You win. I was just looking at her details on the screen.'

I tried to move my chair closer but Roade said sharply, 'You just stay where you are.'

I angled my head but he moved the computer so I couldn't see at all. 'Now then,' he said, well satisfied he was still in control. 'Mrs. Teresa Haverall. Address, 4 Kingdom Grove, Longborough. Age, forty. Next of kin, technically the husband but divorce proceedings in progress.

One child, son aged eighteen, living with father in the village of Lampton. Worked as a hotel receptionist at the Grand Hotel. Separation of the couple, relatively friendly, husband now has new girlfriend.'

He paused then as if I needed time for this information to sink in. I did.

'Why did you say "worked" in the past tense, Sergeant?'

He smiled, savouring the moment.

'A decomposing body was found this morning in the boot of a car in an isolated wood. The number plate had been removed but the car has been identified, from registration marks, as belonging to Teresa Haverall. We don't know any more than that at the moment.'

Although I had suspected she was dead it still came as a shock. I knew this was my moment to get as much information as I possibly could but I couldn't think of a single question. DS Roade, sat back, satisfied with my silence, sensing no doubt that I was struggling to dredge up an intelligent query. Finally I asked, 'Any news on the cause of death?'

'I don't think we can overlook marks of strangulation with a ligature of some sort, maybe a tie. And the pathologist has noted a strange bruise on the back of her neck. He thinks it may be due to a karate chop which may or may not have been fatal.'

'Where was this wood?'

''Bout five miles from Dunsmore.'

'Did anyone see anything?'

'Nope, not that there was anyone around. It's in the middle of nowhere way off the beaten track. We're guessing she was murdered the same night as Jenny Martin.'

'Anything found in the car?' I asked.

DS Roade shook his head. 'Forensic say a good clean-up job was done but they think she was murdered else-where.'

'At Teresa's home?'

'No. The Scene of Crimes have been all over the house—nothing. Nothing at the Martin house, either.'

The murderer was obviously clever, controlled and de-vious. As dangerous as a mad dog but well disguised. Someone you might pass in the street and not notice. But what the hell was the connection between the two women—because I was still sure there was one. It was my final question, I could see Roade becoming restless and glancing at his watch.

Now I'd started thinking in the right way there was so much more I wanted to ask but I couldn't afford to irritate Roade. He was taking a risk, after all. I placed two Mars bars on his desk as I stood up. He looked at them in sur-prise. 'You still like them?' I asked.

'You bet,' he said.

'Thanks a million,' I said. 'I'll be in touch about Nick.'

'We'll catch him anyway,' said Roade. 'But I'd like to be in on it.'

I was at the door when he muttered from the side of his mouth, as if the walls had ears. 'By the way, we do have a suspect.'

He smirked then and faced his computer. You cunning little tyke, I thought, but I didn't show my surprise. I just walked out with my head held high.

I ARRIVED AT Riverview early that afternoon for the baby clinic. I had a feeling it could be traumatic. I needed an update on immunization and current trends in baby care. I'd worked on children's wards in my training and for a short time once qualified, and nothing since has quite equalled the awful responsibility of caring for sick children.

I reminded myself, though, that these were not sick children but well ones.

Each bungalow had its own treatment room but the one on the Amroth-Holland side seemed more cramped. Another work diary was open on a dressing trolley. Three babies were due for immunization plus two mothers listed as general advice regarding weaning. I felt I could cope—just.

I was reading through my practice nurse handbook when the door opened and a tall young man walked in. He was good looking, wearing denim jacket, jeans and Reeboks and sporting his long black hair in a pony-tail. 'Hi. You must be Kate. I'm Neil Amroth. Odd-job man *extraordinaire!*'

'You're Dr Amroth's son?'

He smiled handsomely, his brown eyes watching me closely. He had a wide attractive mouth, great teeth and a slight tan. He also appeared to have a good body. He didn't look a bit like his father. He perched his neat bottom on the edge of the examination couch and said in his deep, well-modulated voice, 'I came in to fix a leaking tap. But it appears to have stopped.' I smiled, he smiled again, and I wasn't quite sure what to say. After a few moments' silence I asked, 'Have you worked here long?'

'I manage to find odd jobs all over Dunsmore and its environs. Much, may I say, to my father's chagrin. I'm one of life's drop outs. I started reading PPE at Oxford but when my mother left home...well I got somewhat depressed and decided to call it a day. I haven't regretted it. In fact I feel quite proud I can turn my hand to most things. Not that my father would ever approve, even if I was earning more than him.'

'Do you live with your father?'

His mouth tightened slightly. 'Oh yes. He has a super house, but of course it's not really a home without my mother. But...we're company for each other.'

'No other siblings?'

He smiled. 'Not that we talk about.' He stood up, flexed his shoulders and then looked over to the tap saying, 'It's still not dripping.'

I couldn't let him go without asking about Jenny. 'I've been hearing about my predecessor Jenny—you must have known her?'

'Indeed I did. I had quite a few chats with her. She was a nice girl, I liked her. But then I like you too. *Au revoir,* Kate.'

As he closed the door I thought: Well, well…there goes a smile that could dissolve concrete. For a mere boy in his early twenties he was all man. The tap had been an obvious pretext to meet me and I couldn't help feeling his nonchalance over Jenny was forced. If she had been having an affair, it could have been with him or indeed any of the doctors or Alan, Mr Practice Manager. She'd had plenty of choice…

My train of thought was interrupted by the sound of a crying baby and my heart sank. They would all be shrieking by the time I'd wielded the needle. When mother and baby actually came in I was all *oohs* and *ahs* and *Aren't you gorgeous,* until—the jab. There always seems an age when the poor baby's mouth opens silently in shock before the wail of protest begins. The mother's eyes fill with tears and it's guilt all round and yet you know how essential it is.

The last mother of the afternoon was a welcome sight. She had come for weaning advice and her baby slept contentedly in her arms. She was young and pretty, in her early twenties, wearing a miniskirt and figure-hugging T-shirt— here was someone who had done her post-natal exercises. Her name was Bethany Lake and she seemed to know far more than I did about weaning. What started out as advice turned into a general chat and it was then that she mentioned Jenny. 'She was so brave, you know. How anyone

could want to hurt her I can't understand. My first baby
died and she spent ages with me. I don't think I could have
coped without her.'

I murmured that it was indeed a tragedy. 'It's strange,'
Bethany said, 'I think she had a premonition, you know.
She had a fall and her face was a bit bruised and I commented on it and she said, "I don't think I'll make old
bones, Bethany." I said something about not being silly
and she laughed and said, "I must enjoy the danger."'

After Bethany had gone I tidied up like an automaton.
So she did know her killer, of that I was convinced. And
so did Teresa. Their point of contact was the college.
Maybe calligraphy was a more dangerous occupation than
I had supposed. Perhaps the answer did lie at the college
and not at Riverview.

I stayed behind for a while writing up notes and just as
I was about to go I heard raised voices and then doors
opening and closing. Something was definitely going on.

ELEVEN

I CAME OUT OF the treatment room to see Neil and Alan going into the consulting room. As I stood there Doctors Thruxton and Wheatly turned up and marched in and as voices became raised I knew for certain that something quite important had happened or was about to happen. I stood there for a while toying with the idea of actually putting my ear to the door but decided that if I was caught it would be nearly as embarrassing as seeing my mother doing a can-can up Longborough High Street.

After I'd been standing there for about ten minutes straining to hear any morsel of the obvious intrigue Alan suddenly swung the door open and called out, 'Kate—come here—you may as well know what's going on.'

All eyes were upon me as I walked into the small consulting room. Alan closed the door behind me. Dr. Wheatly, sprawled on the examination couch, managed to flutter one of his delicate hands at me. Thruxton scowled, Neil stood staring out of the window, his shoulders slumped, and Alan seemed more excited than disturbed. Thruxton muttered: 'Sit down. This is a bloody mess. We may have to close for a few days...that might be best in the circumstances.'

'I don't think that will be necessary,' said Alan. 'We can easily ride this through.' Then he smiled at me and said, 'We have a problem, Kate: Dr Amroth has been taken in for questioning by the police.'

I paused, surprised. Murder, I thought, needed a degree of passion. Dr Amroth seemed to have as much passion as a plate of cockles. 'Surely,' I said, 'they can't really suspect him of murdering two women?'

'Only one woman,' answered Alan. 'His wife.'

'But what about...' I began and then seeing Neil turn and flash me an anguished expression I simply ended on a whispered 'Oh'. After a while I asked, 'Why do the police think Dr Amroth had anything to do with his wife's disappearance?'

This time it was Dr Thruxton who answered. 'Unfortunately they always had some suspicion that...an accident had befallen Helena but of course there was no evidence. Now they seemed to have a revived interest in her whereabouts. There is some suggestion they may want to dig up the gardens here and at Charles's house.'

'I think it's best if everyone carries on as normal,' suggested Alan. 'This...upheaval is obviously going to be short-lived and I think the police are just trying to detract everyone's attention from the real issue, which is who killed Jenny and Teresa.'

'I suppose Dr Amroth does have an alibi for the night in question?' I asked.

I could tell I'd dropped the proverbial clanger when they all stared at me in a prolonged silence. 'I only meant...' I blurted out nervously, 'that with an alibi he...well, they wouldn't suspect him of...anything else.'

'He was with me that night,' said Neil sharply.

'Oh, I see. I didn't know that.'

I kept my mouth firmly shut after that. Not much else was said other than the practice should try to keep home visits down and that everyone should work that bit harder until Dr Amroth returned to the fold.

Thereafter the day was punctuated with patients by visits from most of the staff. Neil was the first to come in.

'Have you got a minute, Kate?' he asked. He looked really unhappy. 'Of course,' I said. He sat down on the chair by my table and said quietly, 'Thanks for not saying anything before—about my mother. I lied when I said I'd seen her... I—' A knock at the door interrupted him. 'Kate, be an angel,' he said hurriedly, 'let me take you out and I can explain everything. Tomorrow? Eight o'clock—I'll pick you up—'

'No,' I quickly interrupted, 'make it outside the Swan in Longborough.'

He nodded and was walking out past Marcus Wheatly before I had a chance to work out why I had so readily accepted.

Marcus walked straight over to the sink with his left hand in the air. 'Have you got a plaster, Kate?'

'Of course,' I said, opening a drawer in my trolley and producing one.

'I cut my finger on a vial,' he explained.

I raised up his delicate hand to examine his index finger. The cut was minute but I dealt with it as seriously as if it had been a severed limb. He still managed to remind me of a prep-school boy and for a while I was in position as school matron. When the plaster was on he flicked back his hair with his hand and said, 'Mind if I sit down?' I knew from the past that doctors could be very squeamish about personal injuries and for a moment I did wonder if he felt faint. He didn't. He just wanted to talk. He was finding the practice hard to cope with, he wasn't sleeping well. He found it hard to be sympathetic with most patients, especially the stressed ones. 'I just can't help it. They whinge and moan about their uncomplicated lives. What the hell am I supposed to do? I wasn't trained as a social worker. At the end of the day I'm drained. They take everything from me. It's no wonder Sara is so unhappy and dissatisfied. She'll leave me one day. Just like Helena. Wives want more of a companion, don't they?'

'I'm sure your wife realizes how stressful your job is.'

'Intellectually of course she does, emotionally she doesn't. She resents it.'

'Perhaps a holiday?' I ventured weakly.

'I wish that was the answer,' he said slowly. Standing up he said, 'Thanks for listening, Kate.'

Later that afternoon Alan Dakers came to see me. He didn't invent some pretext to talk, he just got straight to the point. 'How about a drink together tonight?'

I was overwhelmed, two social occasions in such quick succession—could I cope?

'I can't make tonight, I've got...something to do.'

'Tomorrow then?'

I shook my head and murmured that I was very busy.

'Night after?' he persisted.

This time I nodded. He smiled. 'I thought I was losing my grip there. Once upon a time I would have been snapped up on the first offer.'

I smiled, hoping I looked enigmatic.

I'd just changed and was walking towards the front door when David Thruxton and Ian Holland walked in. They made a strange pair. Thruxton had a warm smile and an air of solid respectability aided by wings of silvery grey hair and pinstripe suits; Ian Holland favoured more casual wear with jumpers of the handmade variety. He was the youngest doctor, keen on computers and seemingly still keen on his job. Sporting a bushy beard and the occasional pair of sandals he was the only one of the four who didn't look like a business man. I could imagine him on summer evenings outside a pub doing a spot of Morris dancing and then going home to vegetable casserole and big hunks of wholemeal bread straight from the Aga. Today though his normally amiable face was creased with anxiety and David Thruxton looked equally worried. Not that they shared their worries with me; they walked towards me, nodded vaguely in my direction and walked on.

THE NEXT DAY I met Dr Thruxton again. He asked if I

would kindly act as chaperone for two female patients. In the few moments before the clinic started we had coffee together. He seemed depressed. By now though I realized not one of the doctors had a sense of humour—in fact they seemed the most miserable medical foursome on God's earth.

'You're started here at a bad time, Kate,' he said as he shuffled papers and tried to tidy his desk. 'Jenny's death has affected us all in different ways. It was so unexpected.' I nodded. And tried to gauge the expression in his eyes. Was he suffering the misery of bereavement or the anxiety of guilt? I couldn't decide.

When the first patient came in I did know why he wasn't the most popular doctor in the practice. She was a short woman in her sixties, overweight but not unhealthy looking. Thruxton gazed at her for a moment and then said, 'Mrs Baines, I see you are still as fat as ever.'

Poor Mrs Baines' embryonic smile faded in an instant. 'I do try, Doctor.'

'Not hard enough. You know the results of being too heavy, don't you?'

She nodded sadly. She'd obviously had the lecture before. I smiled encouragingly at her but her day had been ruined.

David Thruxton examined Mrs Baines thoroughly and questioned her, but by now she was unwilling to complain too much about her arthritic knees or the pain in her back.

'It's your age and weight, Mrs Baines. I can give you painkillers and anti-inflammatory tablets—that's all.'

'Could I see a specialist?' she asked timidly.

Dr Thruxton smiled weakly. 'You're over sixty-five?' he asked.

'I'm sixty-six.'

He shrugged. 'Lose three stone and I'll consider it. See

the nurse here each week and she'll weigh you and report back to me on your progress.'

When she'd gone I said, 'You were a bit hard on her.'

He looked genuinely surprised. 'Was I? She's over sixty-five. It's tough on the aged but there it is. If I referred all my over sixty-fives to consultants the NHS would grind to a halt.'

'You'll be that age one day,' I muttered.

He didn't appear to hear and the next patient was thin as a stick, also elderly but this time suffering from osteoporosis. She, it seems, was too thin. Dr Thruxton's patients couldn't win.

I decided that I didn't like David Thruxton and couldn't help wondering if he wasn't committing murder by medical omission on a regular basis. He seemed to me callous, cold and quite capable of regarding people as nuisances to be got rid of. But no doubt the police were satisfied with his alibi and he wasn't necessarily guilty of anything but having the God Syndrome, as Alan had so aptly described it.

THAT EVENING on my way home from Riverview I called in on Rose Fenny. She was in the kitchen ironing, a great stack of ironed clothes already army-neat on the kitchen table. The smell of damp homeliness reminded me of my childhood, of watching my mother doing the same. Ironing is most definitely a spectator sport in my opinion. Completely soothing. Even more so, as I sipped the large sherry Rose supplied me with.

'I've had a word with CID in Longborough,' I told her, 'and they seem to think Nick is in the clear for the murder.'

'Should he give himself up?' she asked.

'I do think it would be for the best. Once they clear Nick they really will have to put all their efforts into finding the murderer.'

Rose raised her eyebrows and rested her iron for a moment as she carefully folded a waist slip. 'What worries me is...well, say he confesses?'

'Is that likely, Rose?'

She let out a little sigh. 'You hear so many cases about the Old Bill forcing confessions out of people.'

'I don't think Nick would be that intimidated by the police, do you?'

'P'raps not. He is used to being interviewed, after all,' she said, taking a big gulp of sherry and draining her glass. 'My Nick isn't that stupid. Not that I thought he was a murderer either, but when he's out of my sight I just begin to wonder...you know...thinking. I know he can't resist taking cars but violence isn't his scene.'

'You'll persuade him to give himself up, then?'

'Yeah. Why not, love? I mean, he can join his old man, can't he? I did my best, Kate, with the pair of them. Nick rang me today. Says he's going to come back from Birmingham in a day or two, in the early hours, and he wants to talk. What that means is he wants money. I think he's got it into his head to go to Spain—like some high-flying criminal. That's what frightens me about him, Kate. He wants to be a celebrity, famous. Silly little prat!'

Before I left, Rose paid me a week's money. 'I'll be sure to recommend you,' she said.

Which was kind of her, but what exactly had I done? And now I intended to shop him I felt a great sense of guilt. I was fairly sure Nick wasn't going to give himself up and I was equally sure Rose would give him all the money she had to help him leave the country.

Rose stood on the doorstep waving me goodbye. I turned and from a distance, in her short skirt and snug pink top, she looked like a teenage girl.

I drove away feeling a real Judas. My only client now fully paid up and for what?

When I got back to Humberstones' Hubert was waiting outside my office door.

'Your phone was ringing,' he said by way of excuse. 'You need an answering machine.'

'Probably.'

He watched me enquiringly as I sat down. 'What's wrong with you now, Kate?'

'Nothing, Hubert. I'm just not feeling very moral at the moment.'

'What have you been up to?'

His face looked so shocked I laughed. 'Not that sort of moral. I'm just feeling that being a private investigator isn't...well...moral.'

'Don't be daft,' said Hubert fixing me with a glazed sort of stare, 'what could be more moral than finding wrong-doers? I suppose you want it to be a public service paid for by the tax-payers.'

'I knew you wouldn't understand, Hubert.'

'You could try and persuade me over a bevvie at the Swan.'

I didn't need much persuasion. 'I'll be two seconds.'

I changed into jeans and a blouse so baggy it would do me well into the ninth month of pregnancy, if that ever happened, and emerged from my box-room to a very dis-approving look from Hubert. 'Haven't you got any frocks?' he asked.

'Frocks! Hubert, women don't wear frocks any more, especially for drinks at the Swan.'

He muttered a bit about declining standards but I think really he was thinking more about the demise of the stiletto heel, slingbacks and pointed toes.

The pub was empty save for a couple of pensioners play-ing shove ha'penny, a silent couple, obviously married be-cause they stared morosely around them as if looking for someone to talk about, and the landlord whose face lit up when he saw us as potential profits.

I sat in a booth as Hubert went to order drinks. From there I watched a cross-section of middle England recreated. Not a sign of jollity anywhere. My spirits plummeted.

Hubert returned with a double brandy and lemonade for me and a pint of bitter for himself. 'I've ordered chicken in a basket for us both,' he said.

'I'll pay for that,' I said, feeling another pang of guilt at Hubert subsidizing both my calorie and my alcohol intake.

'You will not,' he said. 'I'm old fashioned.'

Two brandies later plus the chicken and chips I burst into song. 'I'm old fashioned, I love the moonlight...'

'That's enough, Kate—people are looking at us.'

'Good. Now, Hubert, whilst I can still enunciate my words, let me tell you about the case.'

He listened whilst I told him about my chat with Roade and with Rose Fenny.

'So you think the answer lies in the calligraphy class?'

'Well, it could do.'

'Doesn't seem very likely some old boy who can teach a bit of fancy copperplate writing could also be doing a bit of serial killing on the side.'

'To non-murderous people, like us, Hubert, of course it seems unlikely. Serial killers are often the most unremarkable people. I mean, they have to keep a low profile, don't they? Otherwise they'd get caught before they achieved serial status.'

'There's no need to be flippant, Kate.'

'I didn't mean to be. I think it's very serious. And I think he's only just started.'

'You're sure it's a man?'

'I haven't found out yet who teaches calligraphy but both victims were attacked viciously and then carried to the boots of their cars, so it would need a strong woman to do that.'

'Or two people?'

'Yes.' Hubert's forehead puckered into a frown. 'Do be careful, Kate. You are inclined to act first and think afterwards. Have you actually got a suspect in mind?'

'Oh yes,' I said brightly. 'The man who inflicted bruises on Jenny—he's the one.'

'Yes. And who is he?'

'Ah. That's the problem.'

I couldn't admit to Hubert I didn't really have a suspect. I had suspicions but no one I could glorify with the title 'suspect'. I waffled a bit then, not answering the question, as politicians do. Saying I'd have to visit her husband again; not that he was a real contender.

But then I remembered how he'd grabbed my arm. Maybe I was wrong. He could be a killer. His grief and depression could well be due to guilt and remorse. Perhaps there *was* something a touch sinister about him. He had, after all, admitted they were planning a separation. Perhaps he had followed Jenny, insisted she come home, murdered her in the house, put the body in the boot, drove the car to the college, left the car and walked home. What about Teresa? a little voice asked. Maybe he thought Teresa was a bad influence, being already divorced and newly single. In a disturbed mind it could make sense to wreak revenge on a person who he thought had led his wife astray.

'As I said,' Hubert was saying, 'even though you don't listen to me—just be careful. I don't like all these strange men phoning you...'

'What strange men? What are you talking about?'

'That phone call just before you came in—"Just tell Kate Neil phoned". Very public school type.'

'I thought you were kidding about the call, Hubert. You're sure it wasn't Alan?'

'He said it was Neil. He wouldn't say that if it was Alan, would he?'

'No, but...'

'What's wrong with Neil, then, who is he?'

'He's a nice chap. I've only spoken to him once. He's just young.'

'How young?'

'Twenty-fourish.'

I glanced at his face. 'There's no need to look at me like that, Hubert. I'm not that interested in him and anyway even if I was I'm not cradle snatching. He is a grown man.'

'Who's Alan, then?'

'He's the practice manager. I quite like him.'

'How old is he—eighteen?'

I began to feel irritated. 'At my age, Hubert, it's difficult to find men of my own age who aren't either married, gay or odd, very odd—'

'That's not true,' Hubert interrupted, 'a bachelor in his early thirties doesn't have to be odd. I didn't get married until I was—'

I felt sorry for Hubert then, he had stepped straight into that one. 'Let's change the subject,' I suggested. 'And I'll buy *you* a drink.' He couldn't get to the bar fast enough.

Although I did rather resent his taking an interest in my potential love life, I was my own worst enemy. Steady, respectable men hadn't appealed before and my longest relationship ended abruptly with masonry falling on to his drunken head. I'm sure he didn't feel a thing. But I did. And it had left me very wary.

Eventually we left the pub, supporting each other. Hubert was somewhat uninhibited and he confided that he was strongly attracted to Danielle. My heart sank.

'Poor old Hubert,' I said.

'Not so much of the *old*. I could still father a child.'

Dear God, I thought, not with Danielle, you couldn't. Even if she was a woman, she was too old.

'Hubert,' I said softly. 'Is your eyesight OK?' He didn't answer. He was far too busy trying to keep us both upright.

Later that evening after I'd managed to flop Hubert onto his bed, covered him with a duvet and staggered back to my box-room, the phone rang. It was Neil. British Telecom now diverted my home calls to the office automatically, which I thought was somewhat clever.

'Kate. I've caught you at last. I'm just checking it's still on for tomorrow evening?'

'Yes, Neil it's still OK.' There was a long pause and I wondered if we'd been cut off.

'Let's make it dinner at the Grand then. I thought it might be fun.'

Dinner at the Grand seemed more of a date than a drink and I suddenly wondered if it was such a good idea after all. And I voiced my misgivings.

'You mean your being an employee of my father's?' he asked softly.

'Well, yes.' And of course the fact that I was several years older than him. But I didn't mention that, hopefully he could have thought I was still in my twenties—hopefully!

'No one need know, Kate. I'll give you a good time—I promise.'

The alcohol had weakened my reasoning powers because at that moment I couldn't think of a single reason I shouldn't have dinner at the Grand and the promise of a good time.

'See you at eight then, outside the Grand.'

'Good night, Kate. I'll see you tomorrow. I'm looking forward to it very much.'

As I fell asleep I wondered if he'd dated Jenny—and whether any man would admit to it in the circumstances.

THE MORNING SESSION went quite well the next day. It was the Well Person's Clinic and anyone could come along, fill out a questionnaire and have various tests including blood pressure, pulse and urine. For a fee the blood could also be tested for cholesterol. It was time-consuming, not because of the tests but because people came who were worried and wanted to talk. One man, Reginald Bott, told me he had come for his health check twice a year for four years and he was plotting his own health breakdown.

'I do everything I'm told to and I don't feel any better. I was forced to take early retirement and I thought I'd be able to really make the effort to be healthy. But look at me now.' I looked. He looked about sixty, quite ruddy in the face, but with a scrawny neck and sparse grey hair, a down-turned mouth and the general air of a man who felt he was on life's downward trend.

'When I first came here,' he explained 'I was full of hope. But now, well, everything's come down around my ears. My wife's a semi-invalid, I'm bored and yet busy, I can't sleep at night for financial worries and then my favourite nurse gets murdered.'

'A tragedy,' I agreed.

'This place is dogged by bad luck. Poor Dr Amroth's wife left him, Jenny's son got killed and now Jenny. It fair depresses me, it does. It's no wonder my blood pressure goes up every time I come.'

'You knew Jenny well, then?'

'She used to visit my wife. Just for a chat and to see if we needed anything.'

'This was till…recently?'

'Oh yes. Her last visit was the week before she was killed.'

'Did she seem worried about anything?'

Reg shook his head. 'Not more than usual. I knew her before her son died, she was so happy-go-lucky. Then af-

terwards she became very quiet and withdrawn. Saying
that, though, she was quite a bit brighter during her last
few weeks.'

'Did she say why?'

He shrugged. 'Not really. But once she patted me on the
back and said: "Cheer up, Reg, live dangerously. I do." I
thought that was a bit out of character because she always
toed the healthy living line. She was the one who helped
me give up smoking. I asked her what she meant.'

'What did she say?'

'She said that living on the brink made you appreciate
life more, and however long she'd got, she wanted to live
with her adrenalin flowing.'

'It sounds as if she knew she was going to die,' I murmured. Reg nodded in agreement.

When he'd gone I thought about how Jenny must have
stood in this treatment room and mulled over the patients'
problems. And her own. Was there a moment when she
realized she might be a victim, and did she care? Is there
such a thing as a natural victim? Someone who deliberately
courts danger? Was the connection between Jenny and Teresa a shared acknowledgement of the thrill of being on the
nearside of death? Surely though that would have remained
unspoken, undetected. Bungee jumping, parachuting, rock
climbing, even pot-holing would, I assume, attract people
who barely concealed their flirtation with the hereafter, but
calligraphy?

When the morning's clinic was over I had a chat with
the Thruxton-Holland receptionist, a woman of formidable
girth but with a sweet young face and a tendency to talk
about the minutiae of life in great detail.

Her name was Maggie, she had two grown-up children,
two 'perfect' grandchildren, a husband who played golf and
a tendency to discuss the condition of her hair in great
detail. I listened patiently for a while. Her hairdresser had

recommended low lights and high lights, a soft perm ('my hair really does take a soft perm well, I was ever so pleased with it but next time she said…') and on and on. She even discussed the state of her dandruff. It was riveting stuff. As a way into the general discussion of hair I mentioned Jenny. 'I believe she had really pretty hair,' I said.

'Oh, she did. A natural blonde. Always kept the same style, a nice little bob. We went to the same hairdresser. Of course her hair was fine and mine's a bit coarse but there it is…there it is.'

There was no stopping her. I daydreamed about having Maggie in front of a bright light; every time she mentioned hair I would snip a bit off. All I could do in reality was grin inanely and bear it and hope that sometime she would fix on something useful. Somehow if her hair had been worth a mention it wouldn't have been so ludicrous, but it was as fizzled as if she plugged herself into an electrical socket.

When I finally escaped and was just about to leave Riverview with the intention of paying a visit to the college I bumped into David Thruxton. 'I'm glad I've caught you,' he said. 'Ros said I really must invite you to lunch tomorrow, the practice wives will be there. Female-only do, but the food is splendid.'

'Thank you. I'd be delighted to come.'

'Jenny used to enjoy the lunches,' he said quietly.

'Everyone seemed to like Jenny.'

He smiled. 'She was with us a long time.'

'How long exactly?'

'Eight years…' He paused, his blue eyes staring at me but not seeing me. 'It's strange how guilty you can feel when someone dies violently—as if somehow we could have done something to prevent it.'

'Such as?'

He shrugged and then held the door open for me. 'I really

don't know, but someone had hurt her and we acted as if we believed her bruises were accidental, merely, I suppose, to save her embarrassment, when if we'd been less squeamish we perhaps could have saved her life.'

'If she had wanted to be saved.'

He nodded. 'I hadn't thought of that.'

As I walked away the thought crossed my mind that he could have been in love with Jenny. Did Ros his wife know? Could Ros have employed a hit man? A hit man paid to do two murders and make them look like the work of a serial killer. I wouldn't know that, until I met them all. It was a lunch date I looked forward to.

TWELVE

I HADN'T TOLD Hubert about my date with Neil Amroth. I felt pleased to be going out and I didn't want him giving me a lecture about the perils of being with a young and rampant man.

There was a feeling of Saturday night about getting ready. First the hair washing, then the bubble bath. Saturday night when I was a teenager had been special. Then I had even painted my toenails but I thought that was going a bit far on a first and probably last date with young Neil the odd job man.

I debated for ages about what to wear. The Grand Hotel wasn't that grand and most people visiting the restaurant didn't dress up. Eventually I decided on a pale mauve blouse teamed with a purple skirt. I dressed it up with dangly earrings and multi-coloured beads and wore a pair of cream sandals that crippled me. I wouldn't be walking far, I reasoned, and could always slip them off under the table if blisters developed after fifty yards. I teased my red hair into a relatively tidy state, noticed my roots were no longer hennaed but back to mouse and sighed that no matter how hard I tried I wasn't going to look as good as a model, even one wearing no make up and dressed in a bin liner and Doc Martens.

I was ready by seven thirty, restless and uneasy. Maybe he wouldn't come, maybe the evening would be a disaster. What did we have in common anyway? Only Riverview. But he had known Jenny and therefore he could be useful. And he was very attractive, which all in all meant that the evening could be a lot more fun than knitting bedsocks.

At five past eight I was convinced he wasn't coming and
the evening stretched before me, all dressed up and feeling
slightly ridiculous. I stared out of my front window. Evening sunlight fell softly on the gravestones, it was warm
and balmy and my restlessness increased. I wanted to go
out tonight, I *had* to go now that I was ready.

Just after ten past eight a black Rover drew up outside.
Neil, I had to admit, looked very smart in a pale grey suit
with a grey and blue striped tie and white shirt. It made
him look older somehow and having only seen him in jeans
I assumed he always dressed that way. I ducked behind the
curtains so that he wouldn't see me looking and when he
knocked at the door I took my time answering. He had kept
me waiting, after all.

'Kate, you look lovely,' he said. He didn't apologize for
being late but flattery was far more soothing than a mere
apology. I praised the car which he said he'd borrowed
from his father, which made me feel as if I was sixteen and
should tell him I had to be home by eleven.

The journey into Longborough was punctuated by silent
episodes; I was definitely out of the dating habit and felt I
should be both mildly flirtatious and wittily entertaining. I
was neither. Neil asked me how long I've lived in Farley
Wood and where I'd lived before. I told him a little about
life in North London and about my mother being in Australia, and then I was stumped. I couldn't of course mention
Humberstones' or Medical and Nursing Investigations.

The restaurant of the Grand Hotel wasn't particularly
busy, but there were fresh wild flowers and lit candles on
every table. The french windows were slightly open and a
gentle breeze and the sound of trees rustling outside combined with occasional insect noises made it feel vaguely
continental.

The waiter was young and foreign looking and he handed

us each a gold-embossed menu that was so large it had to be held open with both hands.

'Would you like me to order for you, Kate?' asked Neil, his blue eyes staring at me over the top edge of the menu.

'I think I can manage, thank you,' I smiled but the smile was fake. I was highly irritated. I'd always felt and probably always will that if a woman can't choose her own meal, even if a menu is written in Urdu, then she should be ashamed of herself. I mean if you don't know what a dish is you only have to ask.

Eventually I chose melon and Parma ham as a first course followed by lobster salad. The wine waiter appeared then and Neil asked with a decisive edge to his voice, 'Champagne, Kate?' I smiled and nodded nonchalantly as if I wouldn't dream of drinking anything less. But when the wine waiter left I murmured, 'Neil, this is going to cost a fortune. I'm feeling guilty, I'm sure you're not that flush with money.'

'I earn enough and I have no one to spend it on. I go jogging nearly every day, skiing once a year and apart from buying classical music tapes and compact discs I'm incredibly frugal.'

'So you don't come here often?'

Neil smiled. 'Christmas, birthdays—my mother liked this place—and to Practice bashes occasionally.'

'You never wanted to be a doctor?'

'Never,' replied Neil emphatically. 'I've seen what medicine has done to my father. Most of the time he's completely exhausted. When Helena, my mother, was around she'd persuade him to relax more but he takes very little notice of me.'

'Do you mind me asking why she left?'

Neil shrugged. 'No, not at all. That's what I want to talk about.'

The champagne arrived then and for a few moments after

the de-corking and the loud pop and the perfunctory interest of the other diners we both fell silent as if remembering occasions in the past when we'd drunk champagne.

'You were telling me about your mother, Neil,' I prompted as Neil stared ahead, obviously deep in thought.

'Yes. My mother—Helena…she was bored and lonely I think. She didn't have a job and I'd gone up to university. They married whilst they were both students. My mother was taking a pharmacy degree but she left after the wedding. Once I'd gone up to university I suppose she felt…redundant. My father would come home at night, fall asleep or do paperwork and of course all the changes in the NHS made so much more work.'

'Where is she now?' I asked.

Neil stared at me, his blue eyes saved from being cold by the long black eyelashes. 'I'd rather not say. She doesn't want my father to know we are in contact.'

'Surely that's unfair,' I said quietly, 'especially now the police seem to think some harm could have befallen her.'

Nick smiled sadly. 'It's up to her. The police will soon realize my father is telling the truth.'

'Even if it means digging up your garden?'

'I respect my mother's wishes. One day she'll come back, I'm sure of that.'

Before the first course appeared I excused myself and went to the Ladies.

The Grand Hotel loo was a four-star one with red flock wallpaper, fresh flowers, abundant mirrors, even two armchairs. One was reserved for the lavatory attendant who sat in a corner reading a romance. She wore a zipped overall which only just held her in, her grey hair was scraped back into a bun and she had a broad, bare face that reminded me of an elderly Russian grandmother. I'd seen her before but never spoken to her. This time I made the effort. First though I placed a large tip noisily into the saucer. She glanced up at me. 'Lovely flowers,' I commented. 'You really do keep the place beautifully.'

'I do me best.'

I was a bit stumped then but I got straight to the point. 'A friend of mine used to work here on reception. I don't suppose you know all the workers, though.'

'I know the women.'

'Her name was Teresa Haverall...'

She stared at me for a moment as if judging if I was half witted. 'You from out of town?'

I nodded.

'Well, me duck. Poor Teresa's been murdered. Battered about the head.'

'I think I'll have to sit down,' I said.

Mrs Attendant put down her book. 'It's a shock, I know. I liked Teresa. She was ever so lively and cheerful. She was one of me favourites.'

'The police don't know who did it, then?'

'No. Haven't got a clue. I mean it must be a lunatic, one of them serial killers like you read about.'

'I expect the police have interviewed you.'

She laughed. 'I wouldn't call it an interview. A young policeman spoke to me—but I don't reckon he thought I knew anything—only took him about three seconds and he was off.'

'What did he ask you?'

'Just if I knew her and what she was like.'

'And what did you say?'

'I told him the last time I saw her she said: "Bella, I'm happier now than when I was a teenager." '

'What do you think she meant by that?'

Bella frowned and shrugged her large shoulders. 'I dunno, duck, do I?'

'Did you see any of her boyfriends?'

'No.' She sounded uncertain.

'No one tall, wearing black?'

'No.'

'Did she mention any boyfriends?'

Again Bella shook her head. Still she seemed uncertain, a little worried. 'You can tell me,' I said quietly. 'I was her friend.'

'Very friendly, were you?'

'Oh yes,' I said, 'very friendly.'

'Well...she did have someone special. Known each other some time. Going to move in together. She was excited about it, said she hated living alone.'

'Did you see him?'

Bella stared at me for a moment. 'It wasn't a man, m'duck. It was a girlfriend. That's the awful bit—she was murdered, too.'

She waited for her information to sink in, then said in a conspiratorially low voice, 'Lesbians, see. Killed by a man who hates them. Just like the Yorkshire Ripper. I mean he hated prostitutes, didn't he? This one hates lesbians.'

'Thank you, Bella, thank you very much.' I put another pound coin in her saucer, she smiled, picked up her book again and said meaningfully, 'I'm sorry about your friend.'

When I appeared back in the restaurant the first course had arrived and Neil looked somewhat peeved. 'I was just about to send out a search party. You're not ill, are you?'

'No, I'm fine. I met someone I knew and we had a chat. Sorry.' His good humour returned after two full glasses of champagne. I lied convincingly telling him that the friend I'd met in the loo had known Jenny.

'What did she say about her?' he asked.

'Nothing much, just that they'd done their nurse training together and she'd heard her son had been killed by a hit-and-run driver...'

'Hey, come on, Kate,' interrupted Neil. 'Let's change the

subject. Drunken drivers are a depressing topic.' He refilled my glass before I had a chance to decline.

'You won't be able to drive home if we keep on drinking.' He laughed. 'Don't worry, Kate, there are plenty of taxis. The night is young and this champers is only the start.' Taking my hand he squeezed it tightly, and his foot touched my ankle. Oh God, I thought, realizing then I should have guessed this would happen. By the time the evening was over I was going to have to fight him off.

By the second bottle of champagne I was talking giggly nonsense about nothing in particular. At the end of the meal we drank brandies from huge balloon glasses and I'd got delusions of grandeur, the beginnings of a headache and the stirring of desire for the young, muscular body of Neil Amroth. A little voice kept saying, *Control yourself. You are a mature woman.* Another voice said, *What the hell! Enjoy yourself.*

In the taxi on the way back to Farley Wood I realized I felt light-headed. Neil put his hand on my knee and I clamped my hand over it very swiftly. He seemed to mistake this for passion and he began kissing me with lots of youthful enthusiasm, and not much finesse. Luckily the taxi driver drove like the clappers and we were back to Farley Wood before Neil's heavy breathing became hyperventilation.

'I'm coming in for coffee,' said Neil. I could tell by his voice he wasn't as tipsy as I was. Indeed, all he seemed to have lost were his inhibitions. I'd lost my legs and stomach somewhere between the hotel and home. 'Please yourself, Neil,' I managed.

I managed to pour the boiling water in the cups but got the coffee into the saucer as well. It was a shambles. Neil followed me into the kitchen where his hands began to roam. He took the cups from me and placed them on the kitchen table. He also began to talk in a sort of husky whisper, sweet nothings, 'Kate, you're wonderful. I'm falling in love with you. Kate—just let me…' His hand had by now engulfed my left breast…

I felt my face flame but recognized that it was not passion I was feeling but some sort of reaction to the lobster. My stomach heaved. I pushed him away and rushed upstairs to the bathroom and locked the door. There I allowed my stomach to heave some more. Neil, thank God, hadn't followed me up the stairs. An audience was the last thing I needed.

It came soon enough. 'Kate!' he shouted. Then I heard the *thump-thump-thump* of his footsteps up the stairs. 'Open up. Are you all right?'

'Neil, I feel terrible. Thanks for a lovely evening but I…' Clutching my stomach I just made it to a kneeling position in front of the loo.

After a few minutes Neil called out again. 'Kate, I don't like to leave you like this. Let me in.'

I managed to answer in a fairly normal voice. 'I'll be fine, really. Please, Neil, just let yourself out. I'll ring you tomorrow.'

'Make sure you do, Kate. I shall be worried.'

I washed my face then, cleaned my teeth and perched on the edge of the bath. Once before lobster had had this effect on me; I had assumed it was a once only reaction. I'd been wrong. The lobster had had its revenge. Perhaps I should become a vegan—future poisoning by fruit and veg seemed pretty unlikely. I decided I wasn't going to come out until I heard him go. Any sweet stirrings of my libido had been well and truly flushed away, all I desired now was my bed and my duvet.

Once I heard the front door close I made my way to bed. I virtually collapsed, slept immediately and woke to the sound of birdsong and soft light falling on my face from a crack in the curtains. My head throbbed, I shivered, my musculature was as knotted as garlic on a string—I could have been dying I felt so ill. I was hoping to sink back into virtual unconsciousness when someone knocked very loudly on the front door. Please, please, not Neil, I thought. I actually liked him and there was no way I wanted him to see the red lumps that now covered my face and neck.

I opened the door a fraction. It was DS Roade. I could see by the expression on his small face that I looked like one of the undead. 'You OK?' he asked.

'I had a late night,' I said, squinting my eyes against the cruel morning sun. 'What's the time?'

'Seven thirty. Can I come in? What's wrong with you? You've got red lumps on your face.'

I groaned aloud, 'Antihistamine will sort them out. Come on in.'

I was still fully dressed and my clothes were as creased as if I'd gone three rounds with a sumo wrestler. I made coffee silently and it was only when the coffee was made I noticed Roade hadn't said why he'd come. In fact I noticed how he looked really glum. I sat down at the kitchen table opposite him. 'What's happened?' I asked.

'There was a car chase last night. The traffic police clocked Nick Fenny doing ninety down the M1. They gave chase and there was a crash…'

'Is he dead?'

'As good as. Severe brain damage. He's on life support but he's not expected to survive.'

Suddenly I felt angry. 'Why the hell did they chase him? Couldn't they have radioed ahead?'

'It doesn't work like that,' said Roade. 'The traffic cops have both been injured as well.'

'When did it happen?'

'In the early hours. His mother's with him.'

'Poor Rose,' I murmured.

'She's already given permission for his organs to be used.'

'Someone will benefit, then,' I said sadly.

We drank our coffee in silence. There didn't seem much else to say. Was it my fault Nick was near to death? Roade looked tired and depressed too. Eventually he said, 'It was a random chase, Kate. The traffic blokes didn't recognize him, they just tried to stop a car that was travelling over the speed limit.'

I sighed, my head still ached. 'Have you had breakfast?' I asked.

His face lit up. 'No, and I'm starving.'

'If I get everything ready can you cook a fry-up? I'll have a shower and you can cook while I'm upstairs.' I put out eggs, bacon, a few mushrooms past their best, and tomatoes.

I could smell the bacon cooking from the bathroom but even in my delicate condition it smelt quite good. By the time I came downstairs, Roade was tucking in. He'd almost managed to clear my stock of food, although he did point to the toast rack to show me he had left me a slice of toast.

Once he'd eaten I made some fresh coffee in a cafetière and as we sat drinking I took two aspirins and a Piriton and asked him how the case was going.

'We've finished questioning Dr Amroth. As far as his wife is concerned we've finished our investigation.'

'And?'

'And he's a devious bastard but we haven't got any evidence to prove she's dead although we are making a lot more effort to actually find her. Missing adults are assumed to be alive especially when there's no evidence of foul play. Hundreds of people go missing every day—what can the police do?'

'So he's not a suspect any more?'

'I wouldn't say that. We can't hold him indefinitely just

because Hook is convinced she's ten feet under some-where.'

'What about the connection between Teresa and Jenny?'

'You mean the calligraphy class?'

I nodded. Roade smiled. 'Mostly pensioners, and the tutor is a frail little biddy of sixty-six. Mind you she keeps a register and they certainly didn't turn up for every class. When they were away they were both away. Neither of them went alone. They sat together, didn't mix much but they weren't unfriendly with the rest of the class.'

'I can't help thinking,' I said, 'that they had more in common than that class. It seems they probably met up on the nights they didn't go to the college.'

Roade smiled knowingly. 'You're right. They did have something else in common.'

'What?'

'Teresa had lost a child too. Years back before she lived in the area. A daughter, drowned in a garden pond, aged eighteen months.'

I thought about that and summed up aloud. 'Two women, both attractive, both quite well balanced, both though with a tragic past, broken marriages and an interest in calligraphy—'

'So,' interrupted Roade. 'Where does that get you?'

'I wish I knew, DS Roade, I wish I knew. But somehow I do know that the death of their children has to be part of the puzzle.'

'How do you make that out?'

'It's all that emotion involved—anger, guilt, recriminations, the desire for revenge...revenge?'

'Yeah, but they would be the ones wanting revenge.'

'I know that,' I said, 'but maybe they were plotting together...'

'Against who?'

'I don't know, but perhaps they felt themselves wronged

and the persons or person found out and decided to silence them.'

Roade smiled. 'Not in Teresa's case. It was summer and she fell asleep in the garden and her kid crawled through a gap in the fence and into the next-door neighbour's garden and then into their pond. It was simply an accident. There was a very thorough investigation and inquest.'

'Oh,' I murmured despondently.

Roade left soon after, thanking me for the breakfast and saying, 'Chin up.' But my chin was down together with my spirits and I sat for a while thankful it was Saturday but definitely feeling gloomy.

At nine I rang Hubert. The phone rang and rang and I despaired. When he did answer I said, 'There you are. I've been trying for ages.'

'I was busy. I've just had a new consignment of coffins delivered. And I phoned you, last night, quite late.'

'I was out.'

'I guessed that. I was a bit worried.'

'There's no need, Hubert. I had a date.'

Silence.

'Hubert, I was wondering if you'd got time for a chat.'

'You're not getting married?'

His voice sounded so aghast I laughed. 'After one date, Hubert, come off it.'

'What then?'

'I'm drowning in a sea of suspects. Nick Fenny is at death's door...'

'How did you know?'

I realized then that I'd stolen Hubert's thunder. *That* was why he had tried to phone me. 'DS Roade told me this morning,' I said. 'He called round.'

'Oh. Well, Kate, you'll have to take it like a man. Your only reason to be on the case has just gone.'

'I'm not taking it like a man, I'm taking it like a woman and I'm not going to give up now.'

There was a long pause during which I knew Hubert was trying to think of something sensible to say. In the end he said, 'You'll have to tout for business. Find someone who thinks the police need a bit of help.'

'Hmm. If I buy you a big cream doughnut, Hubert, will you give me the benefit of your worldly wisdom?'

'You only want one yourself,' said Hubert. 'You know I'm into healthy eating.'

'Please.'

'I'll put the kettle on, then. You're sure you're fit to drive?'

'I'm on my way. I haven't had a drink for hours.'

On the drive over to Longborough I thought about drink-driving and how alcohol can remain in the blood for hours and hours. I really hadn't drunk that much last night but the lobster had managed to postpone a mad passionate night with Neil Amroth. Perhaps I was past it anyway. Maybe a few years of celibacy had addled normal desire. I had read that sexual attraction was merely a case of having the right smell—pheromones. Perhaps he didn't have my sort of pheromones anyway.

Also there was a comment he'd made which interested me. And of course there was Bella's suggestion that Jenny and Teresa were in fact going to set up home together. Did this mean they were just good friends, or was Bella right that the killer may have suspected them of being lesbians? And if so, was he mad enough to believe they deserved to die? More to the point, did Geoff know? Would he admit it even if he did and was he consumed with jealousy? If he hadn't known, would it be cruel to tell him now? Of course it would, I decided. If he was innocent he need never know. If he was guilty, he knew anyway.

THIRTEEN

I STOPPED OFF at the baker's on the way to Humberstones'. I was now hungry but my appetite for sweet things was tempered by seeing quite so many cakes bulging with cream in the window. In the end I bought two iced buns and hoped Hubert wouldn't be disppointed.

'Cheapskate,' he said, as most of the icing peeled off the buns and stayed in the paper bag.

He'd already made a pot of tea and we sat at my desk drinking and eating and not saying much at first. Eventually I said, 'I'm stuck on this case, Hubert. I've only been working at the practice for two weeks and I'm finding it hard to cope. I just can't get round to interviewing everyone and as you said I'm no longer being paid.'

'You could curtail your love life a bit.'

I laughed. 'Love life! Don't be so pompous. I don't think one date in twelve months is going over the top, do you?'

He shrugged, said nothing, rested his hand under his chin and stared at me.

'The trouble,' I said, 'with victims in general is that they know so many people: relatives, friends, aquaintances, colleagues, neighbours. It's like an iceberg. I've only found the tip.'

He wagged a finger at me. 'You're trying too hard, Kate. The first thing you do is start trusting the police more. You have to assume that the men they have interviewed and eliminated are in fact innocent.'

'What if...'

'Assume they're innocent,' repeated Hubert firmly.

'Then what?'

'Then pick one of these innocent men and persuade him you can find out more than the police. So he pays you to stay on the case.'

'Doesn't seem moral, does it?'

'Don't start that again, Kate. You would be doing him a big favour when you find the killer and you'd be preventing anyone else from being murdered. Because he's killed twice and got away with it—why stop now?'

Carefully I wrote down all those people that I knew Jenny Martin had known. That of course included all Riverview staff and many, many patients. Likewise for Teresa; and after all she did work in a hotel so there were dragoons of people there. I stared at the names and thought about the numbers involved and then tore up the pieces of paper in disgust. 'It's no wonder so many murders go unsolved,' I grumbled.

'Now come on, Kate, you can do better than that. You know they had some things in common. Maybe they had some*one* in common. A friend, a...'

'A confidant?' I added helpfully.

'I'm not stupid. I do know a few long words.'

I smiled. 'Sorry, Hubert. I don't feel I'm doing anything well at the moment. It's all like a grey mist. I shall have to go back to the beginning—outside the college and those missing hours.'

'Take it easy with Bill though, won't you?'

'Hubert, I shall be as gracious as if I'm at a Royal garden party.'

He flashed me a quick scowl and he was almost to the door when I remembered the practice lunch. I smacked myself on the forehead in disgust.

'What's the matter?'

'I'm meeting the doctors' wives today. I think they want me as a spy.'

'Well, there's an angle,' said Hubert.

'What do you mean?'

'Maybe that's what Jenny was doing. She found out
something and told Teresa. Someone else found out, and
had to kill the both of them.'

'Hubert, that sounds brilliant. It really is a great idea. All
I need to find out now is who, what, when and why and
then I've cracked it.'

'I give up with you,' he said disgustedly as he left the
room. 'And wear a frock!' he shouted from behind the
closed door.

I DIDN'T WEAR a frock. I wore jeans and a loose dark green
shirt, bought a bottle of white wine and a bunch of freesias
for the hostess and thought to myself anyone bearing wine
would be welcome—befrocked or not.

The Thruxton house in the village of Cottingbury boasted
a sign on the wall saying *Little Haven Cottage*. It was neither little nor, in my knowledge of the housing market, a
cottage. It was a rambling detached stone house in acres of
ground with a courtyard and outhouses. Undoubtedly it was
both very expensive and listed.

Mrs Thruxton greeted me at the door and suddenly I felt
like a Tupperware demonstrator who has arrived minus her
Tupperware. She was tall, slim, with shoulder-length
blonde hair. I guessed it was dyed but it looked natural.
She wore a black and white Laura Ashley type frock with
high-heeled black slingbacks. Her nails were long and red
and pointed. Her face was too long and too gaunt to be
thought pretty but she had real presence and she gave the
impression of being happy with herself. 'Hi, you must be
Kate,' she said, giving me a welcoming smile. 'I'm Rosalind. Call me Ros, though, everyone does. Come on
through, we're all in the conservatory.' I handed her the
wine and flowers. 'Lovely, thank you. Freesias are my all-
time favourites.'

I clumped behind her, down the long hall past two vases

of fresh flowers that well and truly dwarfed my posy. On through a kitchen the size of a dining-room and out into an octagonal conservatory of wicker chairs and vast green plants and a wonderful smell of warm damp compost. Lounging on the wicker sofa and chairs, wine glasses in hand, were four women, all in summer frocks. 'Let me introduce you, Kate.'

I tried to take the introductions in but being a stranger in their camp made me nervous. First came Sara Wheatly. 'Hello, Kate. Welcome to our coven. Let's hope you've got what it takes.' What the hell did she mean? Sara Wheatly had dark, bobbed hair, a delicate face with intense brown eyes and small body parts—head, hands, feet—and a slimness that could have verged on anorexia. The type that men want to protect. Usually I've found they have nerves of steel and it's the big girls that need looking after. I didn't like her one bit and thought her joke (if it was a joke) about witches was in poor taste, the sort of comment that leaves you nervously trying to think of a witty response and not succeeding.

'Take no notice of Sara,' said Rosalind. 'She just pretends to be a bitch. Now then, moving on to our friend near the cheese plant.'

My eyes followed the direction of Rosalind's finger and almost occluded from view by the leaves of the plant was an unremarkable-looking woman, fresh faced and healthy looking, with fairish short hair and a ready smile. She even gave me a wave. 'Hello, Kate, nice to meet you. Alan told me all about you. I'm Caroline Dakers.'

I smiled, tightly. For someone who was supposed to be divorced she seemed remarkably married to me. She must have noticed my expression because she said brightly, 'I expect you've heard Alan and I are divorced. That's true, but we remain very good friends, in fact we like each other more now.'

I smiled again. Alan was fast becoming another fanciable man merely a twinge in my memory. I felt that a bit of animosity between ex-spouses seemed to me to be the more normal state of affairs. Could I really trust a man who couldn't actually cut the marital umbilical cord?

'And next to Caroline,' Rosalind was saying, 'Deborah Holland, known as Debs.'

Debs, in her twenties the youngest of the group, wore a tan sundress from which poked thin white arms and legs. Her dark hair was pulled back severely by two large slides and she reminded me of a startled deer caught in the headlights of a car—half scared to death. She made an effort to smile at me though and said 'Hello' in a shy voice.

Thankfully Rosalind handed me a glass of wine then. 'We only drink white in the day, red is so heavy, isn't it? You could have a soft drink if you prefer.'

'White wine's fine, thank you,' I murmured, beginning to find this lunchtime a real trial. Why on earth had they invited me? Tradition? Or as Hubert suggested, to befriend me and then get me to spy on their husbands? Rosalind took me by the elbow and sat me down on a scoop-shaped wicker chair. 'Let's have a toast,' she announced solemnly. 'Absent friends!'

A murmuring 'Absent friends' echoed round the room followed by a short silence that was broken by Debs who said in her shy way, 'I really miss Helena, you know. And Jenny of course.'

I noticed that poor Jenny only got second place in the pecking order. That seemed odd. There was some reason her death wasn't still the main topic of conversation. The cause of their apparent casualness over Jenny's death did matter, because it seemed to signify a reticence in coming to terms with it. Why? Because one wife at least must have glanced sideways at her husband. Another might have se-

rious suspicions. And Jenny, even in death, would be re-
sented.

As the others began to talk Rosalind, who sat nearest to
me, whispered, 'Just in case you don't know who Helena
is, she's Charles Amroth's wife. She left him four years
ago and we've never seen her since. She just sort of disappeared although I do believe she has written to her son
Neil—I expect you've met him. He's a nice chap but
Charles was terribly disappointed when he dropped out of
university. I mean from PPE at Oxford to odd-job man in
Dunsmore is a bit hard for a parent to take, isn't it? They
barely talk to one another now, although of course Charles
has put work his way. Helena always said Neil was a difficult child but he did go to boarding school at eight so she
really didn't see too much of him after that. Still, he turned
out to be a very capable person, ''can turn his hand to
anything'' as the saying goes.'

'What sort of things?' I asked, feigning ignorance.

'Painting, decorating, plumbing, carpentry, car maintenance.'

'I'm impressed. Obviously a useful man to know.'

'And so good looking,' said Rosalind with a faint lift of
a perfect brow. I felt myself going hot. Please don't let me
blush. I hadn't slept with him and anyway if I had we were
both single... 'Don't you think?' she added pointedly.

I smiled in what I hoped was casual fashion. 'Ravishing,'
I said, 'but just a boy. I find older men more attractive.'
As the words came out I realized with horror they were all
listening and watching me and their faces mirrored anxiety
and suspicion. 'Strangely,' I said more loudly than usual,
'I don't actually like medicos very much. They're so one-
track. Far more interested in their work than the average
man. I prefer...adventurers.'

Ros laughed. 'So do I, but I married a GP. Still we manage, don't we girls?'

The others laughed lightly in unison. I sensed there was an undercurrent of antipathy towards me. Hostility in the air, rising like the smell of damp compost.

'We appear to manage,' said Sara, 'those that are left.'

'Come off it, Sara, it's not that bad,' said Caroline smiling pleasantly. 'You have a secure life, a good standard of living, children at boarding school doing well. Some people would be very envious.'

'Meaning you?'

'I didn't say that. Alan may not be a doctor but he is very involved in the practice. His being so involved wasn't the cause of our break-up but it certainly didn't help. I had to make a life for myself even before the divorce.'

Sara obviously couldn't drop the subject. Sitting forward, tiny head jutting aggressively, she said, 'You are just so content, are't you? A cow in a field could learn from you.'

Caroline looked more crestfallen than angry and it was Ros whose eyes narrowed and from whose lips hissed, 'You bitch! Just because your husband—'

'My husband what? What! Anyway, you're a fine one to talk, you lost your best friend, dyspo that she was, and you've never been the same since—'

'Please don't argue,' interrupted Debs nervously. 'This isn't how we usually behave; what will Kate think of us?'

There was a protracted silence whilst they stared at me as if I were somehow responsible for their bitchiness and that they couldn't give a toss anyway. I emptied my glass quickly guessing that the wine was the only thing that was going to make this lunch bearable.

When lunch did come it was definitely calorie counted. We ate in the dining-room on a splendid mahogany table with a bunch of white lilies in the middle which I thought very funereal. There were prawns and salad, no dressing, no mayonnaise, just lime juice. There was dry French bread and fruit salad and some ghastly low-fat cheese with crispbreads. It was Sara who explained their policy on keeping slim. 'It's just so awful being fat, isn't it? Every day I check my weight, I mean one has to, doesn't one?'

'One does,' I said, po-faced.

Gradually as the lunch wore on the conversation turned to Jenny's murder and Helena's disappearance. The wine which was being drunk quite freely now loosened tongues and they seemed to forget I was there at all. I nodded and smiled and listened. Helena Amroth, it seemed, had left four years ago, very suddenly. The general consensus was that Jenny and Charles Amroth had started an affair some time before and when Helena found out she had left him.

'I know she was drinking heavily,' said Rosalind. 'Vodka, but she'd been doing that for years and keeping it quite well under control.'

'Merely under wraps, Ros,' said Sara. 'How Charles could have let it go on I don't know.'

'I don't think he'd paid her any real attention for years—'

'Come off it, Ros. You're not trying to say he didn't know!'

Ros shrugged. 'It's just that I don't think he noticed until it was brought to his attention.'

'And who did that, I wonder?'

Someone tittered, I think it was Caroline but I couldn't be sure. 'So you think Jenny may have told him?' I asked. Ros glanced at the others as if for agreement and then said, 'Yes. We're pretty sure she did. After he found out he was very bad-tempered for some time, the others were on the verge of trying to buy him out, but then he seemed to pull himself together and he and Jenny were often seen huddled together having meaningful talks.'

'But that doesn't mean she was having an affair,' I said.

Sara gave a slight sneer. 'Of course they were having

an affair. The awful thing is, we should have seen what was happening and done something…'

'Even after his wife had gone?' I asked.

'Yes. Why not?'

'What would you have done?' I asked softly.

Sara caught my drift immediately. 'We didn't kill her, if that's what you're implying! But perhaps we would have persuaded her to resign.'

'I see,' I muttered.

'Do you?' she replied.

'Hey, come on you two. It's in the past now,' said Caroline, 'Charles and Neil have suffered quite enough. The first year was the worst and till…all this happened, they really seemed to be making headway.'

'What happened in the first year?' I asked, unable to control my curiosity. No one spoke at first; Ros began filling wine glasses. I refused any more. I didn't want to forget anything that was said today. Eventually Caroline answered. 'It was all pretty ghastly really. The police thought…they thought Helena's disappearance was suspicious. At one point they even considered digging up the garden…'

'Only because someone gave them the idea that Charles was having an affair and therefore had a motive,' said Sara.

'One thing puzzles me,' I said.

'Only one?' replied Sara. 'My, we are a clever clogs.'

'If you suspected Jenny of having an affair and you disapproved, why did you still invite her to your lunches and still appear to be her friend?'

Sara fixed me with a steady glare. 'Because we really are witches. Perhaps we did cause Jenny's death indirectly. I personally stuck more than enough pins into my voodoo doll.'

Ros laughed. 'Take no notice of Sara. For witches read

bitches. No one disliked Jenny. Charles and her were good friends but we're only guessing that they were having an affair. Helena was my best friend and I still miss her dreadfully, and I'll admit at first we did think something had happened to her. But our first thought was suicide and not murder. Then after that first year we heard…well, vague whispers, and that she was well and happy. We were sad but we accepted it. She'd made a new life for herself and according to rumour she was off the vodka and not at all worried that Charles had found a "friend".'

Ros stood up then and began to clear the table and I saw this as a good time to go. I began to make my excuses. 'Do stay a bit longer,' Debs begged me. 'No one leaves before four. Stay for coffee at least.'

'Just for a short time then,' I agreed.

We all went back into the conservatory. Sara sat next to me and asked in her rather loud voice, 'Do you have a man, Kate? Adventurous or otherwise?'

I smiled, seething inwardly. 'Sort of,' I said. 'He's older than me, heavily into good works.'

'A social worker?' asked Caroline.

'His job does have social and environmental value.' Sara wouldn't let it drop, I could see by the way her mouth moved slightly she had already formed another question in her mind. Before she could speak I said, 'He's the director of a waste-disposal company.' I could read the disappointment in her face. There was no answer to such a job.

Shortly after that I took my leave. I noticed that Debs Holland, apart from asking me to stay, had hardly spoken. She seemed depressed or worried or both. Of course she was younger and newer to the practice than the others but even so I could sense all was not well with her. I'd hardly spoken to Ian, mainly because he seemed to avoid me but also because I hadn't made an effort to talk to him. Perhaps husband and wife were both shy or unhappy. Or maybe they were Morris dancers, only happy when their leg bells were ringing.

About the others I was even more confused. I had assumed doctors' wives incapable of murder but it was an assumption I'd have to rethink. A coven of witches or a band of bitches? Whichever they were I decided I mustn't allow my dislike of Sara and her exaggerations to colour my judgement of the others. Perhaps they had liked Jenny in spite of their suspicions. And of course Jenny did have a penchant for older men. Was it common knowledge in the town, I wondered, that she was extra friendly with Charles Amroth? Maybe Helena Amroth, dried out and recovered, wanted to return home. Was Rosalind prepared to go any lengths to get her friend back? Or more to the point did Jenny want a deeper relationship with Charles Amroth? And if there was a chance his wife was coming back—cured—could he have decided he preferred Helena? But why kill Teresa?

Another niggle at the back of my mind was how it could be proved Helena was still alive. Were there letters? Were father and son in collusion? Maybe Helena did indeed lie dead somewhere beneath the soil.

FOURTEEN

On Sunday I felt at a loss; the day facing me seemed as barren as a sack of sand. I decided to ring Hubert and ask him to share assorted chops from my freezer.

'I'm going on a picnic. Would you like to come?' As I began to look forward to it, he added, 'Danielle will be there.'

'What's happened to Dorothy Tweedle by the way?'

'She's on holiday. Are you coming?'

'Sorry, Hubert, I would have, only I've made other arrangements.'

'Not with that Neil, I hope,' said Hubert as if Neil were Rasputin and Vlad the Impaler all rolled into one.

'No, actually. Someone else.'

He grunted and put down the phone.

Over Sunday lunch, a packet of crisps and a cheese sandwich, I once more listed my suspects. Was there anyone I didn't suspect? Hubert was right, of course, I did need a client, and I steeled myself to see Geoff Martin again. It was one way of spending a lonely Sunday and I might learn something useful.

Driving over to Dunsmore I rehearsed some sort of sales pitch together with a few more questions, questions that I hoped would do more than merely exercise my tongue.

I paused at the front door. There was a Sunday afternoon sleepiness in Dunsmore, a silence about the Martin house. The door knocker made an echoing sound that reverberated as though the house was empty of carpets or furniture. I knocked again. And once more. The thought struck me that he was either away or he'd...topped himself. He hadn't mentioned suicide but he had seemed naturally depressed and defeated and he'd actually welcomed being a police suspect. If Jenny had been having an affair with Dr Amroth it was quite possible the gossip *had* reached Geoff. It was a small place and he'd have to be blind and deaf not to have heard…something. Perhaps he had an alibi for the time Teresa was murdered—perhaps. Trust the police, Hubert had said. Maybe, though, it wasn't a man Geoff was jealous of, but a woman. Teresa, who had suffered, and who shared Jenny's interest in calligraphy.

I turned to walk away. He wasn't in, I decided. Then the door opened and he was standing there, smiling. 'You've come. I knew you would. Have you been knocking long? I was in the garden.'

Without the horse-blanket dressing-gown he looked quite different. Today he wore a navy shirt, with short sleeves showing well-muscled arms, and navy shorts. His legs were of the hairy variety, just beginning to tan. The hair on his head was now neatly groomed and he looked younger, more rested.

In the garden a lounger was placed under an apple tree, the lawn had been freshly mowed and a small mound of weeds had been carefully piled on newspaper. High stone walls surrounded the garden and the trees, bushes and numerous tubbed plants gave it a cool, shady feel—a secluded bower.

'Sit down, sit down,' he said eagerly. 'I've got another lounger in there.' He disappeared into a shed by the farthest wall and came back moments later with a floral-covered sun-bed. They were almost impossible to sit on so we both stretched out and soaked up the sun for a while. It was unusually hot and still.

'We'll have a storm tonight,' he said.

I lay on my back and the glare of the sun made me close my eyes. 'Mr Martin…'

'Call me Geoff.'

'Geoff. Are you satisfied with the police investigation?'

'I'm not dissatisfied, why?'

'Bluntly I'm looking for a client. Nick Fenny as you know was once my client, or rather his mother was, but he's...had an accident and I want to maintain my interest in the case.'

'I see.'

Silence then and I felt like some predatory bird that hovers over a poor worm. I explained my terms and he didn't even blink, he merely nodded. 'OK, then. You're on. I've got nothing to hide and I want the bastard who killed my wife caught sooner rather than later.'

'I still need to ask you a few questions, Geoff.'

'Fire away. And of course, Kate, if you're now working for me I shall expect to see you every couple of days at least.' I muttered in a noncommittal way and then asked how well he knew Teresa.

'I didn't know her well at all. I knew of her. I knew she had lost a child, too.'

'Were you jealous of her?' I opened one eye and leant on my elbow to watch his reaction. There wasn't much. He lay still, eyes closed.

'Of whom?' he asked casually.

'Your wife? Teresa?'

'She didn't see her that often. It wasn't a problem.'

'I don't think you're telling me the whole truth, Geoff.'

'What is this truth that has to be told?' he asked coldly. 'I'm guilty of only one thing and that is loving my wife.'

'What about Charles Amroth?'

He opened his eyes, squinted at the light, closed them again. I hadn't rattled him. This time his voice was measured and calm when he replied. 'If you must know, I had heard the rumours. The man was troubled and unhappy.

Jenny would have felt needed by him. There was nothing sexual in it. I mean he's even older than me.'

'You're sure?'

'Sure as I can be without Jenny here to ask. She was always truthful. Although the more I think about it the more I'm sure she was looking for someone. Man or woman, I don't think it mattered. Just someone who needed her. When in reality the person who needed her most was right here.'

'Was there anyone else whose problems she mentioned?'

'Alan Dakers. Now he is a womanizer. Jenny mentioned him a few times. She felt sorry for his wife Caroline too, they went through a bad patch during the divorce period but Jenny seemed to think they had worked out an amicable agreement. If anything I think Jenny thought she was partly responsible for that.'

I closed my eyes. 'You've had a little time to get over the shock, Geoff. Have you any suspects?'

He laughed drily. 'Hey, you're supposed to be the private dick. Don't you think I've gone over this time and time again? I can't help thinking that Teresa's associates from the hotel are far more likely suspects.'

'Why?'

'Because she told Jenny quite a few of them were "on the prowl".'

'But Jenny died first. Did they have anyone in common at the hotel?'

'Not that I know of.'

I felt then a certain weariness of body and mind. The sun was beginning to fry my brain. I asked the questions perhaps I should have asked at the start. 'Who will benefit financially from your wife's death?'

There was a long pause. Then he looked at me sadly. 'She was insured for ten thousand pounds. Would anybody kill their wife for such a small amount?'

'Only if they were desperate.'

'I've got no money worries. I get regular work and now there's only myself to support.'

'I had to ask.'

'Shall we have a drink? Gin?'

I shook my head. 'I really must go.'

'Why? Do you have some man waiting for you?' Again I shook my head. 'Stay then.'

So I stayed and drank lager shandies and let him talk about Jenny. After a while I asked, 'When your son was killed did you resent the police for not finding the driver?'

'No, I did not,' he said slowly. 'I felt guilty that I hadn't been here. I was working on an article in Spain—just a few days. The police phoned me, I flew back. I couldn't believe it. I just expected the little lad to run through the door. Jenny was sedated for days. She hardly left her bedroom for two weeks.'

He stared up at the branches of the apple tree for a while and tears glistened in his eyes. I felt like a surgeon who'd just done an amputation with no anaesthetic. To ease the awkwardness of the moment I asked if I could see their bedroom and did she have a diary. He said yes to both and then stood up, stretched his arms, patted me on the back lightly and walked into the house. I followed.

It was cool indoors, quite chilly in contrast to outside. We were both temporarily blinded and for a moment had to let our eyes adjust to the comparative gloom after the glare of the sun.

Their bedroom was large, a four-poster bed with a white lacy coverlet dominating it.

'I've still got all her clothes,' he informed me as he opened the fitted cupboards. Inside were row after row of dresses, skirts, blouses and jackets. It was almost like seeing her. I wandered across to her dressing table and gazed at her perfumes still in position.

'I can't move anything of hers,' said Geoff. 'Whilst everything tangible here remains the same I can think as the poem says that she's merely "in another room".'

Jenny's diary lay on the bedside table. It had a cheap plain cover, the sort of diary that the pages start coming out of halfway through the year. Geoff saw me looking. 'Here,' he said, handing it to me. I flicked through it. Mostly empty. When there was an entry it was mostly about the weather. 'Rain today, cold.' Her son's birthday was written in and on that day the weather was more fully described. There was no mention of his death. There were no names, no initials. A diary so private, so bleak. Yet her clothes and the four-poster bed gave me different messages. A nurse yes, practical and down to earth, but that masked what she really was—a romantic. And a romantic has to find romance. And a calligrapher needs to practise. She hadn't practised in her diary. As I put it down I said, 'Tell me about the row with Jenny.'

'What row?'

'The row when you hit her.'

He gave a dry laugh. 'The bruises.'

'Yes,' I said as crisply as a headmistress. He walked across to the window, pulled the net curtain to one side and stared out on to the garden. 'After our son died,' he said quietly, 'Jenny began to sleepwalk. She didn't admit it to anyone at work. She was afraid they would recommend tranquillizers. She was always bumping into things. I think she looked for him at night—well, her subconscious did. I've never hit her.'

I DIDN'T SEE Hubert again till late Monday afternoon. He looked a little flustered but it didn't register until later.

'How was your picnic?' I asked him.

'Fine. Fine.' He stared around my office for a moment as if I had a man stashed away somewhere.

'What's wrong, Hubert?'

He gave me an anguished 'God help me' sort of look and slumped down in the chair. 'You were right,' he said miserably.

'About what?' I was completely confused.

'About Danielle.'

'Oh.'

'She *is* a man. She's on some sort of probationary period living as a woman and then they'll...operate.'

'Do you really like her?'

'Him!'

'Do you really like him?'

'I'm sacking him. He got the job under false pretences. He tricked me.'

'I suppose that's the idea of living as a woman. Trickery's the name of the game until surgeons can make it legitimate.'

'Huh! I feel such a fool.'

'Danielle makes a good woman. I mean, she has got a woman's bone structure and good legs.' I didn't mention the Adam's apple. 'It was an accident of nature, that's all.' Hubert wasn't convinced. He sat sulky and unresponsive.

'You have to admit, Hubert, she's a capable receptionist and the clients like her. Can you really sack someone for being genetically disadvantaged?'

'I'll think about it,' he said grudgingly. 'But I don't want to talk about it any more.'

I made us both a strong coffee, ladled in the sugar for Hubert and offered him my last two chocolate biscuits. He ate them both without a twinge of conscience.

'I've got some good news,' I said cheerfully, trying to raise his spirits above the level of his socks.

'I've got a new client. Geoff Martin has agreed I should carry on investigating the death of his wife.'

He looked up from his mug of coffee and fixed me with one of his most practised baleful expressions.

'It might be very short lived, Kate. I've heard the police are ready to arrest someone for both murders.'

FIFTEEN

'CONFESSED! I don't believe it.' He might just as well have told me the Tories had embraced Maastricht's Social Chapter.

'It's true,' he said, with his first upturn of his mouth that day, and I swear he experienced some perverse delight in telling me. 'Some bloke from the college. He's definitely confessed. And although the police think he's a head case, they are taking it seriously. It seems he knows more about the two women than a mere amateur confessor.'

'I'll ring DS Roade, perhaps he'll tell me more. I still don't believe it.'

Picking up the phone I gave Hubert a somewhat stony stare. He took the hint and moved to the door reluctantly. I felt a bit peeved that I heard so much news second and usually third hand. While the phone rang I reasoned that it was in the nature of the job. I mean I was hardly likely to be anywhere *just* at the right moment but that didn't stop me wanting to be sometimes first in the queue for information.

DS Roade wasn't in his office but Inspector Hook was. Inspector Hook has a face like a day in February, dresses in a symphony of grey and regards me as some sort of irritating but mild condition like haemorrhoids. I tried to disguise my voice but he hadn't made it to inspector by being stupid and the moment I asked for DS Roade he knew.

'Yes. Miss Kinsella,' he said with February in his voice as well. His 'yes' was a 'Yes, what the hell do you want?'

so I mumbled a bit and then said, 'I'm working for Mr Martin now and I'd heard that…'

'You heard someone had confessed,' he interrupted.

'Yes.'

'Someone has. He's still being interviewed.' His voice stayed firmly in the February mode.

'Inspector Hook, in your considered and experienced opinion, did this man do it?'

Hook sighed down the phone and eventually said, 'I don't know.'

'Could you tell me something about him?'

'No.'

'I'm worried he could be my uncle.'

'Well, if he is I'm sure your auntie will let you know.'

'She's dead.'

'Miss Kinsella, you're wasting my time.'

'Call me Kate.'

'Get off the phone, Kate.'

'Give me a clue, please.'

'Find your own clues.'

'I could start a rumour, ring the press.'

Silence.

'Shall I come to the station?' I asked. There was a long pause whilst he thought about that but I could hear him breathing and from the sound of it I guessed I was gradually wearing him down.

'OK. A tip and that's all. Do your own sleuthing. Dunsmore College. Goodbye.' My profuse thanks went unheard as the phone slammed down.

I made a deduction from that. One, the man was from Longborough because otherwise the Dunsmore CID would have been involved. And two, his confession wasn't kosher. If it had been Hook would have sounded more April than February.

By now it was nearly seven. I could make my way to

Dunsmore Adult Education College just in time for the start of classes. Surely there I would find something out and I could talk to Bill again.

I parked alongside Bill's bungalow and then knocked at the door. Bill's wife answered. She looked older than him and where he was round she was thin and slightly stooped. Her hair was a silvery grey, thinning at the temples, her mouth, set on a downward turn, matched her eyes, which also drooped and their bluey tinge stared at me suspiciously. As I explained who I was and that I'd come to see Bill she smiled, which lifted some of the droop. 'Come in, dear. Bill's out. I've been wanting to talk to someone. Things have been getting on my nerves lately.'

We walked through to the front room of the bungalow. The windows were closed and it smelt warm and musty with overtones of lamb casserole. The television was on loudly and a partially knitted sweater lay on the tan-coloured sofa with its cream lace arm covers and matching antimacassars.

'You'll have a coffee, won't you, dear?'

I nodded. Mrs Stone left the room and I noticed her ankles were swollen and she wore her slippers with the heels out. In a few minutes she returned with a mug of coffee. I sipped it; it was hot, creamy and sweet and made with a substance beloved by elderly ladies who shop at the Co-op. It tasted vile.

Mrs Stone switched off the TV, sat down and picked up the piece of knitting, examined it carefully, then fumbled under a cushion and brought out a pair of knitting needles and more wool. She began to cast on. After a while she said, 'I'm glad you've come.'

'Why's that?'

'My Bill makes things very difficult.'

'In what way?'

Mrs Stone continued casting on. 'That night,' she said.

'Which night?'

'The night poor Jenny Martin was killed.'

'Yes?'

'Bill lied. He didn't see anything. Not a thing.'

'Why did he say he did?'

Mrs Stone paused in her casting on. 'He's getting older you see, and tired and lazy if the truth be told. He locked up when the classes had finished. Checked everything like he always does. Then he had a bite to eat and went to his bedroom and watched a video. He has some old war films he likes to watch over and over again. We've got separate rooms see and he doesn't do any more checks after that. He likes to say he does. He's frightened.'

'Of what?'

'Of losing his job. He's well over sixty and he wants to stay on as long as possible. You won't tell the police all this, will you? Because I'm only telling you because I can't live with it. I mean if the murderer is out there—' She broke off to point with a knitting needle towards the college, 'he could come back, couldn't he?'

'So Bill didn't make that late check and he didn't see the tall man in black.'

She shook her head. 'I doubt it very much. He always gets up early in the morning and walks round and he did find the vomit. There were no cars left then in the car park as far as I know. Poor Bill is frightened that the education authorities will blame him. To be honest he's scared of going out late at night. We do get bikers speeding round and a few drunks.'

'Did you hear or see anything?'

Mrs Stone smiled. 'No, dear. I watched television and then I went to bed. Although I did hear something earlier, I suppose it was about seven thirty, usually it's quiet by then because the classes have started. I went outside to see if I could catch any slugs and I heard women's voices—

they were laughing. Then I heard a vehicle driving off. I think they were by the entrance but I didn't see anything.'

'Did *you* think that was odd?'

Mrs Stone gave a slight shrug. 'Not really. You'd be amazed what goes on here. Once Bill caught a couple having sex in the bushes and another time a van drove in and a few minutes later someone stole two computers from the college—you'd really be amazed.'

I agreed that I would. 'Have you heard someone at the college has confessed to the murders?'

'I did hear that, yes. Bill's seen him around. He says he's a creepy type always trying to tag along behind the women. It makes sense, doesn't it. Probably a pervert.'

'If I find Bill could I ask him about this man?'

'Oh…well, I'm not sure. You won't mention what I've told you, 'cos he'll stick to that story through thick and thin. I think he believes it himself.'

I thanked her and left. I found Bill eventually, trying one of the fire-doors. He looked a little sheepish as if I'd caught him doing something he shouldn't.

'I have to check and double check,' he said dolefully. 'These students may be adults but you have to watch them.'

'It's about one of the students I want to ask you.'

'Fire away,' he said with a relieved smile.

'You've heard all about the man who confessed to the murders?' He nodded. 'Tell me about him, will you? It really would be a great help.'

Bill scratched his forehead then rested his hand on the fire-door. 'Where shall I start?' he muttered. 'He's a short bloke, thin, balding but not that old—late thirties, I don't think he's married. He followed the women around like a puppy dog. One or two of the younger women complained but the older women just ignored him. He only came to two classes a week but he always seemed to be hanging around.'

'Did he speak to Jenny and Teresa—did he seem friends with them?'

Bill shook his head. 'I've no idea, me duck, but your best bet is to ask someone in the canteen.'

Before I left Bill I was determined to get a clearer idea of what he did see that night. I didn't suggest to him he might have fabricated evidence but I wasn't sure either that his wife knew exactly where Bill was every minute especially if they had separate rooms. 'Tell me again, Bill, about that night. You have a marvellous memory and your evidence could be vital.'

He looked pleased about that. 'It was like I said. I heard voices and I saw them standing by the red car...'

'How exactly were they standing, Bill?' He stared at me for a moment, blankly. 'How close—snuggling up, at arm's length like strangers?'

He closed his eyes. 'I'm trying to remember,' he said. 'They were close.'

'How close?' I persisted.

'Her head was on his shoulder.'

'And they were talking? Loudly, softly?'

'Well...er. Yes.'

'You don't sound very sure.'

Bill looked puzzled. 'Funny you should ask about that.'

'Why?'

'I only just thought about it. I looked out the window and told you I heard voices didn't I?' I nodded.

'I think I might have made a mistake. Now I think back, see, I can remember it more clearly. I only heard the one voice—a man's voice.'

I looked at him searchingly. 'Did you hear anything of what he said?'

Bill shook his head. 'No, sorry, me duck.'

'And the time, Bill? And how many cars?'

'Two cars. There were two.'

'And earlier?'

'Now look, I know you're only doing your job but all these questions are getting me down. I've told you there were two cars and that was all I saw.'

'Yes, Bill, but what about when you locked up at nine thirty; were there two cars then?'

By now Bill looked flustered and I knew then he wasn't sure. If the other classes had finished at nine thirty and Bill had been prompt at locking up there might well have been the odd tardy student with a car still there. Bill had made it seem so definite—two cars left behind—two cars there at midnight. But of course that wasn't the case. Jenny and Teresa were alive from seven until at least midnight. One or both cars would have left that night and one contained Jenny—dying.

'Just one more question, Bill. Did the man by the car with the woman see you?'

Bill's mouth slackened open and he drew in his breath. 'I don't know about that. He might've done. That's very possible.' He looked suitably concerned and I knew then he was telling the truth about what he saw. But what had woken him was not voices, because I was sure he'd been asleep and low voices would never have woken him, though the sound of a car boot closing would. A harsh metallic sound in the quiet of the night. Then he'd heard voices and looked out the window. What he'd seen, I believed, was a man putting on a show for Bill's eyes, because in his arms he'd held a corpse—ready for the second car boot.

I thanked Bill and he couldn't disguise his relief that I was finally satisfied. He smiled half-heartedly at me and resumed testing the fire-doors.

I found the canteen eventually although the only food and drink was from vending machines and the green Formica tables and chairs remained forlornly empty for over half an hour. When a few students began coming in and searching for change I watched as they avoided all the middle tables, finding instead those nearest the walls.

After a while I approached a table of three middle-aged women who looked as if they might be calligraphists. They weren't. One, a plump woman wearing jeans and a crochet top with glasses on a golden cord that rested on her ample bosom, told me she'd done calligraphy last year but this year was doing art. I asked her if she had known Jenny and Teresa. She told me she knew them by sight. She also knew 'creeping Joe'. His name was Joseph Barnstable and he had tried to latch on to her and her friends but had been cold-shouldered.

'The man was really creepy. He told everyone he was a keen bird watcher but we thought he was more interested in watching other things with his binoculars.' The other two women nodded in agreement.

'Did he ever talk to Jenny and Teresa?' I asked.

'Not exactly,' said one of the women. 'But he did always sit near them and did try to engage them in conversation. They were a nice couple and they were always polite to him. Mind you, I can't believe he murdered them even though he has confessed. Far too much of a coward, I would think—wouldn't say boo to a goose type.'

I left the group to their plastic cups of tea and coffee and drove back to Longborough. I was convinced now that Joseph Barnstable was no more a suspect than Bella the lavatory attendant, but had he seen anything that night? Had he been creeping around the college grounds?

At some point I reasoned both cars were outside the college and it would have been sensible to go wherever they were going in one car. Where to, though? Jenny lived quite near but her husband was at home. If they'd decided to go back to Teresa's home in Longborough then surely they would have taken two cars. Could they have gone there?

Or to someone who would have welcomed a visitor. Alan Dakers? Maybe. Or Dr Amroth? Was he alone that night? If they'd gone to a pub the police would have found that out. But to a private house? Not necessarily, and who was going to admit it even if they had?

I wondered whether it might be worth going to Teresa's house. The police would have removed any vital evidence but maybe I'd find something. Two women can't just disappear for nearly five hours and then turn up dead. But they had and they did. For a kidnapping it was short by any standard. And they hadn't been sexually assaulted. So where the hell had they gone?

TWO DAYS WENT PAST before I heard any more and if I was going to do any breaking and entering to get a peek at Teresa's house I'd need Hubert as lookout and he seemed either very busy or he was trying to avoid me.

It was Hubert though who told me the latest news on 'Creeping Joe'. He'd been released after only a few hours on bail on a charge of wasting police time. Police questioning had soon revealed that anything he knew about Jenny and Teresa had been gleaned by eavesdropping in the canteen at the college. Now it was common knowledge that Jenny had planned to move in with Teresa.

'Poor Geoff,' I murmured.

'Do you think they were lesbians?' asked Hubert, his brown eyes sparkling with interest.

'No, I don't. I think they just wanted to be together for mutual support.'

He didn't look too convinced. 'What exactly do lesbians do?' he asked.

'I don't know, Hubert. Why do you ask?'

'Just interest,' he mumbled.

'I'll tell you what, there is one way we could find out.'

His eyes continued to sparkle so I knew I was on to a

winner. But by the time I'd outlined my plan for sneaking into Teresa's house, his expression had changed. 'This is one of your dodgiest ideas yet. The police could be watching the house.'

'Come off it. Where's your sense of adventure?'

He continued to frown. 'What do you hope to find out?'

I smiled, patted his hand. 'That, Hubert, I won't know until I get in the house.'

'What time?' he asked morosely.

'I'll be in touch. Thanks, Hubert.'

Tuesday was a Riverview free day and I knew I should pay Geoff a visit but I prevaricated. If he hadn't known before that his wife was planning to move out with another woman he would be upset and I wouldn't know what to say. Of course he didn't really need me to say anything but he would want me to listen and somehow that seemed unproductive. So far in this investigation I'd lost one client/suspect and I hadn't yet managed to focus my suspicions on anyone else.

The ringing by my elbow made me snatch the phone up quickly. It was Alan Dakers. 'How about that drink, Kate?' he asked with no sort of preamble.

'When?'

'Tonight?'

'Great. I look forward to it. I'll pick you up about eight.'

'No. I'll meet you at the Swan in Longborough High Street.' He paused slightly. Perhaps he was wondering if I was worth the petrol. 'Fine. See you there. I've got some news, by the way.'

'What about?'

'You'll just have to wait and see. But it's about Charles Amroth. He's admitted...'

'Admitted what?'

'Come tonight and you'll find out.'

SIXTEEN

I WALKED INTO the Swan just after eight. There was no sign of Alan but I could see the back of Hubert's head and next to him Danielle. I crept into a corner booth so that he couldn't see me and wondered how long I could sit there without going to the bar to buy a drink.

Alan arrived about ten past eight. He wore cream chinos and a pale green short-sleeved shirt. I noticed that he walked with a poseur's hand in trouser pocket amble. And he no longer looked intrepid. In fact seeing him out of Riverview made me realize how much I liked Neil. Neil had a vulnerable face. Alan Dakers was far more calculating.

He glanced around the dim interior and I knew he expected me to be there already, which I found irritating. When he did find me, he kissed my cheek, asked me what I wanted to drink and went straight to the bar. Customers were in short supply and it was so quiet that only Desperate Dan's husky tones could be heard and although I tried to catch a word here and there my hearing wasn't that acute.

The vodka and lime Alan placed in front of me was very welcome and he drank half a pint of beer before he even spoke.

'I needed that,' he said eventually. 'Sorry I was late, I had a phone call just as I was leaving. By the way, you look younger than ever out of uniform.'

I smiled. 'Why exactly did you want to see me tonight, Alan?'

'Do I need a reason other than wanting to take an attractive woman out?'

'I'm sure you do plenty of dating, now that you're a free man.'

He laughed, attractively. 'The rumours are all lies, I can assure you, Kate.'

'What rumours?'

'That I'm a womanizer and that Jenny was having an affair with me?'

'I hadn't heard that. Was she?'

He smiled with a cocky brightness revealing how much pleasure it gave him to be thought irresistible. 'No. I liked her but she had a mission.'

'What do you mean?'

'I mean she was preoccupied with finding someone.'

'Who?'

He smiled and patted my hand. 'Hey, this was meant to be a light-hearted evening. Why are you giving me the third degree?'

I finished my vodka in one final swig. 'I'd love another,' I said casually. 'Sorry about the questions but I'm naturally nosy.'

He smiled again at that, picked up the empty glass and walked to the bar. In moments he was joined by Hubert and as Hubert turned sideways I tried to duck back into the booth but I knew he had seen me. Damn...moments later my worst fears were confirmed—he was coming my way.

'Kate, why didn't you—' He stopped speaking abruptly when he saw my expression.

'I'm working, Hubert,' I whispered, like a French resistance worker caught with a Nazi.

'Who is he?' asked Hubert, tossing his head towards the bar.

'Hubert, go away. I don't want to have to explain to him who you are.'

He shrugged and walked slowly away as if he were Thomas and the cock had just crowed three times.

If Alan noticed Hubert retreating from my booth he didn't comment on it. We sipped our drinks in silence for a while until he said, 'Why exactly are you here, Kate?'

I nearly choked on my drink. 'In this pub, do you mean?'

His shook his head. 'No, living in Longborough. I would have thought a spirited girl like you would have worked abroad or lived in a city?'

I thought about this one for a while, old aunt Edie wouldn't do now. 'If you really want to know, coming here was an escape. I was bereaved and I needed a change of scene.'

He nodded and said softly, 'So you're not on a mission, like Jenny?'

'Since I don't know what mission she was on I can't say, can I?' Then I added as flirtatiously as I knew how, 'Come on, Alan, don't tease me any longer. You know I'm curious.'

And it worked. He began to tell me about Jenny's mission.

'Just before the end of term at Christmas four years ago Simon Martin walked out of school a little later than the others—he'd gone back into his classroom to collect his football. He was allowed to walk home alone then as he had no roads to cross. His football rolled into the road and he went to retrieve it. A car careered around the corner, mowed him down and drove on.'

'Surely someone saw it happen.'

Alan shrugged. 'Not really. Simon was on his own, other people were in front, they heard the thud, turned, but the car was already speeding off.'

'No one got the number?'

'No. People were stunned, the car was out of sight by the time they realized what had happened. Simon was killed instantly.'

'What did the police find out?' I asked.

'Nothing. They tried but they had no leads. They decided it was probably a stolen car and a so-called joyrider.'

'And Jenny's mission was to find the driver?'

'Got it. Not at first, though, she was numb and in shock for some time. We were surprised when she came back to work but she was plucky. No, really it was only during the last year she mentioned she was going to find the driver. Ever since she met Teresa, I suppose.'

'Do the police know this?'

'Yes, Kate. I told them.'

'But where would she have started her search? She didn't have anything to go on.'

'Jenny found out something. I don't know how, but she said she had someone local in her sights and it wouldn't be long before she acted.'

'What was she going to do?'

Alan stared at me for a moment. 'You're one of us now, Kate. She was going to kill the driver.'

I was surprised into silence for a moment, trying to work out the implications. Even then I spoke too soon and blurted out, 'How was she going do it? Why didn't her husband tell me this?'

'You know her husband?' asked Alan. 'Why didn't you say?'

'I...um...I met him in London years and years ago and I dropped in to offer him my condolences.'

Alan looked at me warily. I had a strong feeling I'd blown it.

I offered then to buy another drink but Alan said no, he'd get one and I had a minute or two to plan either my exit or how exactly to ask him what Charles Amroth had admitted.

For a while we talked about his ex-wife, the children, then he began talking about the practice. I let him carry on and when he paused said lightly, 'You were going to tell me about Charles—what has he admitted? That he *was* having an affair with Jenny?'

Alan raised an eyebrow. 'Not quite. He's admitted to the police that he was having an affair with...Teresa. And it seems he was the last person to see them both alive that night.'

Now why hadn't I guessed that? Teresa was more his age group, attractive, unattached. And Jenny was the go-between.

Perhaps she *was* a closet romantic having all the pleasure and none of the pain via a proxy lover. Unless of course Jenny had been having her own affair and her friend's involvement just added extra zest to life.

Alan meanwhile fetched more drinks. Alcohol seemed to be having little effect on either of us. His account was plausible but why did I feel so uneasy? Was it because his words sounded so rehearsed? And why should he be the one who knew so much? Jenny must have trusted him completely, but was that trust misplaced? Could Alan have wanted to protect the hit and run driver?

It was near to closing time when I heard someone approaching and there looking over the top of the booth above my head was Hubert. His eyes were as red as a monkey's bum and his voice was a smidgin slurred. 'See you tonight, Kate. Tonight's the night—say no more—about two should be nice and quiet...' Alan at this point started forward eyes ablaze as if he'd met Satan for the first time. I tried not to laugh. 'It's all right, Alan, he's a relative. We go out some nights really late sometimes...we're into studying the night sky...we study the plough and the Milky Way.'

Hubert's face split into a grin and then he fell backwards loudly—he was actually laughing as he hit the deck. How the night sky had suddenly come to mind I don't know and Alan's face showed he didn't believe me.

'Help me up, Kate,' Hubert was shouting.

'Let me give you a hand,' suggested Alan.

I declined his kind offer, helped Hubert into a chair, hissed into his ear to hold his tongue and that I'd see him back at Humberstones' later.

If Alan had lived in Longborough I might have gone back to his place just out of curiosity. As it was, we sat in his car in the Swan's car park, where, in the dark, he kissed me a little half-heartedly, and when I gently pushed him away seemed somewhat relieved.

'Let's just talk,' I suggested.

'What about?'

'Why…you're divorced and I'm not married.'

He held my hand and then raised it to his lips, breathing on it gently before kissing the back as though it had unimaginable charms. I had to admit it was more of a turn on than I expected.

'I'm divorced,' he murmured, 'because my wife…'

He carried on flirting with my hand which I began to think a little odd and on a par with Hubert and feet.

'Understood you?' I queried.

He laughed lightly. 'She thought I was having an affair.'

'And were you?'

'Only a bodily affair—or maybe I should say affairs. My wife couldn't believe I could make love without being in love. We remain good friends. She says I'm immature which is undoubtedly true but as the song says—"growing up is so hard to do".'

'Were you, in fact, having an affair, bodily or otherwise, with Jenny?'

He sighed and dropped my hand. 'Kate. Does it matter to you? It was years ago. We had a fling. Well, a now and again fling. I told her my problems, she told me hers. She was unhappy. We shared a little happiness together. End of story.'

I didn't know what to say. I couldn't ask him too many

questions without arousing his suspicions. Why the hell did I like him anyway? He was a liar and a cheat but was he capable of murder? 'I have to go, Alan,' I said.

'Another time,' he murmured.

At Humberstones' Hubert lay full length on the sofa snoring loudly. I moved his legs to the floor and shouted that I was making black coffee.

Two cups later Hubert was sick, sober and scared. Once the beer had departed his body, his burglary career and my information were in definite jeopardy. I was convinced I would find something out at Teresa's house, so if necessary, I'd go alone, and I told him so.

'Oh no you won't,' he said. After a bit of 'Oh yes I will' it was settled.

We managed to stay awake by watching TV, drinking more coffee and eating biscuits, then I put on a black track suit and trainers, Hubert disappeared and came back wearing a black sweater, black trousers and the oldest plimsolls I'd ever seen. I made no comment, presuming he was as fond of the plimsolls as some people are of teddy bears. Then we left Humberstones' and began walking down the High Street towards the old part of town.

It was a dry night, quite warm. We met no one in the High Street, no one on their feet anyway, just two young men huddled together asleep in a shop doorway. Hubert paused, staring at them for a moment. 'It's a bloody disgrace,' he said sharply. 'This government has a lot to answer for.' He put his hand in his trouser pocket and brought out two pound coins and placed them by the sleeping bodies. A head moved slightly from the pile of blankets and old newspapers. He looked young, about sixteen, thin and with a wary look. Seeing the coins he smiled, 'Thanks, mate, you're a saint.'

We walked on, a bit subdued by our encounter, until we reached the beginning of the old part of town. Here there were several streets of turn of the century housing. They varied somewhat in layout, back to backs interspersed with those with alley ways at the back. After the first two streets of back to backs I realized that we were going to have a hard time getting into a house from the front because the street lighting was excellent and there were no front gardens to hide in. An insomniac somewhere was bound to see or hear us and although many occupants were pensioners there was a fair number of students who could surely be coming home in the early hours of the morning. Burglaries here were a rarity, mostly because local criminals knew there wouldn't be anything in these homes worth doing time for.

Luckily Teresa's house was of the back lane type and as Hubert and I walked down the dark side alley we tried not to tread on tin cans and various bits of rubbish. The air smelt of damp and cat's piss and apart from the occasional distant passing car all was quiet.

I hadn't expected it to be quite so dark, cloud occluded the quarter moon and once we opened Teresa's back gate the garden was as black as a pothole. I made Hubert walk in front of me so that if he fell I could land on him rather than him landing on me.

'Where's the torch?' I asked in a loud whisper.

'In the car.'

I stopped and stared ahead. Well, it would be, I thought. In that moment I knew I'd made an error of judgement. This was all a ghastly mistake. But it was too late to turn back. And maybe I would find something in Teresa's house that…I took one step and stumbled in the darkness. Treacherous giant pots seemed to guard every yard towards the back door. I walked on, my feet crushing to death several snails on the way, each snapping of the shell sounding loud as a pistol crack.

Eventually we arrived at the door to the kitchen. I could

make out, just, the slated roof of the kitchen extension. Adjacent to the kitchen door was the ground-floor sash window, curtains drawn.

'What now?' asked Hubert.

'We could force the back door,' I suggested cheerfully.

'Don't look at me,' said Hubert as he leant against the wall. 'I've had it—I'm tired.'

'I'll do it, then,' I said and even as I said it I knew I was making a mistake. I'd seen doors broken down on television, some beefy policeman taking a run, side on, at a door. I pushed the door with my hand. The dark paintwork felt old and peeling; maybe the door was weak. It was worth a try.

I steeled myself for impact.

'I can't watch this,' muttered Hubert.

'Close your eyes, then.'

I thrust my shoulder against the door. The pain was excruciating, so much so I thought I'd dislocated something. I couldn't cry out so I muttered 'shit' a few times and felt better for it.

'Leave it to me,' said Hubert and he loped off bent low like Quasimodo about to leap from belfry to balcony. He was looking for a flower pot and in moments he found one, told me to stand back and smashed the back window with it. The sound of breaking glass caused us to catch our breath and pray.

No lights came on, no one shouted 'What the hell's going on?' Hubert found the safety catch and opened what was left of the window and I scrambled in straight over the back of a chair, luckily, an armchair, and landed on the floor.

For a few moments we both lurched around in the dark and then I found a lamp and placed it on the floor, hoping the light would be less noticeable from outside. Hubert and I both sat on the floor for a while trying to get our bearings.

The room was long and narrow, with pale green walls decorated with various toning prints. A dining-room table and chairs were placed at the far end by the front window. The long dark green curtains with large pelmets gave the room a coolly elegant feel.

At our end of the room were filled book shelves, a two-seater sofa and an armchair in cream plus a coffee table with a posy of wild flowers in a pottery vase. As soon as I saw the flowers, day fresh, I guessed someone was in the house.

'We have to get out, Hubert,' I whispered frantically.

'After all that! Why?'

'We're not alone.'

It was then we heard heavy footsteps approaching the front door.

'It sounds like clogs he's wearing,' whispered Hubert by way of light relief. The door opening sounded like 'our' front door and I snapped off the light. We waited silently, hardly daring to breathe. We heard every step along next door's hall and then silence.

Just for a few seconds we experienced the euphoria of relief. Then we heard the car, the doors slamming, the heavy footsteps. And the shout of: 'Open up, it's the police.'

SEVENTEEN

HUBERT AND I flashed each other desperate looks. Again came more banging on the door followed by another 'Open up, it's the police.'

We started to run, stumbling out through the door, Hubert getting out first, pushing past me and dashing up the garden like a sprinter on speed. I rushed on blindly falling at the second pot plant then tried desperately to move off again. I was too slow, the police fell upon me as fast as flies on jam.

They dragged me to my feet and I was trotted through the house whilst one PC cautioned me and I protested my innocence in a loud voice. 'You don't understand...'

'Tell us about it at the station,' said the younger of the two PCs. His helmet seemed far too large for his small head and he wore rimless glasses that shone in the dark making him seem more sinister than I hoped he was.

Once I was in the back seat of the police car the other PC returned to the house and I sat there mumbling that when I got to the station I wanted to see either DC Roade or DI Hook.

'You'll be lucky,' said PC Shiny Specs. 'They're both tucked up in bed.'

I muttered about wanting my solicitor but then remembered I hadn't got one.

The other PC, older, although built like a wrestler, gave me a cheerful 'Haven't we done well' sort of smile, making him appear more user friendly. He drove off saying, 'Done many other jobs, love? You don't look much the average burglar to me. Still, it takes all sorts to make a criminal.'

'I'm not a criminal,' I said indignantly. 'I'm a private detective.'

They were still laughing about that as we drove into the station.

I'm in luck, I thought, when I saw the station sergeant was a man I'd met before. He acted though as if he'd never seen me in his life, took my details with a stony face, ignored my protestations of innocence and told the two arresting officers to take me to a cell.

'In the morning I'll get DCI Hook to interview you,' he said as the two PCs started to bundle me away. 'In the morning' echoed in my head. When in the morning? Where was Hubert?

The cell was cold, and bare apart from a concrete pallet, a thin mattress, two blankets, a pillow and a naked light bulb high up in the ceiling. What did you expect, I asked myself, lamps, duvets and a four-poster? It smelled of disinfectant and urine and as the door closed with a dreadful mechanical finality I shivered and felt tears stinging my eyes. I told myself I couldn't break down yet for God's sake, they'd only just shut the cell door. Some people, some criminals smelt this smell and felt the cold and the awful loneliness for weeks, months and years. I'd be out in the morning. I'd be out in the morning. I practised repeating that to comfort myself. It sounded good.

I wrapped the blankets round me, propped myself up on the 'bed', my head against the wall, and tried to think positive thoughts. Such as when did I last read in any newspaper of a private detective coming to trial for burglary? They must be at it, I thought. Or perhaps being intelligent they never got caught.

If I could have slept I would have been disturbed. The first sound of footsteps and the hatch opening made me think I was being released. It wasn't freedom that beckoned, it was merely to make sure I hadn't been spirited away, or hanged myself or merely snatched some sleep. The face that looked at me on the first occasion was young and quite good looking. I gave him a regal wave to hide my disappointment. The next 'visit' a female face appeared, middle aged, round faced and with a friendly smile.

'I'm the police matron—Mrs Brightman. Are you all right? Would you like a hot drink?'

'Yes, please,' I replied gratefully, thinking that I would never have believed such simple questions could be so comforting.

The cocoa that came in a plastic cup ten minutes later was hot and sweet and I savoured every mouthful. After that I settled down to sleep and prayed as I drifted off that the morning would come quickly.

At eight Mrs Brightman brought me tea and toast. I was allowed to go to the loo and quickly wash my hands and face. Then a constable arrived at eight thirty to take me up to the interview room where Hook and Roade sat waiting for me with faces as blank as deactivated androids.

'Sit,' said Hook.

I sat. And waited. Hook stared at me. I stared back for a while but then I looked away. Interview me, I thought—ask me something, anything. Eventually I said, 'Inspector, I'm sorry about this. I was perhaps a little over enthusiastic in pursuing my investigation.'

'That's an understatement,' he said frostily. 'What exactly did you hope to gain?'

'Only information, Inspector. I wasn't planning to steal anything. I thought maybe I'd find a diary.'

'One that we'd missed?' he asked and the sarcasm was obvious from his eyebrows to his larynx.

'I was stupid,' I mumbled.

'Could you say that again?'

'I was stupid.'

I caught Roade's eye then and he smirked and if I'd had

a Mars bar with me I'd have rammed it down his throat.
My anger at his silly self-righteous smirk made me bold.

'Inspector, I did not enter that house with criminal intent,
I made an error of judgement and I'm sorry I smashed the
window but since the combined forces of Longborough and
Dunsmore CID seem to have made very little headway I
can't help thinking that one more person's perspective on
the case wouldn't come amiss.'

Hook's face suffused with colour, then he paled leaving
a white area around his lips. Every muscle in his face and
neck tensed with anger. I watched the change in his face
as if observing a rare medical phenomenon.

'You've done it now,' whispered Roade with obvious
delight.

'The charges are,' intoned Hook, 'one, breaking and entering, two, criminal damage, three, resisting arrest—'

'I didn't resist arrest,' I interrupted in a state of growing
panic. Perhaps Roade was right—I had done it now!

A knock at the door and a mumbled request from an
unseen person in the corridor spirited Hook away. And left
Roade and me staring at each other across the table. He
began shaking his head and tutting.

'I won't give you another Mars bar if you don't talk to
me properly,' I said.

'He's determined to charge you,' said Roade. 'So don't
be flippant. You're in deep shit. That crack you made about
not making headway on the case really got to him. He can
be a nasty sod. If I were you I'd cry and grovel and try
and butter him up. You might, if you act well enough, get
off with a caution.'

'Why exactly is he so sensitive?'

'Perhaps he wasn't breast-fed long enough.'

'You know what I'm talking about, Sergeant Roade.'

Roade sat forward and placed his elbows on the table.
'It's Charles Amroth or to be more exact his missing wife.

Four years ago Hook was certain Amroth had killed his wife. She was an alcoholic and the marriage had been dodgy for years. Once their son had gone off to university she got much worse. When she disappeared Hook was working in Dunsmore and on his way to being promoted to chief inspector, but he was over-zealous. No evidence was ever found that Amroth had killed his wife, the son said he'd had letters from her but couldn't produce any. Amroth himself seemed relieved she'd gone and shortly after there were rumours he and Jenny were having an affair.'

'Do you think they were?'

'I'm not sure, maybe.'

'It is possible though, isn't it?' I said. 'Bereaved people often behave out of character. They'd both suffered loss, they worked in the same place, they had opportunity. But then I've been told he was also having an affair with Teresa.'

'That was only recently we think. It sounds as if Charlie was "me darling" to them both. Hook would love to nail Amroth but there's no evidence.'

'No forensic?'

Roade shook his head. 'Not so far. Nothing worthwhile.'

'Where have you looked?' I asked.

'Everywhere, including the house you broke into. There's nothing.'

'So you think maybe Jenny and Teresa were killed out of either Dunsmore or Longborough.'

He nodded. 'The trouble is they were killed cleanly, taken unawares—'

The door opened suddenly and Hook stood there still looking angry. 'You, Kinsella—get out. The super doesn't want the adverse publicity. Go. Roade, take her home, make sure she gets there and tell Humberstone he's lucky to have friends in high places.'

Roade took me by the arm and led me out of the building as fast as if it were in imminent danger of collapsing. Once in the car I managed to catch my breath. 'What the hell was that all about?' I asked. One minute I was in danger of a court appearance and a criminal record, the next I was being led off the premises in one almighty hurry. Roade shrugged, as mystified as I was. 'Search me. He probably won't tell me either. He'll be in a mood now for days, he'll make my life a misery.' I patted him on the knee and he blushed a deep crimson. As Roade drove off I had to ask him one more question. 'Do you think more than one person killed Jenny and Teresa?'

'I don't know. Forensic think a karate-type chop was used on the back of their neck and then they were strangled.'

'I see. And the diaries of both women?'

'What about them?'

'Nothing in there?'

'Yeah, that is a bit strange. Both of them seemed obsessed by the weather, a load of trivia—dripping taps, that sort of thing.'

'A code?'

'Why?'

I shrugged. I realized that I probably had two pieces of information the CID didn't have. The first, that Jenny wasn't quite dead when she was first bundled into the boot of the car. The second, that Jenny and Teresa were on a predatory mission.

As Humberstones' came into view I thanked DS Roade for the lift and for the information. He raised an eyebrow at that. I don't think he realized he'd given me any.

'See you,' said Roade, as he dropped me off. 'Stay lucky.'

Hubert waited for me by my office door. He looked relieved.

'I didn't know you could run that fast,' I said.

'I didn't know you couldn't.'

'I fell over a plant pot, Hubert. I can run. You wouldn't win a George medal, would you? You just abandoned me to my fate.'

Hubert scowled. 'I'll cook you some breakfast,' he said, 'and I'll explain.'

'I've had toast.'

'Have some more then.'

Over toast and coffee Hubert said, 'I had to make a quick decision, go back for you and risk us both being caught or stay free and help you from the outside.'

'I bet you went to bed.'

'I did not. I was making phone calls. How do you think you got out?'

'I heard, "friends in high places".'

'Precisely, Kate.'

I waited for him to explain, I sipped my coffee and waited.

'Well?'

'Think on this, Kate. Would you do a favour for the man who buried your mother?'

'I see. The superintendent's—mother.'

'Higher than that,' said Hubert proudly. 'Let's forget it now, shall we? Did you find anything out?'

'I'm traumatized, Hubert, by my ordeal. You seem to be taking that very lightly.'

'One night in a cell is no big deal, Kate. What did you find out?'

'I found out that the police have no evidence. They suspect Dr Amroth of three murders.'

'Three?'

'Hook is convinced Helena Amroth is dead.'

'Do you think she is?'

'I don't know but I'd hazard a guess that Jenny and Te-

resa thought she was alive and I can't help feeling their
''friendship'' with Amroth had an ulterior motive.'

'You've lost me.'

'I think Jenny suspected Helena of being the hit and run
driver.'

'Why should she do that, was there any evidence against
her?'

'Just circumstantial—Helena's being an alcoholic then
disappearing soon after the accident made them put two
and two together. Then someone reinforced their suspicion
and then two and two definitely made four.'

'Does this get you anywhere? Has Dr Amroth got an
alibi for the night of the murder?'

'It seems he was at home with his son, but I did what
you suggested.'

'What was that?'

'Presumed the police would have checked that out very
thoroughly.'

'Neil doesn't live in the house—you do know that?'
Hubert had one of his cocky expressions.

'You know jolly well I don't. No doubt you'll explain.'

'Technically Neil lives at home but during the summer
months he stays in a summer-house at the bottom of the
garden. So maybe his father wasn't in the house when Neil
said he was.'

'How did you find this out? From your friends in high
places?'

He ignored that remark. 'I also found out, Hook nearly
got the elbow for police harassment. Amroth filed a formal
complaint. Hook, it seems, was so convinced of Helena
Amroth's death that he was prepared to sacrifice his career
for it—he wanted to dig up the garden and had dug up part
of it until he was stopped.'

'Did no one look for her presuming she was alive?'

'Her son did, he went to London and made enquiries and

even got the Salvation Army to search for her. There were one or two leads but they came to nothing.'

Is it that easy to just disappear? I wondered. Had Jenny and Teresa found her and was it true Jenny wanted the ultimate revenge? Helena was obviously the catalyst but where was she now, and had she killed both women or had them killed?

Then I remembered Charles Amroth. *If* he had killed his wife and successfully hidden the body or disposed of it and Jenny and Teresa found out where Helena's body was, maybe he'd had to silence them. But would they have told anyway? If Helena's death was what Jenny wanted and Charles was a friend to them both—was he in any danger from them?

Hubert must have seen I was low spirited, and he patted me on the shoulder. 'There's only one answer, Kate—you have to find Helena Amroth dead or alive.'

I stared into his prune-coloured eyes wishing I could find the answer there. 'I agree. But how?'

'Someone knows where she is. A friend, relative. Someone…'

EIGHTEEN

MID-MORNING IT BEGAN to rain, the bouncing off the pavement sort. Even though it was Saturday Longborough High Street soon became deserted. I had to do something. Hubert said he had paperwork to do as he was planning a revamped information pack with a new selection of hymns and did I have any 'requests'? I didn't.

At lunch time I rang Geoff Martin and arranged to call at the house in the afternoon. He sounded depressed and said it was about time he saw me and that he wasn't too impressed with my efforts. What the hell did he expect?

At the house he suggested we sat in the kitchen. Outside the rain fell steadily from grey skies and Geoff looked pathetic again, especially since he hadn't dressed or shaved and the horse blanket was back.

'It's getting worse, not better,' he said as he slumped at the kitchen table. 'I'm hardly working, I can't sleep. When I do drop off I dream about Jenny, sometimes Simon too.'

'Geoff, I know this may upset you but I have to ask…' He watched me warily like a dog expecting a cuff. 'Why don't you ever mention revenge, why aren't you more angry? Did you expect Jenny to die?'

'Of course I didn't,' he answered sharply. 'Why do you say that? I've got enough problems staying on an even keel without you suggesting that in some way I didn't care…that I expected it.'

'Did you in fact talk to each other at all?'

His right hand clutched the side of the kitchen table and after a few moments he began to drum with his fingers.

When he didn't answer I asked, 'What's the matter? Have I touched a nerve?'

'Too bloody right. I'm raw—can't you see that—you hard-hearted bitch. Oh, it's all right for women, they have their friends. Who have I got? No one. No bugger wants to talk to me. I wanted to be a suspect, did you know that? They let me talk, they made me talk.'

'Were you angry when Simon died?'

'Of course I was angry. I would have laid down my life for both of them.'

'Would you have killed the driver of the car?' He paused, placed his hand over mine, pressing it into the table. 'Oh yes. And so would Jenny.'

I tried to pull my hand from under his but the pressure was vice-like. Suddenly I felt scared of him. He stared at me, sensed my fear. 'You're supposed to look for the truth but it makes you uncomfortable, doesn't it? The truth is rarely palatable.'

'Geoff, I want to find out who killed Jenny and Teresa. You obviously do too but I'm sure you're hiding something. By not telling you're hindering the investigation; after all, we do want to find the person or persons responsible.'

'I'm paying you to do that,' he said coldly. 'That shows my intention. I have nothing more to say.'

He released my hand then. 'I need a drink,' he said. He stood up and walked to the kitchen unit, opened a cupboard and took out a bottle of brandy. Before he closed the door I saw it was full of booze. He poured two brandies into sherry glasses, handed one to me and drank his in one huge gulp. Then he poured himself another. I sipped mine slowly in silence not knowing quite what to say next.

Eventually I said, 'How much progress had Jenny made finding Helena?'

'Who said she'd made any?'

'I think she knew where Helena was staying. And I think you know too.'

'Think what you like,' said Geoff petulantly. 'Nothing matters any more.'

'Of course it matters. Whoever killed Jenny and Teresa must be brought to justice.'

He refilled his glass then and tried to do the same to mine but I placed my hand over it and shook my head. He drank so fast a trickle of brandy flowed down his stubble and when his hand began to shake I realized he'd probably been drinking all morning.

'I'd better go,' I said.

'Do that.'

As I stood up to go he stared at me. His eyes, I noticed now, were slightly bloodshot and the tiny slivers of red should have warned me of danger. 'Try not to drink too much,' I urged him.

'You stupid bitch—don't you give me advice!' he shouted as he got to his feet unsteadily. So unsteadily that the chair he'd sat on fell to the ground. I don't know if it made a noise because by this time he was lashing out at me. 'Get out you bitch—come here again and I'll...get fucking *out!*' His hand caught my cheek and I half stumbled to the floor. The shock winded me but then he began kicking me in the back. I crawled towards the door. He was extending his vocabulary now, screaming a variety of abuse at me. I knew I was in terrible danger on the floor, I scrabbled to my knees and began screaming. He paused in his kicks and his tirade and in those seconds I was up and running. I didn't waste time flinging doors shut I just ran down the hall out of the garden to my car where in the pouring rain I fumbled awkwardly in my shoulder bag for my keys. I glanced towards the open front door. He stood there calmly watching me. As I found my keys I had the satisfaction of giving him a two-finger salute.

I drove off at speed and it wasn't until I got to Humberstones' that I examined my face in the car mirror. There was swelling and the beginnings of a bruise under my right eye, my wet hair looked pasted to my head and my mascara had run on to cheeks whose blood supply had temporarily gone elsewhere. Really I hadn't felt much at the time, only shock, but now I was beginning to feel pain. And I was starting to get tearful. It would only upset Hubert if he saw me like this so I sat in the car park for a while and then drove back to Farley Wood.

Once in the house I snivelled for a while, made a cold compress for my face using a pack of frozen peas in a wet flannel, drank some cheap sherry, dried my hair and tried to decide what to do next.

When the phone rang I hoped it was Hubert. It wasn't, it was Neil and I found myself telling him what had happened.

'I'll come over,' he said, 'I'm on my way!'

In thirty minutes Neil was at my door. He put out his arms to me immediately and cuddled me, then with his arms around my shoulders he took me into the house. He smelt of soap and after-shave and I must admit I was glad I hadn't phoned Hubert, he would only have nagged.

Neil made tea while I sat at the kitchen table and told him I'd gone to see Geoffrey Martin because I felt sorry for him.

'Do you think he killed his wife?' asked Neil.

'I didn't but I'm not sure now. Although I do think he would have killed the car driver who mowed down his son if he'd found her—' I broke off as Neil looked at me sharply. He shrugged. 'Strange about my mother, isn't it? Some people suspect she left suddenly because she'd run down Simon Martin, others believe my father killed her four years ago. What do you believe?'

'I'm not sure. Is your mother alive? Have you really had letters from her? Has anyone seen them?'

Neil laughed. 'Come on, Kate, I told you my mother wrote to me. I certainly wasn't going to let anyone else read those letters—even my father. They were totally personal. My mother's alive and happy, she didn't drink and drive and if she'd had a car accident she would have stopped.'

'Unless she panicked?'

Neil smiled good-naturedly. 'She wasn't the panicking type. My mother is the cool, collected sort.'

She would be on a full tank of vodka, I thought. Most people can stay pretty laid back, if well anaesthetized with alcohol.

Neil stayed for dinner, which he insisted on cooking, and afterwards he looked round the house and offered to do lots of odd jobs that needed doing. 'Only if you agree to go out with me again though,' he said laughing.

I didn't need my arm twisting and we arranged to meet on Tuesday evening. Just before leaving Neil said, 'Please be careful of Alan. I know he likes you but not only is he a womanizer he also likes killing animals—did you know one of his hobbies was hunting?'

I shook my head. When Neil eventually left, I thought getting beaten up was almost worth it.

LATE ON Sunday morning I called in at Humberstones'. I'd made a few notes on the case and I wanted to see if there was anything I'd missed. I had of course lost yet another client but I'd come this far and I wasn't going to give up on the case now.

My notes were scrappy but everyone I'd talked to was there. One name and one fact stood out as the most important; Bill Stone's final and I hoped truthful statement that he'd seen two cars after midnight on that night.

Nick however had said that the Golf was the only car there. And on that point he had no reason to lie. Therefore Jenny's car didn't leave that car park until Nick stole it. Why? Why leave one car behind earlier? Who did Jenny phone that night? Who was the most obvious person—her husband! Or maybe Charles Amroth? Teresa had to come by car because she lived in Longborough but Jenny could easily have gone on foot, the college being only ten minutes' walk from where she lived. The only reason she would have taken the car was because she wanted to go somewhere after the evening class. Was the plan to return to Dunsmore and then for Teresa to drop Jenny back at the college? And then Teresa would either go home or...or go to see her lover? What was Charles Amroth's alibi for that night? And why didn't I know?

I sat and mulled through my so-called evidence, not getting very far, when I heard Hubert coming up the stairs. He looked as glum as a pigeon fancier whose prize pigeon has failed to return.

I'd forgotten for a moment about my bruised face and his glum expression quickly turned to a surprised one. 'What happened, Kate? Who did it? Come on, tell me— I'll sort him out.'

'Calm down, Hubert, it was an accident. Really. Too much cheap sherry, I walked into the side of a door.'

'You're lying,' said Hubert, 'I know you well enough now, you're lying.'

I denied it of course. He continued to look at me suspiciously and walked round me in a circle, trying, I suppose, to see my face from all angles, or merely unnerve me.

'Do sit down, Hubert.' He sat opposite me and lifted my chin so that he could assess the damage. 'Don't fuss, please, Hubert—it's nothing.'

He continued to look at me thoughtfully and then said

slowly 'Didn't you say Jenny had bruises occasionally and when you found the man who gave her those bruises you'd have the murderer?'

'Hubert, you know I talk rubbish at times.'

'It's not what you say, Kate, that worries me, it's what you do and who you meet. When did it happen?'

'Yesterday.'

'Why didn't you ring me?'

'Because I walked into a door?'

'I tried to phone you,' said Hubert. 'You were out.'

'That's enough, Hubert. Let's drop it, shall we? I need help on this case, a bit of common sense and intelligence.'

He managed a gratified smile at that and I went over the hit and run scenario and said a little bit about Jenny's wish for revenge and suspicion of Helena Amroth.

'What about her husband: is he bitter and twisted?'

'He is now.'

'Where is this Helena Amroth?'

'That's just it, Hubert, I don't know.'

'She's the answer to everything, isn't she—if she's alive.'

''DI Hook is convinced she's dead.'

Hubert shook his head. 'That's a bad trait in a detective. An open mind, that's what's needed. Maybe he's too sure Charles Amroth is a killer and that's blinded him to the more obvious suspects.'

'Such as?'

'The husband.'

'I don't think he did it, Hubert, I do think he, Jenny and Teresa were intent on finding Helena...'

'Maybe they did find her.'

'Oh God, Hubert. I've just realized that if they had found her and Geoff knows where she is...what has he got to lose by killing her?'

'Someone must know where she is. Her son.'

'He might, but he says he doesn't. And why should she be living near here?'

'Why not?'

I stared at him in surprise. 'Hubert, you're brilliant,' I said excitedly. 'I could kiss you.'

'What did I say?' he asked with a quick grin.

'It's crystal-clear now,' I said. 'Well, almost. Helena Amroth is alive and well and living somewhere locally. Jenny and Teresa found that out, Geoff too, and they were planning to kill her. All that stuff I heard about Jenny saying she was ''living dangerously'' makes sense now. What could be more dangerous than planning to kill someone?'

'How, though?'

I shook my head. 'I suppose they wanted to plan a murder they could get away with, a perfect murder. A reciprocal murder...they were planning to mow her down.'

I got so excited at this point I jumped up from my chair, gave Hubert a hug and jigged up and down.

'Hang on, Kate, don't get too excited. If three people planned to kill Mrs Amroth—how come two of them are dead?'

NINETEEN

ON MONDAY MORNING I carefully applied make-up over my bruise before setting off for Riverview. I needn't have worried, no one noticed anyway.

Dr Amroth was back at work and seemed relatively cheerful. David Thruxton was in a foul mood. Two patients had left in tears, a receptionist had threatened to leave and Ian Holland had been heard muttering to himself and seemed quite seriously depressed.

The morning passed quickly and just after twelve Charles Amroth went off to do home visits leaving Ian Holland in his consulting room. Of the four doctors Ian, although the youngest and outwardly the most relaxed looking, didn't seem a very happy man. On a few occasions I'd noticed his breath smelt strongly of peppermints. Maybe I was wrong about the Morris dancing.

In the few weeks I'd been at Riverview the only time Ian Holland had spoken to me was to refer patients. Today I decided I'd try to rectify our non-communication by taking him a cup of coffee and staying until he was forced to talk to me.

I made two cups of strong coffee, knocked loudly on his door and walked in. He was at his desk signing prescriptions. He looked up and a vague look of puzzlement crossed his face as if wondering who exactly I was.

'Coffee?'

He nodded and I placed the coffee in front of him.

'Do you mind if I have my coffee in here, Ian?'

It wasn't a question because I'd already sat down. Today he wore a green-and-white-flecked hand-knitted sweater that was already wearing at the elbows. He ignored both me and my coffee and for a while I began to feel distinctly uncomfortable. Then telling myself that private investigators and practice nurses should have the constitution of an ox and a hide to match, I said, 'This coffee needs a lift— you haven't got anything to go in it, have you?'

'Whiskey,' he said quickly, opening the top drawer next to him, taking out a gold-capped flask and placing it in front of me. I smiled and poured us both a generous measure. It certainly improved the coffee but still he studiously avoided looking at me.

Although I knew he was popular with patients I sometimes wondered why. He always seemed rather shy, especially of me, and he tried to avoid eye contact whenever possible. He was conscientious and I knew he was kind and tried to explain patients' conditions whenever possible. His real talent, though, lay with the children. He wasn't shy with them and he always treated the mothers with respect; and he spoke to them in language they understood.

He suddenly put down his pen, uncapped the flask and drank steadily.

'I hate this place,' he said, staring into his coffee cup. 'I don't like being a GP much either. Would you go into nursing if you had your time again?'

I smiled. 'No, but tell me what's wrong with being a GP.'

'It would take too long. Increased bureaucracy, the gradual breaking down of the NHS, a work-load that would kill a donkey…a depressing amount of suffering and a number of patients who would try the patience of Job himself.'

'They should suffer in silence, shouldn't they, and be grateful,' I said in jest. Ian managed a half-hearted smile.

'Perhaps it's this place,' he muttered. 'Murder, disappearances, affairs, interviews with the police. I find it…enervating.'

'It interests me,' I said, which sounded better than just being nosy. 'Have the police given you a hard time?'

'I wouldn't say that exactly. The first few days were the worst—non-stop questions then. Finally they seemed to think the alibis were if not cast-iron at least stainless steel, and then they left us alone.'

He swigged again desperately on the whiskey and I avoided looking at him.

'I can go days without a drink so don't get the wrong impression. I'm not an alcoholic...yet. I'm working on it. It's so common among doctors now I think it should be classed as an occupational disease.'

'You mentioned ''affairs''—I'm intrigued.'

He seemed relieved I'd changed the subject but stayed silent for a while.

'Did you mean the affair Jenny was having with Charles Amroth?' I prompted.

He laughed. 'Jenny may have been keen, but can you imagine Amroth working up much steam? No, I meant...another affair.'

I waited for him to explain but he didn't. 'You can't just feed me a titbit like that, Ian, and then leave me in the lurch.'

'More whiskey?' he asked.

I nodded. The coffee had been drunk by now but to keep him company and to keep him talking I would at least appear to drink it.

Then, abruptly standing up, he turned and walked the few paces to the window to stare out at the neat soulless flower beds, stroking his beard in the way people stroke a cat, for comfort. 'I didn't tell the police. I don't know why,' he murmured as if forgetting I was in the room.

'What didn't you tell them?'

He said quietly, 'I was in London the day Jenny died, I told them that of course. I went for an interview for a job in Papua New Guinea—I thought it might be more civilized there. My wife met me at the station about nine—' He broke off, staring at the garden.

'What exactly did you omit to tell the police?' I asked.

He turned then to glance at me as if trying to diagnose how trustworthy I looked. I obviously passed this test.

'This is confidential,' he said as he resumed staring out at the garden. 'Although I do have to tell the police now, I should have told them in the first place but I thought it might make them even more convinced that the answer lay in this practice. I assumed that soon they would leave us all alone and look elsewhere for suspects. But they keep on harassing Charles and I'd rather they heard it from me, before Charles hears about it, second or even third hand.'

'Charles?'

'Yes. I saw them outside the National Gallery. David Thruxton and Helena Amroth.'

'You're sure it was her?' I asked, puzzled. 'I didn't think you knew her.'

'I've seen photographs. She's altered but it was definitely her—she's a very striking woman. I've been wondering what to do ever since. I mean, this really could break up the practice. Poor old Charles under a cloud for so long and his partner busy screwing his very much alive wife.'

'And Ros's best friend,' I muttered.

'I have to tell them, don't I, Kate?' he said flatly.

'Who knows about this—your wife, presumably?'

'No,' he said sharply. 'She doesn't know and I don't want her to know. She's beginning to think the practice is jinxed anyway.'

'I can understand that. When do you plan to tell the police?'

'Today. The strange thing is I think I saw them getting on the train that evening. It may have been imagination, though—I only saw their back views and I didn't see them get off.'

He turned slowly, sat down at his desk and resumed signing prescriptions. I picked up the coffee cups and saucers and murmured, 'Good luck,' but he didn't look up as I left.

Back in the treatment room I checked my diary for the next afternoon then, flicking through the pages absentmindedly, I noticed Jenny had made two entries about a dripping tap. Two, I thought, *two!* It made sense; Jenny's diary, the one I saw at her home, wasn't her only diary. All that weather trivia was in an open diary, she had another diary, one that was far more personal, more revealing. Or at least she had had one, once.

I drove back to Longborough just in time to see Hubert and Desperate Dan walking towards the Swan. I felt a surge of irritation and mild jealousy. It wasn't so long ago that the only person Hubert took to the Swan was me. I felt as discarded as a fag end and I sat in my office watching from the window to see if they came back together. They did. I then waited for Hubert to come up my staircase. He would have seen my car in the car park but I waited and waited and still he didn't appear.

Just after three I rang Geoff Martin. He sounded both surprised and sober.

'I'm sorry,' he said, 'it was completely out of character. Drinking is a new pastime and I know it brings out the worst in me. I've been feeling very ashamed—'

I cut his apology short, now was the time to get tough with him. 'Jenny's diary—I want it. I'm at my office.'

'You've seen her diary.'

'Come off it, Geoff, I know she had another one.'

'How do you know?'

'I just do. I'll be expecting you in about half an hour.'

'What if I don't come?'

'I report you for common assault.'

'I don't have much choice, do I?'

'None at all, Geoff. I think you've hindered this investigation for long enough.'

A few minutes later Hubert came up. He looked like the man who'd just won the only prize in a national lottery. I smiled coolly.

'Danielle understands me, Kate, she really does...' He paused as he saw my expression.

'I've got Jenny Martin's husband coming to see me, Hubert. I'd like you to sit in on the interview.'

'Why? You scared of him? Was he the one who—'

'No, he wasn't,' I interrupted, 'but I may need a witness.' Hubert looked pleased at that. 'When's he due?'

'Any minute, and I'd like you to make him wait downstairs in the hall for a few minutes when he does arrive.'

'Aye, aye, Captain,' said Hubert giving me a salute and mumbling about the Caine Mutiny and the disappearing strawberries which I took to mean he thought I'd gone power crazy.

I kept Geoff waiting for ten minutes on the ghastly armchair at the bottom of my stairwell and by the time I came to collect him he looked paler than usual.

'You must be a hard woman,' he said, 'to work here.'

'As the proverbial nails, Geoff.'

Hubert stood in the corner of my office facing my desk and Geoff got a shock as he walked in. I must admit in his funereal black and with a weird forced smile on his face Hubert did look like an understudy for the Prince of Darkness.

'What's he doing here?' Geoff asked. 'I didn't expect a third party.'

'Hubert is my friend, associate and landlord. He knows everything.'

Geoff looked at Hubert with a nervous frown and they both stood eyeing each other like two apes about to begin

a supremacy battle. Then after a few seconds of full con-
centration Geoff's face relaxed, Hubert lost his slightly in-
ane grin and the level of tension dropped palpably. It
seemed as if they had both claimed an inward supremacy,
and that being so they didn't need to prove anything.

I turned round my office chair so that Geoff's view of
Hubert remained and then put my hand out. 'The diary,
Geoff,' I said firmly, 'I know you have it.'

He smiled with satisfaction. 'I did have it, Kate, but not
any more. There is no way I would have let the police read
her most personal thoughts. I would have chewed it and
swallowed it first.'

'What did you do with it?'

'It was bonfire time.'

Shrugging as if this was no great blow, I said, 'Just tell
me what was in it that you were so ashamed of, and I'll
forget about the other matter.'

'You are a bitch,' he said coldly.

Hubert moved forward then, saying, 'Watch it, mate!'

I flapped my hand at him so that he returned to his orig-
inal position. 'Jenny's dead,' I said softly, 'nothing can
touch her now.'

Geoff sighed deeply and supported his head between his
hands. 'You're right, I suppose. What does anything matter
now? It was about a year ago Jenny found out Helena was
not only alive and well but having an affair with David
Thruxton. That made her very bitter. Ros was her favourite
among the doctors' wives and Jenny had always been
friendly with Charles Amroth, she felt sorry for him. She
knew the gossips said they were having an affair but it
wasn't true. Jenny discreetly introduced Teresa to Charles
and their romance bloomed, but very quietly. Inspector
Hook and his cronies as you know had long suspected Amroth of getting rid of his troublesome wife. Their affair was

secretive and stayed a secret until...until the murderer
found out.'

'So what was in the diary, Geoff?'

'Dates, times, arrangements...thoughts.'

'What sort of thoughts?'

'Killing thoughts. The adultery Jenny viewed as treach-
ery and as confirmation that Helena was just the sort of
person to be a hit and run driver. She became very bitter.
She wanted Helena dead. Teresa did too. After all, with
Helena really dead she would have been free to marry
Charles.'

'And what about you, Geoff? What did you want?'

'I wanted the same as Jenny and Teresa. Helena killed
our son, I was convinced of that.'

'You wanted her dead?'

He nodded, raising his eyes and staring at me bleakly. 'I
wish to God she was dead. Jenny and Teresa might both
be alive if she were.'

'I'm puzzled. Why isn't she dead? What stopped you?'

Geoff laughed drily. 'We were too long in the planning.
Much too long. We found out all about her, where she
worked, where she lived, what name she used. We followed
her, occasionally together, sometimes separately. We got to
know her movements, even what time she pulled her curtains. It was almost a hobby, we'd never been happier.'

'Where does she live, Geoff?'

He smiled knowingly. 'Not far away. She has a job, a
rented cottage, a car, paid for no doubt by David Thruxton,
and I'm sure he kept an eye on Neil for her. She had the
ideal arrangement.'

'Surely Ros guessed what was going on?'

He shrugged. 'Who knows.'

I thought there was a strong possibility she might and
indeed was now one of my top of the range suspects. I
recapped aloud Geoff's admission and then bluntly asked,

'How exactly did you plan to murder Helena? I take it you had planned the perfect murder?'

He stared at me for a moment, eyes glittering with a fervour I usually associated with religious maniacs. 'You know everything now. I've got nothing to lose by telling you. We watched, we waited and we were patient. Too bloody patient. We intended to run her down just as she'd run Simon down. Not just one car, sometimes all three of us drove separately. We guessed that if we were caught a jury would have trouble convicting any one person of the actual death. Three cars or two cars mow someone down— who can tell whose were the fatal tyres? Somehow though it never seemed to be the right time and murder seems easy in theory but not so easy in practice. Perhaps we enjoyed the hunting too much, knowing where our prey was, being able to move in for the kill at any time. We left it too late.'

'Did you tell anyone else of your intentions?'

'Of course not. And I shall deny this conversation.'

'Someone must have known, Geoff, or at the very least guessed.'

'Possibly,' he murmured. 'I do hold myself responsible for Jenny and Teresa's deaths, you know. We should have killed the bitch while we had the chance. Still, it's not over yet, is it? It's not over.'

As he turned to go he saw Hubert, somewhat paler and leaning against the wall for support. 'Ah, Dr Death. No doubt you think you ought to rush straight to the police. Remember, though, without the diary there's no evidence that we were planning anything at all.'

'What about the night of the murders?' I asked.

'Jenny rang me to tell me the class had been cancelled and did I want to come with them because that night may have provided a good opportunity, but I had deadlines to meet.' He broke off to laugh harshly. 'Dead—lines, funny, ha ha ha. Anyway, I did fall asleep and when I woke at two a.m. and Jenny wasn't home I imagined she'd been caught. So I burnt the diary. Then I rang the police and waited for them to come. But they brought me news of quite a different kind.'

'Tell me where Helena is now,' I said softly.

He stared at me sullenly for a few moments. 'Why should I make things easy for you. You're a private detective, do what you're paid to do—detect!'

There was nothing more to say to each other. He turned then and left the room.

When we heard the last of Geoff's footsteps on the stairs, Hubert almost staggered to the chair. 'That's made me feel queasy,' he said. Then he patted my hand. 'You have a lot to put up with, Kate, in your job. Nasty character. I need a drink.'

'I don't think he was always like that, Hubert. Him or Jenny. I think thoughts of revenge kept them sane.'

'Sane! You've got some funny ideas, Kate. I think he's as mad as...a rabid dog.'

'What are we going to do, Hubert?'

'Have a drink.'

'No, after that.'

'Go to the police, of course.'

'To say what?'

'Just to tell them what we know. They can decide what to do about it.'

'I'm not happy about that, Hubert, you know how slow they can be. After four years Hook still thinks Helena Amroth is under flower beds somewhere. What's he going to say to her—be careful crossing the road?'

'He might want to bring her in on suspicion of murder.'

I frowned. 'True, Hubert, he can only bring her in though if she hasn't been splattered on some lonely road.'

'What are you trying to say, Kate?'

'We should follow him, that's all. Find out where she lives and warn her.'

'That's all! He's a maniac with nothing to lose!'

'Yes, Hubert, but if you think he's mad, think on this—there's someone out there who is even madder and more dangerous. Someone who also thinks they have nothing to lose. Someone who doesn't just think about killing, but does it.'

TWENTY

WE HAD A DRINK—a large coffee. And I planned tactics. 'All we have to do is follow Geoff, because he knows where Helena lives, and then we warn her.'

'Sounds simple,' said Hubert frowning. 'Too simple. Anyway, he could have gone straight from here to...wherever she is.'

'I think he'll wait for a while until he makes his move. He's left here in a determined state but give him time to think and he'll revert to his more cautious self.'

Hubert grinned. 'You think you're a real little Clement Freud, don't you?'

When I began to laugh and told him he was priceless, his expression became puzzled and slightly wounded. 'What did I say?' he asked.

'Hubert,' I said, 'you keep me sane. I'm just thankful you're not one of those psychology-quoting pseudo-intellectuals.'

'Are you trying to say I'm thick?'

'No, Hubert. You're just the best sort of...partner there is.'

His face tinged up somewhat from mere pasty to mottled pink, and he smiled. I'd made his day. And although I wouldn't tell him, he'd made my year.

Late evening I drove to Dunsmore with Hubert beside me. He'd bought a picnic in a proper picnic basket, a copy of the *Funeral Director* and, for me, a copy of the *Daily Telegraph*.

'I am impressed, Hubert,' I said, 'especially with the newspaper.'

'It's good on crime and this case in particular. According to their reporter, Charles Amroth is still under suspicion. There's a suggestion that he was in some sort of sexual relationship with both women.'

'A *menage à trois?*'

'That too,' said Hubert. 'And there's photos of all the women involved.'

In Dunsmore traffic was slight, most people having long since gone home. The tree-lined avenue where Geoff Martin lived was particularly quiet. I parked the car about three doors down from the Martin house and from there we had a good view of the front entrance. I presumed he couldn't see us, unless he was watching from upstairs with a pair of binoculars.

It was now nearly seven, clouds were gathering and the wind was whipping up slightly. 'What time do we eat, Hubert?' I asked. He raised his eyes to heaven as if I should be concentrating on more important things but nevertheless he leant over and began opening the basket. He'd handed me a curry pasty wrapped in foil and potato salad in a plastic tub, and I'd just acquired a plastic fork when Geoff Martin's car sped out of his drive. I practically threw the food over my shoulder, started the car and we were off as close behind him as I could manage.

He drove into Dunsmore's main road and I thought for a moment he was going to stop as he had been signalling left as he neared a parade of shops, but then he cancelled his indicator and drove on and out of town. At the next crossroads he turned right going towards Weston-Cumby, a village of film-set cosiness, where buying a barn cost a fortune and house sellers would rather not sell their house at all than sell to the wrong type of person. This was the village in which Charles Amroth lived.

I'd heard that Charles lived in a house overlooking the duck pond at Weston-Cumby and as Geoff slowed down,

I stopped by the village pub and watched him drive towards the largest house in the village.

'Some house,' said Hubert appreciatively. 'I bet it's listed. Georgian by the look of it.'

It was elegant. Stone pillars guarded the wrought-iron front gate, the surrounding low walls were covered in clumps of blue flowers and creeping ivy crept up the sides of the front door towards the windows.

We sat and watched as Geoff slowed to a halt and then he too just sat and stared at the house.

'What the hell is he up to?' I asked.

'No idea. Have a curry pasty?'

I nodded but by now they were crushed and forlorn looking and Hubert's expression matched the state of his pasties. 'They were a lot of trouble—now look at them—pathetic.'

'He's on the move,' I said excitedly as Geoff left his car and began walking towards the house. Moments later the front opened and he went inside.

'Come on, Hubert, we'll go round the back and have a look. I mean if he tells Charles about Helena there could be trouble.'

He grabbed my arm. 'Better to wait, Kate—you don't want to blow your cover yet, do you?'

Although disappointed I knew he was right. Charles, after all, might not have been that surprised about his wife having an affair with his partner. He might have been more surprised to find out his practice nurse was a private investigator. It wasn't likely that it would end in fisticuffs anyway.

Back in the car we waited and waited. I read the *Daily Telegraph*, Hubert sat engrossed in the *Funeral Director*. I stared for some time at photos of Jenny, Teresa and Helena. Teresa, elfin faced, looked to be in her twenties; the photo of Jenny also was years out of date. Helena interested me most. She was tall, long faced but attractive with fair hair piled on to her head, wearing a navy polka-dot dress and carrying a trug full of flowers. The background to the photo was fuzzy but it appeared to have been taken in the front garden of the house in Weston-Cumby.

Eventually, as it began to grow dark, Geoff appeared, walking briskly towards his car. I left it till he was nearly out of sight before following him.

He drove straight back to Dunsmore, parked his car carefully in the garage and went indoors. Both Hubert and I felt really dejected, until I thought about what he'd just done. He hadn't gone to discuss the weather. He'd been a harbinger of bad news, but why? Charles would have found out soon enough once Holland told the police. Why tell him now?

I repeated my question aloud to Hubert who suggested being a woman I should know.

'What's that got to do with anything?'

'He's acting like a bitchy female, isn't he? Taking delight in telling him.'

'Maybe, Hubert. But he could just be trying to implicate him so that when Helena is found dead suspicion is more than likely to fall on Charles.'

I STAYED AT HOME on Tuesday morning spending the time rehennaing my hair in preparation for going out with Neil that evening. It did cross my mind that it might not be too cheerful a date, if his father had told him about Geoff's visit. I didn't mind listening if he wanted to talk although I certainly didn't want to play the substitute mum. I wanted to be more *femme fatale*.

The afternoon at the practice passed quickly. There seemed to be no new gossip but there was an atmosphere of expectancy as if I wasn't the only one to know what was going on. It was David Thruxton's afternoon off, Ian

Holland kept himself firmly in his consulting room but I did wonder just how many people he'd sworn to secrecy after me. I supposed it was like that with most people, once you decide to tell one person a secret there's no point in not telling others.

I was just leaving the practice at five when the phone rang. It was for me. Ros wanted to see me as soon as possible—like this minute. She sounded distraught and had obviously been told.

'I'm on my way, Ros,' I said, 'but wouldn't you rather Sara was there or Ian's wife?'

'I want you. Those bitches would only crow and say I told you so.'

As I approached the house Ros opened the door. She'd been crying and drinking, her mascara had made two black rings underneath her eyes, her hair matched her distracted expression as though she had run her hands through it over and over again. I followed her into the hall and she stopped for a moment by one of her vases of flowers. It obviously irritated her for she swept it to oblivion with one almighty sweep of her hand, screaming 'Bastard! Bastard!' as she did so. Somehow I didn't think she was talking about the vase.

In the kitchen we sat at the long pine table. The cream-coloured Aga, fat and squat, dominated the kitchen and seemed to represent all that had been lost by being solid, reliable, strong and ever-present. Ros poured each of us a huge gin and tonic. I don't drink gin but in these circumstances I felt I could force one down.

'I'm going to have my revenge,' she said between clenched teeth. 'You know of course what's been going on?' I nodded. 'I don't know what's hurt me more, my husband's treachery or hers...the bitch! What really devastates me is my own stupidity. I mean how can I have *not* known?'

'Where did he say he was going when he went out?'

She stared at me, the anguish in her eyes making her look demented. 'Golf, the masons, one or two medical seminars. You name it, he was there…or supposed to be. He'd ring me if he was away. I bet that viperous conniving…*bitch* was lying there beside him even as he spoke to me.'

Ros began to cry then and I put my arm around her, feeling as ineffectual as if offering an aspirin to someone about to have their legs amputated. She cried for some time, mopping her tears with paper tissues from a box in front of her then, as they became sodden, aiming for a wastepaper bin in the corner of the kitchen and missing. Eventually her sobs gave way to sniffing and gulping, but her breathing was still ragged and uneven. She swigged down more gin and tonic and then said softly, 'I'll kill them both.'

'Are they worth going to prison for?' I asked.

Ros didn't answer that question. 'It's her… I can't believe she'd do that to me. We were best friends, for years. I'd told her the most intimate details of our lives…no wonder she was drinking heavily—cow…bitch…' I could see she was struggling for more terms of abuse so I added whore, strumpet and Jezebel for good measure. She managed a wry smile, spread her hands in a gesture of helplessness and said, 'What am I going to *do*, Kate?'

'Divorce him, find yourself a lover, demand a huge settlement—bleed him dry financially.'

'That's not enough,' Ros answered calmly. I found her composure more unnerving than her tears. 'How long had it been going on? That's what I want to know. For four years I half suspected she was dead or living abroad. I felt that had she been alive she would have contacted me by letter, postcard—some way.'

'Charles must be very upset too. After all, he's been suspected of killing her.'

'Pity he hadn't.'

'Where exactly is David now?' I asked.

Ros managed a dry laugh. 'Well, he's not upstairs in a trunk, if that's what you think. He's gone, maybe he's gone to her, I don't know and I don't care.'

We sat in silence for a while. Ros drank steadily and didn't seem to notice that I'd stopped. Eventually she said, 'How long? How bloody long?'

'For what?'

'How long before she left here had it being going on? I mean I was seeing her once a week at least. How many others knew, I bet Sara knew! She always had a knowing smile on her face. I can't bear it—not the thought of me being the last to know.'

'I don't think anyone knew...except—' I broke off but it was too late.

'Except who?' demanded Ros.

'Except Jenny,' I said reluctantly. 'And her friend Teresa.'

Ros opened her mouth and then closed it again. 'Surely not, oh God I don't believe it. David wouldn't have killed them...he wouldn't...' She tailed off, perhaps realizing that until a few hours ago she hadn't suspected him of adultery and now there grew the suspicion of murder.

Tears filled her eyes and began to run down her cheeks. She wiped them away roughly with the back of her hand. 'He must have loved her very much to commit murder,' she said.

'Don't jump to conclusions, Ros. I mean, did he have the opportunity? Where was he the night they both died?'

She thought for several moments then said, 'He'd been to London that day, a BMA meeting...or at least that's what he told me. I was half asleep when he came home. I told the police he was back by eleven thirty...that was what he told me. I'd been in bed an hour or so, it seemed about right. He could have done it, couldn't he?'

'If he did, think about this, Ros. Why did he kill Jenny and Teresa? Was it to prevent them telling you? To save you pain?'

'It's kind of you to say, Kate, but I don't think that entered his head. More likely he worried about losing his job at the practice. And of course we're still paying school fees…'

Thinking of her children brought more tears and I felt relieved when we heard the sound of a car crunching up the drive and then loud knocking on the door.

'I don't want to see anyone,' said Ros firmly.

'Shall I see who it is?'

By the time I'd walked into the front sitting-room there was a repeated knock and a gruff male voice saying, 'Open up please, it's the police.'

As he'd said please I opened the door. Two men in plain clothes stood there, both in grey suits, looking sombre and both complete strangers. The elder of the two stepped forward. He was large, with a pot belly and a thick-set face which matched his thick-set neck, but he had a friendly smile and lively blue eyes. 'I'm DCI Hyton and this is DI Blackamore,' he said, 'we've come to see Mrs. Thruxton. And you are?'

'I'm Kate—the practice nurse. Mrs Thruxton is very upset at the moment, could I just warn her you're here?'

'You go ahead, dear.'

Poor Ros paled when I told her the police wanted to speak to her and she whispered, 'You will stay, won't you? I don't want to be alone with them.'

I nodded. I was only too relieved it was Dunsmore CID and not Hook and Roade.

I wasn't quick enough in getting rid of the gin and the glasses and they gave us a faint look of surprise. Blackamore was a dead ringer for someone but it was only after a few minutes that I remembered who—a young Christopher Lee. He had the face of man plagued by demons and doubts.

Ros reluctantly gave permission for them to sit down. 'We won't keep you long, Mrs Thruxton,' said Hyton arranging his bulk on the rather narrow chairs, 'really it was your husband we wanted to speak to.'

'He's not here,' said Ros giving them both a 'don't argue with me' look.

'Have you any idea where he is?' asked Hyton patiently.

'In hell as far as I'm concerned, Inspector.'

'Which branch of hell would that be, Mrs Thruxton?'

Ros sighed deeply. 'He's with his mistress, the bitch, Helena Amroth. I really don't know where and I don't care.'

'I see,' said Hyton. 'Could you tell me where he was yesterday evening?'

At first I thought she wasn't going to answer but then she said quietly. 'He had a phone call about ten, he said it was a patient. He left the house soon after and I presume he went to the Amroth woman.'

'Had you had a row?' Blackamore asked.

'Of course we'd had a row, I don't always look like this. It was only last night I learnt of my husband's affair.'

'And you haven't seen him since?' Hyton queried with an apologetic smile.

'No. I have not seen him since and I would prefer not to see him ever again.'

There was silence then and I noticed that the two detectives had suddenly acquired very serious expressions. Ros noticed too.

'What's happened?' she asked. 'Why are you looking for him? He didn't murder Jenny and her friend. He liked

Jenny. He might be a treacherous bastard but he isn't a murderer.'

'We didn't say he was, Mrs Thruxton,' said Hyton quietly. 'His morals are no concern of ours but his welfare is.'

'What do you mean? What are you talking about?'

Hyton paused to loosen his tie slightly. 'This afternoon we called on Geoffrey Martin at his home. We found him, but not alive. He'd been battered to death. The police doctor puts a preliminary time of death at between two and four a.m.'

TWENTY-ONE

I FOUND IT hard to believe Geoff was dead. An out of sight sudden death doesn't cause quite the shock you expect. With no body to confront there was only my memory of Geoff being very much alive. It just didn't seem possible. I did wonder if he had put up much of a fight. Had he perhaps thought, at that moment of confrontation, that death was preferable to living without wife and child?

Events seemed to crowd in on me. I needed time to sort out what was going on. David Thruxton had disappeared and was now the chief suspect with Charles Amroth jostling for the position. Inspectors Hyton and Blackamore had left soon after breaking the dramatic news. Ros, strangely, had become calmer after hearing of Geoff's death and decided to ring Sara Wheatly after all.

I'd left the moment Sara had arrived; I knew the drinking would go on into the early hours and I'd already had a large gin and tonic.

As I drove into Humberstones', Hubert appeared in the car park and practically attached himself to my hubcaps he was so keen to talk to me. The church clock struck seven and it began to rain.

'Have you heard?' he asked me before I'd even managed to lock my car. 'The CID have been round, they want to talk to you, they're not happy. Hook said he would personally drum you out of Longborough if you weren't here when he came back.'

'When's he coming back?'

'He didn't say. And you had a phone call from Neil, he says, "Can you make it tomorrow instead?"'

I had to admit I'd forgotten about my date with Neil and it hardly seemed important. My second client dying was far more relevant.

By this time I was getting soaked so we ran in and Hubert insisted I came up to his flat.

'You can have a bath if you want. I thought I'd get us a takeaway tonight—Indian or Chinese?'

'I think the Chinese has gone bankrupt.'

'Indian then.'

Hubert rushed off, presumably before I changed my mind, and I started running the bath and then decided to go up to my box-room for some fresh clothes. The phone rang while I searched: it was Neil. 'I'm sorry about this evening, Kate, but, as I'm sure you know, Geoff Martin has been murdered. Initially they suspected my father but I think I've convinced them he didn't leave the house last night. Poor old Pa is in a bit of a state, as you can imagine.'

'It must be awful for both of you,' I said. 'What's happening about the practice?'

'Marcus and Ian will keep it going and Alan's going to get in a locum and some night relief.'

Suddenly I remembered the bath. 'I must go, Neil, I've got a bath running.'

'I'm jealous,' murmured Neil. 'I'll see you tomorrow about eight at your place.'

Luckily Hubert had an oversize bath and the water wasn't running down the stairs to meet me. I chose various luxurious foams, oils and body shampoos and added a bit of each to the bath water, then I lay back and tried to order the various events. Thinking in the bath is amazingly easy. So too is falling asleep and I had to force myself to concentrate.

All my thoughts went back to that night when Jenny and Teresa drove off from the college in Teresa's car. Jenny had rung Geoff and he'd turned down the invitation to go hunting Helena. What about Teresa, though? She couldn't have felt the strong desire for revenge that Jenny and Geoff experienced. Did Teresa in fact go her separate way that night? Where would she have gone? To her lover—where else? Did they have an argument? Did Teresa realize it was all getting out of hand and that she was being used as a pawn to get information out of Charles Amroth. How much did he know anyway? He was intelligent enough not to admit to the police he'd seen Teresa that night. Was the plan that Jenny should go off on her own and then return for Teresa? Why should Teresa even be in on the plan to mow down Helena? Because…she had a vested interest! Helena's death would free Charles to marry her…

'Kate—you must be clean by now. Food's in the oven.' Hubert's voice destroyed my chain of thought but I knew now I was getting somewhere. I had to talk to Charles and if necessary 'come out' and tell him I was a PI. Not that I'd actually got a client any more but I reasoned that cracking this case would up my profile and more work might come flooding in—might!

Over chicken dupiaza, king prawn curry, onion bhajis, pilau rice and naan bread plus several cans of lager Hubert and I discussed the case.

'I'm ever so confused,' said Hubert.

'It's a confusing case. Jenny was attacked but was still alive for a while, that points to the murderer being disturbed, or merely hurrying. Also, if she was on her own simply hanging about to watch Helena's coming and goings surely she would have got so bored she wouldn't have waited until nearly midnight?'

'Maybe she went to see Charles as well?' suggested Hubert.

'Maybe she did just that. But they were killed at slightly different times. We know Jenny was attacked first but where was Teresa at the time? Unless of course there were

two people involved. According to Roade's interpretation
of the forensic report he seemed to think the strangling and
the blow to the head were virtually simultaneous and neither victim put up much of a fight.'

'So?'

'So, they were taken by complete surprise.'

'What about Jenny's last word?' asked Hubert as he
mopped up the last of his curry with some naan bread.

'I can't really give that much credence. I mean it seems
so strange that if she was capable of speech she didn't just
say who did it.'

Hubert shrugged. He was like me, lots of questions and
supposition but no answers.

He began clearing away and stacking the plates. 'The
thing is, Kate,' he said, pointedly handing me a tea towel,
'you already know where to find Charles Amroth and so
do the police—you've got to find Helena because the CID
must be near to finding her. They may already have done
so.'

'Hubert,' I said, 'you're dead clever.'

He gave me an old-fashioned look. 'Better than being
just dead, which seems to be on the increase around here.'

'You're right about Helena. I've been thinking she really
can't be far away. Ian Holland thought he saw her and
David getting on the train, so if he didn't see them getting
off, they went on past Longborough. If we check the sta-
tions further up the line, not more than fifty miles away,
then we can see what we come up with.'

'We?' asked Hubert eagerly.

Shortly after we'd washed up and cleared away we collapsed on to the sofa like two sumo wrestlers after a blow-
out but we did manage to stir ourselves to scan a map of
the railway system. There were three possible stops—Melton, Naresworth and Bendarrow.

'What do you plan to do?' asked Hubert. 'Keep driving round each town until you find her?'

'Of course not. I've a much more sophisticated method than that.'

'Which is?'

I paused. What the hell was I going to do? 'I'll think on it, Hubert, after the coffee and mints.'

'You'll be lucky,' said Hubert. 'You can make the coffee.'

It was while the water was boiling I wondered where Helena was brewing her coffee. She had to live somewhere. It was likely she'd found a place to rent and it was also likely she had a job. Neil had said something about that...she'd begun a pharmacy course but never completed it. She could be working as a dispenser or as a chemist's assistant. Well, it was a long shot but worth trying.

THE FOLLOWING AFTERNOON Hubert and I set out to the first town on our list. Melton surprised me by having a multi-storey car park, a cinema and a leisure centre. Compared with Longborough it was a veritable metropolis. There were at least four estate agents in the town, luckily all in the centre and all doing some letting work because actually selling houses had now become a rarefied occupation—similar to archeology or wild-boar hunting. 'I'll go in alone,' I said as we neared the first estate agents. 'If you're with me, Hubert, I won't be able to lie with a straight face.'

As I walked in I was conscious of the fact that Hubert was still peering through the window but as a young man rushed towards me I managed to ignore him.

'Madam,' said the young man smiling with a keenness I found unnerving, 'can I assist you?'

'I do hope so,' I said. The salesman was about twenty and too young for his grey pin-stripe, the trousers of which lapped over the top of his shoes as if he'd recently shrunk. He wore a red tie, had the eyes of a religious zealot and the hair of someone who'd been reduced to his mother cutting it. Before I could speak again he was telling me how much cheaper it was to buy rather than to rent. I cut him short.

'I'm a contact tracer,' I said, flashing him a quick glance at my UKCC card. He looked puzzled. 'I find people who...may have picked up a nasty disease. They have to be warned, you see...' I let that sink in and he gazed around the office as though looking for someone more senior. There were two women typing, with heads down.

I described Helena, saying I'd heard she was renting in the area and wondered if they had anyone of that description on their rental register.

'Short or long lease?'

I shook my head. 'I've no idea, but she could have been renting for some time.'

'How long?'

'Two or three years.'

'She'd know she'd got a disease by now, wouldn't she?' he asked.

'Not necessarily.' Then I added in a low serious voice, 'It does depend on the disease.'

He began checking. I explained she could be under an assumed name, I described her, I guessed she may have changed her name to Helen even called herself Mrs Thruxton. Ledgers and files and accounts books were gone through but there was no joy.

It was five thirty by the time all four estate agents had been fruitlessly visited. Hubert was fed up with wandering about and wanted to go home.

'Just one more town,' I wheedled. 'It's still light and they could be open late.'

I drove on to Naresworth which was a much smaller

place. There were two estate agents; one was closed. Hubert by now had grown sullen. 'This is ridiculous, Kate. I want to get back. I'm on the bleep tonight.'

Hubert was often 'on the bleep' for night-time deaths, especially those in nursing homes. I began to get disheartened. 'Just this last one, Hubert, it doesn't close till seven.'

Before he could argue I had rushed into the office of Telling and Bellman and the one sales negotiator, glad of something to do, sat me down and began checking his computer. Hubert kept walking past the window, pretending to be interested in the house details displayed there.

As the salesman, whose name was Darrel, pronounced Dar-rel, continued to search on the computer I became more and more dispirited. Helena could be using any name, and of course false references.

'You do take up references?' I asked Darrel.

Darrel smiled. He was a man of long parts: long legs, long hands and long eyelashes. He wore his dark hair in a pony-tail, but best of all, he really was worried about this woman with the unnamed disease who it seemed could be contaminating one of his properties.'

'Don't you worry, Miss Kinsella, we'll find her. This is serious, isn't it?'

'It certainly is—a matter of life or death. Could you check your clients' references?'

'It'll take time but I'll get there and if she's with Telling and Bellman I'll find out.'

I murmured my thanks, told him he was wonderful and that mankind itself would be grateful. He smiled, as if knowing that all along.

About half an hour later, with Hubert pressing his face against the window and telling me to hurry up, Darrel said, 'Hey, what's this? There's a reference from a doctor in Dunsmore for a lady called Miss Helen Chadwick...'

'That's her!' I cried out. 'It must be.'

Darrel read out the reference which stated Doctor David
Thruxton had known Miss Helen Chadwick for many years
and she was honest, reliable, et cetera.

'Bit funny he didn't know she had a disease—being her
doctor.'

'Doctors these days,' I said with a sage nodding of my
head.

'It's quite isolated, stone, a barn conversion. One bedroom, sitting-room, kitchen, bathroom, central heating—not
bad for the price...' Darrel went on in full flow but I was
already on my way to the door and blowing him kisses and
telling him I'd be sure to recommend him to all my friends.

Hubert knew by my face I thought I'd found her. We
looked Lyrestone up on the map. Five miles away, that was
all. It was eight thirty now and still supposed to be light
but clouds had gathered and it was beginning to rain. Just
a measly trickle at first but after a mile or so it came down
vertically and I had to drive cautiously along narrow one-
car roads with sudden twists and bends which deserved the
description 'Godforsaken'. Field and the odd farm here or
there were all we saw, then suddenly we were in the village
and through it and searching for Firs Barn.

I drove on for about two miles but there was still no sign
of, or to, Firs Barn Cottage. Swearing and cursing and with
Hubert shh...shh...and tut-tutting in my ear I stopped
abruptly at a gated field and started back towards the village. And then I saw it, a turning, as narrow as a footpath,
with a sign.

'We've found it, Hubert,' I announced triumphantly.
Hubert, silent at first, soon said, 'I'm not hanging around
outside like a stray dog. I'm coming in with you.'

'Of course you are, Hubert. I wouldn't leave you outside
in the rain.'

Firs Farm had long since become derelict, the roof was
gone from the farm house and the outbuildings were door-

less and with crumbing walls. Only the mud seemed fresh and new. We drove past the farm and on about half a mile and there to the left of a small orchard was Firs Barn Cottage. The lights were on. Helena Amroth, alias Helen Chadwick, was in. Behind thin curtains I could see shadows moving. Two shadows.

TWENTY-TWO

MESMERIZED FOR a few moments Hubert and I watched the tableau as the rain slipped unchecked down the windscreen; the figures still, then moving away, coming back, standing together, hugging.

Hubert suddenly moved into action, snatched up my car blanket to shelter us from the rain and as he held it over our heads for protection we began to walk towards our quarry.

The cottage was one storey, stone built, but not particularly smart or cosy. Even in the gloomy rain I could see there were no roses or ivy creeping around the porchless door, and no flowers grew beside the path. Our footsteps crunched damply in the rain and the door was opened after one knock.

I don't know who was more surprised—him or me. For there in the doorway stood Charles Amroth, his mouth open until he managed to stammer, 'Good God—Kate! What on earth are you doing here?' He then saw Hubert emerging from the shadows.

'Who's he?' he demanded.

'I think we have some explaining to do,' I said mildly, amazed at my outward composure.

'If you must,' said Charles coldly. 'You'd better come inside.'

Helena stood by the window. The room matched the thin curtains. The furniture consisted of an ancient brown mock-leather settee, one floral geriatric-style chair and a drop-leaf table containing the remains of a meal, an empty bottle of wine and two glasses.

'Who are these people?' she asked Charles sharply. She looked much older than her photograph. Her fair hair had been tied back loosely, she wore no make-up and she had obviously been crying.

The introductions were made, I explained that nursing was merely a way of funding my investigation agency and that though I was once involved in the murder case, now, I had no client and had merely tracked Helena down to warn her that she could be next in line.

The atmosphere remained as frosty as an ice bucket's bottom. Finally it was Helena who spoke. 'I'm well able to take care of myself, Miss Kinsella. And always have been. Nothing has gone on that I don't know about. I've been persecuted and so has my husband for matters over which we've had no control.'

So carefully did she speak it was almost as if she had prepared her speech—a quality of resignation was there, almost a summing up for the defence. Charles Amroth smiled sadly at his wife.

'My wife and I have a lot to discuss, Kate. I'd be grateful if you'd go now. And it may seem harsh but I'd prefer it if you didn't return to Riverview—we'll employ an agency nurse until...we're more organized.'

Hubert and I left then completely silent and demoralized. As we drove away I said, 'Well, that's that. I don't understand what's going on. How long has he known she's been living there? Do you think she's about to confess to the police? Did you notice how cool she was? Lots of determination, that woman—'

'She scared me,' interrupted Hubert. 'I reckon she killed Jenny and Teresa because they knew about her hit and run driving. I suppose she thought that was the end of it but of course Geoff knew too, so he had to die.'

'What about Charles though, was he in on all this? He's

let the police think he killed his wife simply to take suspicion and interest away from her, but why?'

'What do you mean, Kate?'

'I mean, Hubert, their marriage wasn't on the rocks it was in quicksand. Why would he risk everything to protect a wife he didn't love any more, who had a drink problem, who'd left home anyway and who was having an affair with his partner?'

'Well, I don't know,' said Hubert miserably, 'and to be honest I'm past caring. I'm tired, thirsty and it's all far too complicated for me. But...'

'But what?'

'Just because he didn't love her any more didn't necessarily mean he would want her to go to prison. Maybe it was a bit of self-interest, he wouldn't have wanted the practice to fall into disrepute, would he?'

'Would you murder someone to protect Humberstones'?'

There was silence while Hubert thought about it. And the silence said it all—he was giving the question serious consideration.

'I'd like to say I wouldn't commit murder but I might be tempted. After all, Kate, what else do I have?'

'Hubert, I'm surprised at you. I thought you were a very moral man.'

'I am,' he agreed, sounding crestfallen as though he'd disappointed himself. 'I'm just saying I might be tempted, that's all.'

'Of course they do have Neil to think about. How will he feel when he finds out his mother has been living locally and not seeing him.'

'Did he go to boarding school?'

'Yes. From the age of eight...'

'Well, then. Public-school kids get very self-reliant.'

'Yes, but his mother leaving home like that has obviously affected his career. He was at Oxford and it disturbed him enough to have to give up his degree course.'

'Perhaps he was looking for an excuse to leave.'

'Maybe...'

'Can we please stop talking now, Kate,' said Hubert. 'I just want to sit back and relax and know you're concentrating on your driving.'

As I drove towards Longborough I tried not to dwell on the fact I'd lost my job. I had quite liked it. I would miss the patients. And my improved social life. I remembered then about Neil. With all this going on probably it was best I didn't see him again. I'd give him a ring later and...report sick or something.

Hubert began cooking omelettes on our return and I dashed up to my office to collect my notes on the case. The phone rang just as I closed the office door. Ignore it, I thought, but I couldn't. It was Neil.

'Kate, I have to see you tonight. Can you come over? I'm worried sick about my father. I really do need someone to talk to.'

'I'm just about to eat, Neil, but I'll come after if you're that desperate to see me.'

'Thanks, Kate. See you soon.' His voice rose a little in what sounded like relief.

Hubert wasn't pleased when I returned. 'Omelettes have to be carefully timed, Kate—but you wouldn't know that would you?'

'I can cook omelettes,' I said. 'I was delayed by a phone call.'

'Who from?'

'Neil Amroth.'

'I'd stay away from that family, if I were you. In some families ill luck runs through the generations as fast as rabies and I reckon it's catching.'

'I'm seeing him later. The poor lad sounds really up-tight.'

'"Poor lad", indeed,' sneered Hubert. 'You just want to hold him to your bosom, but not for maternal purposes.'

I feigned indignation and told him I had to go for the sake of the case.

'Sake of the case! Come off it, Kate. Leave it to the police now. They must be quite near to arresting someone.'

I thought about that as I chewed my leathery omelette. 'I don't think they've got the evidence, Hubert. Perhaps they know but they can't prove it. I'm convinced they were both killed in the grounds of the college. By the time they found out where the car had been parked that night any real forensic evidence would have been destroyed by the coming and goings of students, cars, bikes, et cetera. Forensic evidence isn't of much use if it's been trampled on a hundred clumping feet.'

'Fingerprints?' asked Hubert.

'I'm not sure, but the police would be cock-a-hoop, wouldn't they, if they'd found any? Someone was waiting for them—expecting them. Nick said the car was open with the keys inside. I've got it!' I broke off excitedly. 'The murderer was already in the car. He gave Jenny a karate chop to the neck and...'

'Hang on, Kate, wouldn't Teresa have seen this?'

'Not necessarily. She would have been concentrating on unlocking her car, starting the engine... She looks sideways to wave goodbye to Jenny and sees her slumped in the driver's seat. She switches off the engine, rushes over to her friend's car and...it's curtains for poor Teresa.'

'That's all guesswork though, Kate. Couldn't he have been waiting in the bushes?'

I nodded. 'You're right, Hubert. It's all guesswork. But maybe I can get some info from Neil. They alibied each other for that night. I think maybe Charles had grown weary of Teresa or maybe she was too demanding. We assumed he didn't love Helena but maybe he did, perhaps he wanted her back. Knowing that Jenny suspected Helena of killing her son and having lost interest in Teresa, he followed them—'

I broke off, realizing there was some basic flaws in this argument and before Hubert cottoned on I made a hasty exit.

ON THE WAY to Weston-Cumby I noticed for the first time it was *en route* for Naresworth. Was it significant? I wondered.

As I drove into the village itself with its two miniature street lamps, one either side of the duck pond, I was as pleased as if I'd found an oasis in the desert. Really, to call Weston-Cumby a village was an exaggeration. There didn't appear to be a shop or even a church. The Amroth house wasn't overlooked and the other few cottages were small as though they were once part of an estate and the Amroth house belonged to the squire.

The lights were on downstairs and I drove straight to the front of the house and stopped. I was about to close the car door when Neil appeared. 'Good of you to come, Kate, park your car round the back near the summer house—just lately we have callers at all hours.'

The path at the side of the house went on and on until eventually I could see the shape of the summer house raised up on huge concrete slabs and lit by a carriage lamp. I'd imagined something approaching the standard large shed. This was a Tyrolean-style 'shed', with a balcony and hanging baskets, brass cowbells and painted wooden tubs of glorious flowers. I parked in a small gravelled parking area and could see that to the right of the summer house was a garden pond. I walked towards it, ignoring the rain, and stood for a while staring at the pond lush with reeds and

greenery. Lily pads floated on top and a garden gnome had cast his tiny fishing line in the rain-speckled water. I was childishly fascinated by the whole atmosphere of the place and stood trying to imagine it on a warm moonlit night...
'Lovely, isn't it, Kate?'

Neil slipped an arm round me and pulled me close. 'Come on I'll show you my castle.'

The inside was lit by candles, some in bottles some in holders. The room was large with partitioned areas. A round pine table with two chairs in one corner. Two black single futons folded up and ready for use as chairs made use of the centre of the room. A free-standing book case against one wall was packed so full that it overflowed as books stood in piles beside it.

'I'll show you round,' said Neil.

He led me, still with his arm round my shoulder, to the kitchen area. 'The galley,' he said. 'I put the sink in myself.'

To the left of the sink was a Baby Belling oven and cupboards above and below. On the right was a small fridge from which he took a bottle of white wine.

'You'll have one, Kate?' I nodded; rarely do I refuse a drink. Wine in hand, he led me to another partition and his bedroom, a three-quarter bed alongside a line of boxes covered with white sheeting.

'Unfortunately I have to keep most of my gear in here. I've got a small van but that's not big enough for everything I need. Still it's home.'

'What about the loo and bathroom?' I asked.

'Just here,' he said, opening what I'd thought was a cupboard but was in fact a loo and shower.

We sat down then on opposite futons and Neil said, 'I'm so pleased you've come, Kate. I knew you would in the end.'

'You sounded worried on the phone,' I ventured. He

shrugged his wide shoulders. He was wearing a navy track suit and Reeboks. I'd worn my black track suit and I couldn't help wishing I looked a little more alluring.

'The police have harassed us continually. It's lucky I suppose they don't come during surgery hours but someone in the practice is questioned every day. The CID have been here this evening looking for my father. I told them we lead separate lives but they continue asking the most stupid questions.'

'Like pigs sniffing truffles,' I suggested.

He laughed. 'Exactly. I couldn't have put it better.'

'What are they most interested in?'

'They suggest that we're lying when we say we didn't leave the village the night of the murder. The impression they give is that my father and I cooked up our alibi between us. That one or both of us killed all three victims. Meanwhile the real killer must be far away by now.'

'What's your theory?'

'My theory for what it's worth is that the murderer's real victim was Geoff Martin. Jenny and Teresa were a warning.'

'A very heavy warning,' I said swiftly. 'And why should Geoff be a victim?'

'His job.'

'Journalist?' I said in surprise.

'Jenny used to tell me he often got pretty hot news items.'

'I thought he dealt mainly with business articles—making the most of your building society, that sort of thing.'

Neil smiled. 'Business stories cover more than that: drugs, stocks and shares, takeovers. I think he was on to something really major, or at least according to Jenny he was.'

'You and Jenny were quite friendly then?'

'I did work at her house from time to time. Geoff wasn't

much of a handyman. I put up some shelves, fixed a leaking tap, even did a bit of point work on their side wall.'

'What do the police think about your theory on Geoff?'

'I think they were grateful I'd given them another line of enquiry. More wine?'

I nodded. It was the best wine I'd ever tasted. So good that I knew this glass should be my last.

When Neil came back with the bottle he seemed in lighter mood.

'Let's stop all this heavy stuff, Kate. I live with it. Let's talk more about you. What were you like as a schoolgirl?'

I was a bit surprised by the question and hoped he wasn't going to suggest I wear a school uniform.

'As a schoolgirl I was ravishingly beautiful, it's only the passage of time that's withered me.' He laughed at my little joke. 'No, actually, Neil, I was mousy and nondescript. I wasn't much of a student either. I went to an all girl's comprehensive in North London where the science teacher was so hairy that each lesson I would sit with my best friend Liz trying to count the number of hairs on the parts of her body we could actually see. Consequently I don't know a fulcrum from my elbow or a molecule from an amp. The maths teacher merely told us to read the maths text book and so anything beyond single digits also remains a mystery.'

'You were happy, though?'

'Not exactly happy, Neil. Obsessed.'

'What with?'

'Our future sex lives. So much anticipation and I can't help thinking we were conned. What about you, Neil?'

His eyes clouded suddenly. 'I was sent to boarding school at the age of eight—' He broke off and stared ahead.

'That's young,' I said, 'but when you were older it was OK, wasn't it?'

'No, it was never…OK. I was depressed, though no one

recognized it. I only cried once when my mother left me there—"You're a man now," she said. So I went through years of misery, pleading with my parents to allow me home. It fell on deaf ears. Academically I was doing well and my father wanted me to go into medicine but I couldn't do it just to please him, could I?'

I nodded in agreement. Neil's blue eyes now looked as bleak as his father's. 'You came home in the end though,' I said, trying to offer vague and rather crude consolation. He stared at me; beneath his lips I could tell he was gritting his teeth in anger as the muscles of his mouth began to twitch slightly. He stood up abruptly and began pacing the room. 'I came home because I was disturbed by my mother leaving. She hates me, she always has.'

'I'm sure that's not true.'

He stopped pacing for a moment and glared at me. 'And what do you know about this family? You and your jolly pleb school with a kind mother waiting at home with tea and scones. What do you know about anything?'

I didn't answer. He was getting angry now like a drunk gets angry and there's no arguing with that sort of anger. I just sat there, like one of Hubert's corpses. He began pacing the room again, up and down like a demented animal in a zoo.

'Why did you have to mention school days, why couldn't you have been miserable at school? What were you hoping to do? Amuse me? Make me jealous? Can't you see my parents hate me? I had to build this place to stay here. He said there was no alternative—I had to go. I said there was. So I built this place, it was my idea. And the job. I like him to see me walking round with spanners and hammers—it pleases me to humiliate him. I don't like to be thwarted, Kate, in *any* way.'

A little voice whispered in my head then but it wasn't issuing instructions it was saying: oh God oh God, he's stark staring mad. I took a deep breath. He was a human being, sick but still fairly rational.

'Neil, sit down, take it easy, we were enjoying ourselves before. Don't get so upset. We can talk about something else if you want.'

He continued to pace up and down but more slowly now. His features contorted occasionally but his mouth had relaxed slightly. Eventually he came to rest beside me on the futon. And I knew I'd left it too late to do a runner.

'I feel better now, Kate,' he said as he put his hand on my knee. I tried to ease away from him.

'I'll make some coffee, shall I, and then I must be going.'

'Why must you be going?'

'My landlord expects me home. He's waiting.'

Neil smiled and in that slow deliberate smile I saw the venom and the cunning. The wine rose in my throat and came into my mouth. I swallowed it back. The hand on my knee had moved up to my thigh. And I knew, as surely as that hot hand crept up my thigh, he was going to rape me...and then kill me.

TWENTY-THREE

NEIL'S HAND STAYED clamped to my leg, his eyes were staring ahead blankly. I daren't speak, and although my heart hammered away, the rest of my body seemed to have disappeared. I felt as if I were brain and heart and nothing else. I could hear the rain intensify for a moment and then steady to a gentle patter against the roof. Thoughts rushed through my head, not major moments in my life but consoling things like he hadn't raped Jenny and Teresa—no, but he'd attacked from behind. First rule then: don't turn my back on him. Second rule: be cunning. Third rule…third rule…oh God…plan a diversion!

He suddenly came to life. 'Kate, let's go to bed. I need to sleep with you.' He clamped an arm around my shoulder and stood me up. Somehow my memories of all the rape accounts I'd ever read came flooding back. He didn't have a knife or a gun, he hadn't hit me yet. He hadn't even threatened me. Yet I was terrified. I wanted to live. If I fought would it be worse for me? Would it inflame him, make him more determined to have me? If I was passive would I seem like the ideal victim just waiting…to die afterwards. He'd told me he had to have his own way, he meant that literally. He couldn't bear to be thwarted. I had to appear willing.

As we walked towards the partition behind which lay the bed, I stumbled and cried out, 'My ankle, my ankle—I've twisted it!'

He stopped, saying calmly, 'I'll carry you, Kate.' The ease with which he picked up my sturdy body was an awesome reminder of his physical strength. He laid me gently on the bed. 'I'll massage it for you.'

'No,' I said sharply, then added with as much pathos as I could manage, 'It's so painful, I'll do it myself, but thanks anyway.'

I began massaging and snivelling slightly as if I were trying to be brave. Keeping my ankle at a very odd angle I urged him, 'Look, Neil, see, it's deformed. I think it's broken.'

'Nonsense,' he said. 'It's just sprained. Lie down, I'll raise it up on a pillow.' As he reached behind my head for a pillow I threw myself off the bed and rushed towards the door. I didn't have a chance. He felled me in an instant and began dragging me back by my 'sprained' ankle. 'You lying devious bitch. I thought you were different—' He broke off to haul me on to the bed. This time he wasn't gentle. His hand rested on my throat. 'Make a noise and I'll kill you now.'

He sat on the bed, one hand on my throat staring at me. I tried desperately hard to breathe quietly. Strange, I thought, how in situations like this decisions still had to be made. Life or death decisions. Should I keep looking at him? Should I look away? Would close eye contact be considered staring and inflame him more, or now it make him hesitate?

'I can't breathe properly,' I said, eventually. 'I'm choking.'

He didn't answer but lowered his hand to my right breast where it rested like a lead weight. I guessed that to even try to fight back now would lead him into an angry frenzy. I had to try a different tack. I placed my hand over his and began gently caressing it. 'I really like you, Neil, let's just enjoy ourselves, shall we?'

His response was sudden and terrifying. 'Whore... tart...bitch!' He struck me across the face and began tearing at my track suit as if trying to pull the actual fabric apart. His hands were ripping down the bottom half, then swiftly, one hand came to rest on my neck—squeezing. I was choking, suffocating, drowning, all at once. There was blackness in front of my eyes—my life didn't flash before me but I did see Hubert and I knew he'd never forgive me for being so stupid.

My hands flailed looking for a weapon, I grabbed wildly, pulling off the sheet that covered the boxes and then throwing it over Neil's head. In that split second I read the words on the box—in blood-red crayon in the right-hand corner, it said BALL COCKS. Ball cocks and not bollocks was the last thing Jenny saw. It was here she was attacked... I felt the blow to my jaw as if my head was being torn from my neck and then nothing...

Nothing, until I found myself being pulled upright and dragged along. I allowed myself to slump as if I was still unconscious. I wasn't going to make it easier for the bastard. My jaw throbbed, blood trickled from my mouth, my neck ached painfully and I was sure all my teeth were wobbling free inside my mouth. The thought of being put in the boot of the car was as terrifying as if he were going to bury me alive. And I knew the cavalry wouldn't be coming in the final reel with the trumpeter sounding the charge.

The rain on my head and face revived me; I slumped further down. He dragged me up. I started to retch. He relaxed his grip slightly, giving me what I knew would be my last chance—we were near the pond. As I bent over making loud puking noises I grabbed the garden gnome and thrust it at his shin with all my strength, scraping downwards. He staggered back with a howl of real pain. Then I began to run. I knew he wouldn't let a mere bashed tibia stop him. I ran as fast as I was ever likely to run, out towards the duck pond and the village.

I turned, he was coming after me, limping but quite fast.

I ran on and on out past the duck pond into the main road. When in doubt, my mother told me, scream *Fire!* Summoning all my strength I did just that: '*Fire! Fire! Fire!*' He was closing on me. I continued to scream. It seemed ages before there was any response but suddenly cottage lights were going on, a window opened. 'What's up?' a man's voice carried loudly in the night.

'Ring the police,' I yelled. I heard a car driving up. I was in the middle of the road but I didn't care. I couldn't do any more. I slumped to the ground.

It was the lights that woke me. At first I thought it was the car. Then I focused. Helmeted men stood round me and the lights belonged to a fire appliance. I moved my head slightly—three fire appliances.

'Don't move, love. You're all right now. The ambulance is on its way.'

'And the police? He tried to kill me.'

'There's no fire then, love?'

I tried to shake my head but my neck hurt too much. The fireman took off his jacket and I thought he would put it round my shoulders but he didn't, he laid it across my legs. My track suit bottoms were gone. I was sitting there in full view of the Dunsmore and District Fire Brigade in my up-to-the-waist type sports knickers, and I hadn't shaved my legs. As I tried to laugh at this predicament I felt my tooth loosen and put out my hand to catch it. I wouldn't be smiling any more for a while; it was only a crown, the stump being a little fang left to peg it on. I wanted to laugh again. Relief surged through me like a quick blood transfusion.

The ambulance men arrived then, checked me over minutely like mechanics looking for faults, put me in a neck collar, swathed me in blankets and then lifted me into a wheeled chair. The ambulance man was just delivering his reassuring speech when a shot rang out. Please let him be dead, I thought. We all looked in the direction of the Am-

roth house. Then as if rallied by the sound of gunfire the
police arrived. They were armed and began surrounding the
house at speed. A loud-hailer was quickly fixed up and a
sonorous voice proclaimed, 'This is the police. Come out
with your hands up.'

I giggled at the originality. I was just hysterically happy
to be alive. Nothing could daunt my euphoria. Until I saw
DI Hook coming towards me. By now the ambulance men
were considering lifting me into the ambulance. I closed
my eyes. Perhaps Hook wouldn't say too much if I acted
half dead.

'How is she?' he asked the ambulance man.

'She'll be fine. A bruised chin, bit of resulting whiplash
from a punch on the jaw, general bruises, a tooth knocked
out, a bit of shock. Could even have a hair-line skull frac-
ture—otherwise no probs, vital signs satisfactory.'

'You have to hand it to her,' muttered Hook. He obviously thought I really was half dead or deaf. 'She's a private investigator and she's dedicated. You have to admire
that even though you know she's a misguided amateur and
a bit on the thick side. She'd walk on fiery coals to nail a
suspect. Some coppers wouldn't do that.'

'What's going on inside?' asked the ambulance man.
'Should I wait for a while for more casualties?'

'Why not? Shouldn't be long. The marksmen aren't going to grow old waiting. He could be dead anyway.'

I sat there with my head stuck up in a collar, swaddled
in blankets, feeling like a trussed turkey and Hook had the
nerve to call me a bit on the thick side. I wanted to explain
but I knew I couldn't. I'd been the victim of a pretty face
with attractive pheromones. But I should have guessed,
with my experience I should have recognized an oddball
when I saw one. Other women had been taken in by him,
though, and I was extremely lucky to have survived.

The man on the loud-hailer was getting impatient. His

speech was getting faster now and he began to sound more and more like British Rail. It was almost unintelligible.

I opened one eye thinking Hook had gone. He was standing over me. 'You should have left it to us, Kate. We were on his trail, we just didn't have enough evidence to convict him. That's the trouble with amateurs, they think police work is all intuition and derring-do but it's painstaking gathering of evidence that matters. All you've gathered, Kate, is the pain. You should pack it in before you get killed. Poor old Humberstone is nearly demented, you know. When we told him we suspected Neil Amroth he was already getting out the right size coffin for you.'

'Liar,' I said calmly, hoping it wasn't true. I smiled to show I didn't believe him.

'Ye gods!' he said, reeling back a step. 'You've grown a fang.' I closed my mouth quickly. With a hand covering my lips, I said, 'Please ring Hubert and tell him I'm OK.'

'I'll tell him you're in the casualty department. Good luck.'

Hook strode off and suddenly search lights were trained on the Amroth house, flooding both the house and the duck pond with light. It had stopped raining now. I guessed it was all over, for minutes later armed men began to move from hidey holes everywhere.

I watched the action as though it had nothing to do with me, as if it were a film set. After some minutes Charles Amroth was brought out. I could see blood seeping from his chest, his ashen face corpselike in the eerie light.

Armed police shared our ride to the general hospital. They'd been assigned to take down Charles Amroth's 'dying declaration'. He seemed to be dying but he certainly wasn't declaring anything. I watched as the ambulance men speeded up his intravenous fluid, took his vital signs and then after a few moments begin to intubate him.

Watching the fight for Charles's life I felt my euphoria

sag with my adrenalin levels. I began to shiver and I couldn't stop and then I began to cry.

Even on the trolley in the Accident and Emergency department being examined by a young female houseman I couldn't stop. 'It's just a reaction to shock,' she said kindly, as she examined me limb by limb. I apologized profusely between sniffing.

A young nurse held my hand until Hubert came. 'Your dad's here,' she said brightly.

Hubert stood and stared at me for a moment. He'd gone a paler shade of off-white. 'I'll get your dad a chair,' said the nurse quickly. She came back immediately with a chair. 'There you are, Mr Kinsella—rest your legs.'

Normally I would have found that funny. But I didn't that night. Hubert, patting my hand awkwardly, said, 'You do look bad, Kate. How's Dr Amroth?'

'Worse. He's shot in the chest.' I began to cry again. After a moment's sniffing and gulping I managed to say, 'He was deranged, Hubert. Why didn't I recognize him for what he was?'

'A nutter?'

'No, a psychopath. I'm giving up the agency. Near-death experiences aren't all they are cracked up to be. Every case I do I seem to land up in Casualty. They'll be charging me soon.'

'That's more like it, Kate.'

'Like what?'

'You've stopped crying.'

I had, but I didn't feel any more cheerful. 'Hook said I was as thick as a plank.'

'I'll thump him for you,' said Hubert, trying hard to jolly me along.

'I was taken in, Hubert, by a pair of sparkling blue eyes and tight Levis. If I can't be objective I shouldn't try to be a detective. I once did my mental nurse training, I mean I should recognize a...'

'Madman,' suggested Hubert.

'No. Someone with psychopathic tendencies.'

'Well, you didn't, did you? Do you think they'll let you out tonight?'

'I'm not staying anyway, Hubert. I want to go back to Farley Wood.'

'You'll do as the doctors tell you.'

'I'll do what I want, Hubert. Discharge myself if necessary.'

An hour later I didn't have the pleasure of discharging myself. They hadn't got a bed for me anyway. According to the staff nurse I spoke to, Charles Amroth was undergoing surgery and his chances were fifty-fifty.

I borrowed a blanket and Hubert ushered me to his car and insisted I stayed in his flat overnight. By now I was too tired to argue, too tired to cry. I just wanted to be left alone.

Hubert made me Horlicks which I hate but forced down and put me to bed in his spare room. I kept the bedside lamp on and lay staring at the ceiling. Occasionally the sound of the phone ringing or of Hubert opening the door startled me.

'Go to bed, Hubert,' I managed to murmur.

The next time I looked up and saw a black shape at the door I screamed. Hubert was wearing a navy dressing-gown but in my half-asleep state I thought he was Neil poised with his shotgun.

'For God's sake, leave me alone.'

'Just checking,' he said. 'I'm staying on guard tonight.'

'Whatever for, Hubert? Just stop fussing and leave me alone.'

He mumbled something. Wearily I sat up in bed. 'What's going on?' I asked.

'He's not dead. Neil Amroth isn't dead. He got away.'

TWENTY-FOUR

'I DON'T BELIEVE IT. I just don't believe it. He was in the house. No police force could be that careless.'

'I'm telling you he got away. It was dark at the back of the house, he slipped away across the fields. The fire brigade coming first may have had something to do with it. Gave him time to escape.'

'I'm staying here until he's found then. I'm not moving from this bed.'

Hubert reassured me that he'd stay on guard and I tried to get back to sleep. A Group-4 cock-up I could understand but not this. I slept fitfully, aware of every bruised muscle, my jaw stiff—my fang conspicuous in my mouth like a nasty foreign body. And my crowned tooth missing. I dreamt that Neil was still coming after me.

When the phone rang the next time I sat bolt upright and alert.

'It's for you,' said Hubert from the doorway. 'It's Inspector Hook.'

Stiffly I negotiated my way out of the bed. I'd aged twenty years in an hour. If Hook had rung to harangue me I decided there and then I was giving up the agency. I picked up the phone.

'I'm sorry I have to ask you this, Kate, but we need you.' I raised my eyebrows at Hubert. 'We've got young Amroth holed up with his mother and David Thruxton. He's threatening to kill them both unless you put in an appearance.'

'Why me?'

'Why not?'

'Two reasons, Inspector Hook. One, I'm scared to death of him. Two, I've lost my front tooth.'

'It is a lot to ask. But this time we won't miss him. And Roade has got your tooth.'

'I'll need Super-glue.'

'Expense is no object. Will you come?'

I hesitated. For all my flippancy, I was really scared. When I didn't answer Hook said, 'Please, Kate. He's calm at the moment. We don't want anyone to get killed, do we?'

No, we don't, I thought, least of all me.

'I'll come,' I said eventually. He began to give me instructions for finding the way but I cut him short. 'I do know how to get there,' I said. It was only a very minor triumph.

I dressed quickly, refusing to look in a mirror. Hubert was as jumpy as a hungry flea and I felt sick with apprehension. He drove me to the village and we hardly spoke, but as we neared the cottage he thought it an appropriate time to give me advice.

'Now don't rile him, whatever you do. Agree with him. Don't try to be heroic...'

'Just going there is heroic. I feel sick, my mouth's dry, my legs are reduced to just the marrow and you say don't try to be heroic. Never again, Hubert, never again.'

Police cars were parked well back from the cottage, where lights glowed softly, and although the sky was beginning to lighten I could see no armed police in evidence.

Hook appeared from the shadows to greet me. 'Thanks for coming, Kate. He's calm at the moment.'

'I can't see any armed men,' I said, my eyes scanning nervously the trees and bushes that enclosed the cottage.

'They're well hidden. This time we'll be sure.'

'What about my tooth?'

Roade appeared then, smirking as he handed me the mea-

sly crown plus some Super-glue in a large envelope. I
stuffed it quickly in my pocket. I wasn't going to be doing
much smiling anyway.

A few moments later a senior officer from the Dunsmore
CID spoke over the loud-hailer. 'Neil. This is Superintendent Archer. We have Kate here for you. She's willing to
come in but only if you throw out your gun.'

I whispered to Hubert who stood by my side, 'He's an
optimist.'

It seemed a long time before anything happened. Then
the front odor opened to reveal Neil standing behind a
cowed David Thruxton. With an almighty push Thruxton
was sent sprawling to the ground. No one moved. The voice
of Superintendent Archer cut through the silence.

'Keep on the ground, sir. Just crawl towards us. That's
it, sir.'

He crawled forward. As he came nearer I could see one
eye was swollen and closed and blood trickled from his
mouth and nose. Eventually he was half dragged behind a
car and out of my view.

Hook disappeared for a time, to talk to David Thruxton
and then returned saying, 'Neil's agreed to pass the gun
out as soon as you get to the front door. All I can say is,
our marksmen are well positioned and, well…it's up to
you.' I nodded. My mouth was so dry. Hubert stepped forward. 'Kate. Come on. I'll take you home. He's not worth
it.'

'I've come this far, Hubert,' I croaked. If this was brav-
ery I decided I didn't like the feel of it but when Roade
showed me the bullet-proof jacket I was to wear I felt
somewhat more courageous, and anyway I couldn't afford
to look a wimp in front of all these men.

I was helped into the jacket and then I began the short
walk to the front door of the cottage. It had looked like a

short walk before I took the first step but once I'd started it felt a long long way. I kept expecting to hear the crack of gunfire but all was silent save for my footfall on the gravel.

At the door I stopped. It opened slowly a few inches only, then in one simultaneous action, the gun was thrown out and I was dragged inside. A lamp had been placed on the floor so the room was in muted light. Helena sat head down on the sofa. Neil, pale and sweating, yanked me roughly on to the sofa beside her.

'You two have met. You two treacherous bitches.'

I swallowed hard. Told myself I must keep him talking and every word I said must be thought out. Carefully rehearsed. Keep my voice low and calm.

'Neil,' I said. 'I know you think that about us but perhaps you should be the one to explain to us the folly of our ways.'

'Folly—huh! That's a good one.'

I held my breath waiting for his angry explosion. Instead he laughed drily. This time I'd got away with it. Next time I knew that if I chose the wrong word it might be my last.

Helena began sobbing, trying to stifle the sound with a cushion she held on her lap for comfort.

'Shut up, shut up!' yelled Neil in our faces. 'I don't like that. I wasn't allowed to cry, remember—remember, do you?' Surely, I thought, all this wasn't about him going to boarding school!

Neil stood back slightly, everything about his face and body alert and expectant. He was like a rattlesnake still rattling but poised for the strike when it stopped. I had to say something to get him to talk, so I said carefully, 'Sit down, Neil. The police will wait for us to come out, you know. We can all walk out of here together.'

'Too cosy,' he sneered. 'Do you really think it's going

to be like that?' Then abruptly he turned to pull the curtains aside and look out. He stood side on though, so no marksman could get a decent view of him. For some moments he just stood there deep in thought.

Could we both charge him? I wondered. I touched Helena's leg and she looked up into my eyes. Her face was pale and tearstained and she'd bitten her lips in an attempt to keep herself from crying out, but it was her eyes that showed her real state of mind. They were blank. She'd given up. She fully expected to die.

Neil swung round from the curtains. He was now holding a hand gun and smiling triumphantly. 'Did the police really think I'd give up my only gun?'

'Why, Neil?' I asked, aware that my voice wavered. 'Why all this, what's it all about?'

'Ask the bitch next to you. She knows. Come on— Mother dear—time to confess, isn't it?'

Helena gazed into her son's eyes but fear seemed to have paralysed her and she didn't answer. Neil moved forward and yanked her head back by her hair. She moaned softly.

'I'm waiting. Tell Kate all about it. Tell her how you hated me. Tell her how my father killed my real mother...tell her!'

Helena began to speak then, tears trickling down her face.

'You're wrong, Neil—very wrong. She died a natural death—a brain haemorrhage. I didn't even know your father then. I did my best to be a good mother to you...'

'Your best! That's rich. What did you do? Insisted I went off to boarding school at eight years old. You knew I was disturbed. Good God, I was ill...depressed. Did you care? Of course you didn't...'

'I couldn't cope with you, Neil. The tantrums, the stealing, the bedwetting, the lies, the running away...'

'That's enough of that. Did my father want me to go?'

Helena gulped, pressing the cushion to her mouth. I put my hand in hers. 'No,' she said eventually, 'he didn't want you to go.'

Neil began to pace up and down mumbling to himself. It took me a few moments to hear his exact words, which were:

'I didn't mean to kill him he shouldn't have come at me. I didn't mean to pull the trigger and if he hadn't got in the way…it was all his fault all he had to do was keep quiet and listen…'

'Your father's not dead,' I said softly. 'The doctors think he'll make it.'

Neil paused in his pacing to stare at me. 'I love my father…sometimes. He's been good to me. He wanted her back. Once she'd gone I had to come home, didn't I? I had to be here for him. One day I knew I'd find her. I'd got it confused and twisted in my mind about my real mother. I had no memories of her death until…'

'Until when, Neil?'

He stared at me, the same stare his father had given me once, as if not remembering who I was.

'I went to see a hypnotist in Oxford…' he began, then stopping, he pulled aside the curtain and stared out.

'What did you find out, Neil?' I murmured.

He turned to face me. 'I was nearly three, I'd wandered into their bedroom in the night. I'd just got to the bedroom door when I heard them shouting. My father was holding my…real mother, shaking her. She slumped down and then Daddy was on the floor beside her kissing her and banging on her chest. Oh, I know intellectually he didn't kill her but he was shaking her before. He had some responsibility.'

'But you still loved him?'

'Of course. I mean I didn't remember what I'd seen until

I was grown up but it was all there in my subconscious…festering like some slow-growing abscess. When he brought Helena home I was nearly five. I did resent her and I have to admit that I played up, so that she would go away—instead, I was sent away. Years of misery then, of not being close to my father, but I survived. None of it was my fault after all. And then came the accident—' Neil broke off, crouching down on his haunches, holding the gun in the palm of his hand, staring at it.

'What accident, Neil? What happened?'

'Simon Martin's death. That's when Helena left home. Could she have picked a worse time? Could you, Helena? Could you?' She gazed at him, her eyes filled with tears. 'It was coincidence, that was all. I had to get away. I was going mad.' Neil smiled, the sort of smile I once thought charming. Now it seemed inappropriate and evil.

'You should have stayed, Father needed you, but of course you had interests elsewhere, didn't you? Didn't you? Answer me.'

'David was kind to me and discrete. The scandal of the accident would have wrecked the practice. I didn't rush from your father straight into his arms—I lived in Spain for two years—I hardly saw him.'

Neil's expression tightened, he gripped the gun in one hand and with his free hand he clenched and unclenched his fist again and again. 'My, my, how that must have rankled. In all that time though you couldn't even be bothered to send a postcard or a letter…I had to lie to save my pride.'

'I thought a clean break would…be best. I did worry about you both.'

Neil laughed, a dry harsh laugh and as he laughed his eyes glimmered with rage or hatred, I wasn't sure which.

'The only person you ever worried about was yourself and your resentment of me,' he said, 'Did you think I didn't know you wanted a child of your own? That's why you hated me...'

'That's not *true*, Neil!' Helena cried out. 'I didn't hate you! How could I stay after what had happened? I blamed myself for that. I knew Simon, I liked Jenny. How could I stay?'

'My father had to stay.'

There was silence then, broken by Helena's ragged breathing, a clock ticking somewhere out of sight and the first sounds of the birds' dawn chorus. How much time had passed I didn't know. The police outside no longer mattered. The world seemed to have shrunk to this room and talk of death and the prospect of dying.

'My father lost his peace of mind and you, because of one mistake,' said Neil, slowly stroking the barrel of the gun with one finger.

I suddenly felt very sick and shivery, I held on to Helena's hand as Neil continued to talk.

'He should have stopped but it was the child's fault running out into the road. Father had to think of all of us. He told me that, he also told me you two had been drinking together and rowing. A patient had rung him and he'd gone out in the car. He couldn't have stopped. The impact was so great it was obvious the child was dead. He couldn't have done anything.'

I managed to speak then. 'So it was your father who was responsible for Simon's death?'

Neil nodded. For a moment his eyes became blank but then he focused on me. 'Yes of course. We tried to ignore the gossip about Helena but you didn't drink and drive, did you, Helena? Neither did my father, or at least, only the once.'

Now that Neil was talking more I had to ask the question, 'Why did you kill Jenny and Teresa?'

'Why indeed,' answered Neil dully. 'I didn't plan it. That night my father entertained Teresa. Jenny came to collect her. Jenny had been busy following Helena. I'd read her diary at the house when I was doing some odd jobs. I'd known a few weeks, that's all. I realized if they harmed Helena it might come out that she was not the driver. And anyway I didn't want Helena to go to prison—I wanted it to be as it was before. Teresa was the real obstacle—she wasn't good enough for him. She was a trollop—she was just playing with his affection. He didn't love her of course. He wouldn't have married her. I wasn't prepared to allow my father to marry again. I thought with those two out of the way Helena could come home and we'd be a family again.'

'And Geoff Martin? Why did he have to die?'

'I reasoned once he was over the shock he might go after Helena. No one guessed, you see, that it was my father who killed Simon.'

'And David Thruxton? Didn't you see him as an obstacle?'

'He knew all along. He liked the practice, he didn't want to lose his relatively easy life. Once Jenny and Teresa were out of the way I could have dealt with him.'

I fell silent for a while. It was growing lighter outside. My mouth was dry, my leg muscles tight and knotted. I wanted this to be over.

'Shall I make some tea?' I asked.

Neil stared at me and then smiled. 'Helena can make the tea. Go on, Helena—I'll watch you.'

Trembling, Helena stood up and with uncertain footsteps walked towards the door. I couldn't get a view from where I sat of the kitchen but I heard the tap running and the noise of cups and saucers being moved. Neil had the gun at waist level pointing her way.

'Neil,' I murmured. 'Tell me about the night you killed Jenny and Teresa.'

He glanced towards me then turned back to watch Helena. After a few moments he said, 'It simply happened. My father was saying goodbye to them both. I was watching. The phone rang, I heard them say to him to go inside and answer it, and I waylaid them. Jenny had already started the car engine. I asked if they would like to see my garden pond. Teresa was reluctant but Jenny said, "Why not?" So Jenny drove the car down to the summer house. My father obviously thought they were driving off. Jenny stood looking at the pond and the tadpoles while I took Teresa in to see the inside of my home. I killed her almost immediately. Jenny came in then and I was a bit panicky...sort of excited too. I had to kill her as well. I waited till I thought my father was asleep and then I quietly drove the car back to the college. I'd put Teresa's body in the boot of her car. And I was just about to deposit Jenny in hers when I saw someone watching me from the bungalow near the car park. I held Jenny up for a while talking to her, then I put her in the boot. I drove off in Teresa's car, and abandoned it in woodland a few miles away. Then I jogged home, had a bath, washed my clothes and went to bed for an hour or two. My father assumed I'd been in bed all night.'

I sat almost mesmerized by the matter of factness of murder. Helena came in with the tray. Her face matched the colour of the milk. She placed the tray on a side table.

'You can be mother,' said Neil.

Helena began pouring the tea from the pot with shaking hands. 'No milk for me,' I said, and as she handed me the cup I tried to signal with my eyes I was going to try something. She looked at me still terrified and uncomprehending. Neil sat down underneath the window, took his cup and put the gun on the floor beside him.

As I held my cup and saucer my hand trembled and the cup chinked noisily on the saucer. 'I think I will have milk,' I said, moving forward to the table with the cup still in my hand. If Neil realized what I was going to do his face didn't show any concern, his cup was at his lips and as he swallowed I threw the whole of my scalding tea in his face. I heard him cry out, heard cups crashing around me, grabbed Helena by the hand and suddenly we were out through the front door and running. I didn't look back—but I did hear the shot.

FOR A WEEK I stayed in my cottage in Farley Wood. Hubert came every day to see me. I visited the dentist but found that once I could smile again I didn't have the urge.

Roade and Hook came once and were more than pleasant. They had been suspicious of Neil all along but were short on evidence although they were amassing medical information. From the age of seven he'd had psychopathic tendencies but that is no crime and he'd never been in trouble with the police. He'd died instantly but his father was expected to live. It seemed Charles had known his ex-wife's whereabouts at all times but she couldn't cope with Neil, and Neil was the main reason for the break-up of their marriage. Helena and Charles had done all in their power to prevent him from finding Helena's whereabouts. For many years she had been terrified of him but Charles had always found excuses for his son's behaviour. Charles felt that with Neil near by he could protect his wife, whom he still cared about, and keep a watchful eye on Neil's mental state. His first concern on coming off the ventilator had been for Neil. Perhaps their son had loved them too, in his own twisted way.

Physically and mentally I now felt exhausted. I didn't sleep well: the nightmares kept me awake, I wasn't interested in food although Hubert tried to tempt me with strawberries and fresh salmon.

'You're in a post-violence depression,' Hubert told me with a worried expression. 'You should see a doctor.'

I ignored him. He threatened to bring Danielle to see me. I even ignored that.

'I'm a failure,' I said. 'I'm giving up. I'm leaving Longborough. I'll pack up the office on Monday.'

On Monday I arrived at Humberstones', and walked slowly up the stairs and into my office. On my desk sat a huge vase of flowers and beside them an answering machine—new and sparkling and with a flashing light to indicate a message. I switched it on. It was Hubert.

'Hello, Kate. This is Hubert speaking,' he said as if I were that stupid. I waited, expecting a message of goodbye and it's been nice knowing you et cetera but there was nothing. Blank. Zero. Silence.

As Hubert walked up the stairs I began to laugh, a little hysterically but it was a laugh.

'What's so funny?' asked Hubert. 'I thought my farewell speech was pretty good.'

'I expect it was, Hubert—but it didn't come out. All that came out was "This is Hubert speaking."'

'Bloody thing,' said Hubert, giving it a bang with his fist and then looking disappointed when there was no response.

'Where did you get it from, Hubert?'

'A car-boot sale. The bloke who sold it to me said it was top of the range. It cost me a tenner!'

I began to laugh again. 'You're priceless, Hubert. I'd miss you so much.'

'Does that mean you'll stay?'

I nodded.

He beamed, his face all smile and pallid creases. 'Come on, Kate, I'll buy you chicken and chips down the Swan.'

'How can I refuse?' I said. 'After all, Hubert, I'm counting my blessings. Food, drink, a decent pub, an answering machine that doesn't work, body parts still intact and you for a friend. What more could I ask?'

Hubert shrugged. 'A few thousand in the bank?'

I smiled and linked my arm in his and we made our way downstairs together.

THE CONCRETE PILLOW

RONALD TIERNEY

First Time in Paperback

A Deets Shanahan Mystery

Shanahan wasn't keen on working for an addict.

They couldn't be counted on for either their perceptions or their payment. But something about Luke Lindstrom made the Indiana private investigator take the case.

Perhaps because he remembered when Luke and his brothers were the local high school basketball superstars. Maybe because adulthood had only brought them failure—and untimely death. Mark took a fatal dive off a balcony. Matthew fell off a cliff. That left Luke…and John. Until John takes a deadly tumble.

Now Luke decides to find out who wants him dead—before the killer succeeds. And while Shanahan is all too aware of how tough family relations can be, he's discovering that in Luke's case, it's just plain murder….

"Shanahan is a terrific character, feisty, even noble."
—*Publishers Weekly*

Available in March at your favorite retail stores.

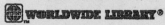 **WORLDWIDE LIBRARY®**

PILL

Dust Devils OF THE Purple Sage

Barbara Burnett Smith
A Jolie Wyatt Mystery

First Time in Paperback

BACK IN THE SADDLE AGAIN

With one solved murder behind her—a worthy credit for any fledgling mystery writer—Jolie Wyatt is now working as a newscaster for a local radio station. And the news is as hot as the blazing Texas sun: an escaped convict, a local boy named James Jorgenson, is believed to be heading straight for Purple Sage.

When a college kid is found dead, everyone thinks Jorgenson did it, even Jolie's teenage son, who vows to catch the killer of his longtime pal. But Jolie is riding a different trail that's leading her straight to a killer. She may even get a new way to experience the murder mystery—as a corpse.

"[Jolie] Wyatt is a charming, strong-minded contemporary character..."
—*Houston Chronicle*

Available in April at your favorite retail stores.

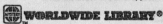

WORLDWIDE LIBRARY®

DUST

A LOVE TO DIE FOR

CHRISTINE T. JORGENSEN
A Stella the Stargazer Mystery

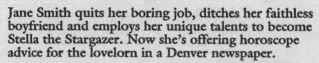
First Time in Paperback

MURDER IN THE STARS

Jane Smith quits her boring job, ditches her faithless boyfriend and employs her unique talents to become Stella the Stargazer. Now she's offering horoscope advice for the lovelorn in a Denver newspaper.

The ink is barely dry on her first column offering advice to a lost soul looking for "a love to die for" when she stumbles upon the body of the owner of her favorite lingerie shop—stabbed to death with a pair of scissors.

Add a police detective she *almost* liked before he accused her of murder, toss in her own uncanny sixth sense and an expressive pet chameleon, and her future is a bit unpredictable...especially with a killer gazing at Stella.

"Stella's quirky humor, human frailties...will endear her to many readers." —*Publishers Weekly*

Available in March at your favorite retail stores.

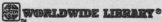 **WORLDWIDE LIBRARY** ®

LOVE

By the bestselling author of *FORBIDDEN FRUIT*

FORTUNE
ERICA SPINDLER

Be careful what you wish for...

Skye Dearborn knew exactly what to wish for. To
unlock the secrets of her past. To be reunited with her
mother. To force the man who betrayed her to pay.
To be loved.

One man could make it all happen. But will Skye's
new life prove to be all that she dreamed of...or a
nightmare she can't escape?

Be careful what you wish for...it may just come true.

Available in March 1997 at your favorite retail outlet.

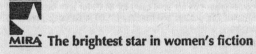

MIRA The brightest star in women's fiction

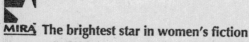